ABDUCTED

By Ken Warner

Contents

ABDUCTED

Prologue

Thirty-five years ago

Martha McClure got in her car and started the engine. She waved to her friends through the window and drove down the street.

She'd been best friends with Tiffany and Abigail through most of their college years. But after graduation, she'd moved back home to live with her parents. Tiffany and Melissa had stayed in Topeka and rented an apartment together. Martha had wanted to join them, but her parents were old-fashioned and insisted she live at home until she got married.

This was the first time she'd been back to Topeka to visit them. She lived over four hours away, so she knew it would be tough to get back here again anytime soon. They were doing well—they'd both secured decent jobs, and they each had a boyfriend. Martha had had the time of her life catching up with them all weekend. She was determined to convince her parents to let her move to the city.

She took the on-ramp and merged onto Interstate 70. As she traveled west, the traffic thinned out. It was already very late, and the sky grew darker as the bright city lights became dimmer in her rearview mirror.

For the next few hours, she was lost in thought, trying to figure out the best way to talk her parents into letting her move out. She was an adult now, so she *could* just get up and go. They had no legal right to stop her. But she knew that her father, at least, would never speak to her again if she did that. She wasn't ready to risk that.

Finally, she reached her exit. She turned onto the state route that would take her home. It was a clear night, and there were no other cars on the road. She could see the Milky Way clear as day.

Suddenly, she noticed clouds forming out in front of her, directly above the road. They came out of nowhere, gathering quickly, as in a time-lapse video. She saw lights flashing in the clouds, almost like lightning, but there was no thunder.

The clouds were moving toward her. As they got closer, she could see there was a bright ring of lights inside of them.

Martha panicked. When the lights were almost directly above her, she turned down a side road and accelerated. Looking in her rearview mirror, she could see that the lights were following her— and gaining fast.

Suddenly, her car died, and her headlights turned off. Martha screamed in alarm. She managed to get the car to the side of the road.

Getting out of the car, she looked to the sky and saw that the ring of lights was now directly overhead. Martha said a prayer, crying freely now—she was scared for her life. But the next moment, everything went black.

Chapter One: Interrogation

Present day

Sydney Hastings walked into the lobby of the CIA Headquarters in Langley, VA. She checked in at the front desk, and the receptionist instructed her to have a seat in the waiting area. She took a seat in the empty room, nervously eyeing the armed guard stationed near the entrance.

Officer Babcock had invited her here—no, "invited" was not the right word; it was more of a summons. Brian Kwan had confirmed that refusing the invitation would be futile because then Babcock would have them arrested.

And so here she was. Brian was late, of course.

Sydney had made sure to arrive only minutes ahead of their scheduled appointment. Brian had predicted that Babcock would keep them waiting—a power play intended to make them nervous. This was already going to be a huge waste of time, so she didn't want to let it last any longer than absolutely necessary.

The compound was not open to the public, but they had been expecting her. She had only had to provide her ID for the guard at the gate, and that was that.

Getting here hadn't been difficult. The Malor had obliterated

Washington, D.C. itself, but the damage did not extend beyond the beltway, which would have been her route here anyway. Driving directly across the city had always been slower when that was still possible.

It was surreal, though, driving near Ground Zero. Only a week had gone by; the idea of the city being *gone* was still impossible to process. It was the nation's capital, for God's sake—how were they supposed to get past this?

There had been nearly a half-million confirmed deaths between the attacks on Miami and D.C., but the number kept increasing every day. Sydney found it difficult to comprehend—so many lives lost in a matter of seconds.

She had nightmares almost every night, reliving the attacks; she'd been present on the Othali ship for both, utterly helpless to do anything to save all those people. Although she'd begged them to do something, the Othali could not interfere. Doing so would have exposed them to the Malor, who were vastly more powerful; they would have destroyed the Othali ship.

Sydney lived outside the city, as did her mom. But several friends and colleagues from the hospital where she'd worked had lived inside the destruction zone and were presumed dead. Thousands of people were still listed as "missing," but they had found a handful of survivors in the wreckage—one hiding in a bank vault, of all places. Apparently, those things could withstand a nuclear blast.

But she knew the nature of the Malor weapon meant that they would never find any remains for most of the victims. The discharge would have vaporized them.

"Ms. Hastings?"

She'd been so lost in her thoughts that she hadn't noticed the man approaching. He was wearing a gray suit; she thought he looked like an agent.

"Yes?" she asked.

"If you'll accompany me..?"

She followed him through a maze of corridors. He finally opened the door to what was clearly an interrogation room. She moved inside, and he left her there, closing the door.

There was a table in the middle, a chair at each end; mirrors lined one wall. Sydney took a seat.

It was quiet here, the hum of the air conditioning the only noise. She stared at the mirror for a minute and thought she could make out a shadow moving beyond it a couple of times—a one-way mirror, she assumed. She fought the urge to give the middle finger to whoever was watching from beyond.

Minutes passed, and there she sat, alone with her thoughts.

Finally, the door opened. Officer Babcock walked into the room and took the seat across from Sydney. He placed a stack of manila folders on the table.

"So, Miss Hastings," he said. "Thank you for agreeing to meet with me."

"Like I had a choice."

"Miss Hastings—Sydney, is it? Do you mind if I call you 'Sydney?'"

"Sure. Do you mind if I call you *shithead*?"

Babcock let out a long sigh.

"Miss Hastings. Do you know the present whereabouts of Jaden and Malia Kwan?"

"Not a clue," she said. "Well, I'd imagine they're somewhere in interstellar space by now."

"So, they left the planet on the alien ship."

Sydney said nothing. She had no reason to believe he wouldn't already know this.

"Is it true, to the best of your knowledge, that the DNA fragments found beneath the Great Pyramid—the ones from which the twins were created—were left there by those same aliens, thousands of years ago?"

"So I've been told," she said. "But you'd know more about that than I would, right? You were the one in charge of that *project*, weren't you? That's all they were to you—a project. As opposed to living, breathing human beings."

"*Half*-human," he replied. "And a project that cost the American taxpayer an enormous amount of money."

"You're a bastard."

"Miss Hastings, you knowingly transported minors across state lines, without their parents' consent—"

"Yeah, because you *shot* their parents!"

"—and you harbored known fugitives," he continued as if she hadn't spoken. "You're facing at least a handful of federal felonies. I would consider your situation carefully if I were you."

Sydney glared at him but said nothing further.

"That's better," Babcock said with a smirk. "Now. What is it the aliens—the Othali, is it? What is it they wanted with Jaden and Malia?"

"What is that supposed to mean? Their mother is an Othali—she went with her people, so of course, she took her children with her!"

"Hmm. And there was another Othali here, on Earth, for all those millennia, was there not?"

"Bomani, yes."

"And where was he all these years?"

"I have no idea," said Sydney. "He was captured by the Germans in World War II, along with Melissa. But then she thought he'd died when she escaped. At some point, he moved to Bermuda to be near the power station there. But I don't know how long ago that was, or where he might have been before that."

"Was Melissa Kwan in touch with this Bomani prior to the invasion?"

"No. I just told you, she thought he was dead."

"I see. So, you never witnessed any interaction between Bomani and Ms. Kwan?"

"Am I speaking English?"

"And Bomani departed the planet with the rest of the Othali?"

"Yes."

"You saw him go?"

"Well... no, I guess I didn't. But he was on the Othali ship the last I saw him, and only Brian and I came back to earth on the shuttle. I assume he left with the Othali."

"Is it possible he left on a different shuttle?"

"Sure, anyone could have left; they had several shuttles. What are you getting at?"

"Is it true that the Othali craft is a *warship*?"

"That's what they said."

"Interesting."

"What?"

"They crossed half the galaxy to come to Earth in a *warship*. That would seem to imply aggressive intent, would it not?"

"Are you insane? The Malor *destroyed their planet*. They were lucky to escape!"

"You believe they are a peaceful people."

"There's no evidence to the contrary."

"They had a warship."

"Yes, because they'd explored other worlds and found planets the Malor had destroyed. They were able to figure out what had happened and feared it would only be a matter of time before the Malor found *their* planet. So, they prepared."

"Yet they arrived here at the same time as the Malor. That's quite a coincidence."

"It was no coincidence at all! That signal from the Miami power station drew them both here—the Othali *and* the Malor—but *separately*."

"As they say. But how do we know that? Perhaps the Othali were working with the Malor to destroy this planet."

Sydney found it difficult to refrain from screaming at this man.

"That's just absurd. The Othali *fought* the Malor. They led the operation to take out their engines. They did everything they could to help *save* us."

"Is it true that the Malor have been sending scout ships here, to Earth, for many years—centuries, perhaps—prior to the invasion?"

"That's my understanding, yes."

"And at least two Othali remained here, on this planet throughout that entire time, is that correct?"

"Yes, Melissa and Bomani. They were the only Othali left."

"Is it possible that one or both of them contacted the Malor scouts? Or, perhaps one of them used one of the power stations to send a signal to the Malor centuries ago, prompting them to send the scouts in the first place?"

"Bomani did say that he'd heard about the crash in Roswell and paid attention to the reports of other alien visits," Sydney told him. "But he'd never heard of the Malor—the Othali hadn't yet discovered them when he came here with the other colonists. So, I'm pretty sure he didn't know anything about the scouts—only that they weren't Othali."

"Mm-hmm."

"You really think Bomani had some involvement with the Malor invasion?"

"Either he or Melissa Kwan."

Sydney shook her head.

"Look, I don't know anything about Bomani. I met him for the first time when we found him in Bermuda. I spent only a matter of minutes with him. But I know Melissa Kwan very well. She would never have plotted with an alien species intent on destroying our planet."

"You say you knew her well, yet you never realized she wasn't human?"

Sydney didn't know what to say to that.

"It was Melissa Kwan who left the DNA fragments beneath the Great Pyramid, was it not?"

"Yes."

"And then she waited *thousands of years* for mankind to develop the technology necessary to bring those fragments to life, correct?"

"Yes."

"And for all those centuries, she masqueraded as a human being, living in various societies, fooling everyone with whom she came into contact into believing she was one of us? Including you?"

Sydney only nodded.

"Is it not possible, at least, that a woman with that kind of patience, not to mention tenacity, could have been harboring other secrets as well?"

Sydney made no reply.

"And not to mention this Bomani character, about whom you admit to knowing next to nothing."

"I just don't see how it makes any sense," Sydney said, feeling a little like she was trying to convince herself now, too. "Jaden set off that signal, and that's what attracted the Malor. They already knew of our existence from the scout ships they'd sent. The signal seemed to announce that we'd achieved some level of technological advancement, meaning that we'd be ripe for them to plunder. That's what they did, right? They'd used up all the resources on their planet, so they traveled the galaxy going from one world to the next, exploiting them for their own survival?

"The Malor didn't need Melissa or Bomani or anyone else to do that. They could have—and would have done the same thing even if the Othali had never existed."

"Yet it was the Othali who created that power station. We do not possess the technology to send such a powerful signal so far into space so quickly. *And* it was an Othali who triggered the signal. Is it possible Jaden Kwan did that at his mother's behest?"

"No—it was an accident! He just touched the thing, and it went haywire! I was there—Jaden didn't know what he was doing!"

"Hmm."

"No, you listen to me—I'll admit, you've got me second-guessing what Melissa's role might have been. But there is *no way* Jaden— or Malia—had anything to do with the invasion. The night you shot their parents, they left their house believing they were normal human teenagers. That much I know for sure."

"But they knew Malia possessed seemingly supernatural abilities, and Brian Kwan had just revealed to them that they were the product of the DNA found in the Giza complex."

"Sure, but—"

"Brian Kwan may have been in on the plot," said Babcock, excitement in his voice now. And Sydney finally realized where he was going with this whole charade. "He could have relayed Melissa's instructions to Jaden—her instructions to activate the pyramid and send the signal."

"No. Not possible. I was with them—both of them—Jaden and Brian—the entire time. From the moment we met Brian, until the instant we took off in my truck, and your helicopter took Brian away."

"Every moment, you say," said Babcock. "It would have taken only seconds for Brian to pass instructions to Jaden. It may not have been verbal—he could have handed him written instructions when you weren't looking."

"But Brian didn't know about the Malor then! He didn't know Melissa wasn't human or that she had anything to do with leaving the DNA under the pyramid! He believed the DNA came from ancient Atlantis!"

"Perhaps," Babcock conceded. "Yet he still could have been an unwitting accomplice. Melissa Kwan could have left him specific instructions to give to Jaden when he came into contact with the power station."

"You're just looking for an excuse to arrest Brian," said Sydney. "That's what this all comes down to."

"I don't need an excuse," he retorted. "Brian Kwan committed more felonies than you did—in addition to transporting minors across state lines and harboring fugitives, he broke into a top-secret government facility and stole highly sensitive government assets!"

"He rescued his niece and nephew from *your* torture chamber! That's hardly criminal!"

Babcock stared at her for a moment.

"We're done here," he said, rising to his feet and collecting his unused manila folders. "You're free to go."

"Wait, what?" she said as he opened the door. "You're letting me go?"

"It's certainly not my choice," he said to her over his shoulder. "But you've got friends in high places, it seems. You've been granted a full pardon."

He stalked out of the room, leaving the door open behind him.

Sydney jumped to her feet and ran out into the corridor, but Babcock was nowhere to be seen. She made her way toward where she thought she'd come in but only managed to get lost in the labyrinthine building.

Finally, she ran into a security guard who provided her instructions back to the main entry.

The midday sun blinded her as she emerged from the building into the parking lot. She found Brian's Mercedes parked next to her truck. She tried calling him, but it went to voicemail. She decided to wait for him—she wanted to know what the hell was going on. She was pretty sure Babcock would be the one interrogating Brian, too.

Chapter Two: Stranger in the Night

Sydney didn't have long to wait. Brian came strolling out of the building only fifteen minutes later.

"Hey," she said, sliding down from the hood of her Explorer. "That was fast."

"Yes," he replied with a grin. "I learned right before arriving that we've both been granted a pardon, so I knew Babcock's interrogation was toothless. I didn't answer most of his questions.

"But why don't we stop for coffee, and we can compare notes?"

"Sure thing," she said. "Is there a Starbucks nearby?"

They got into their cars, and Sydney followed him out of the complex. As they approached the gate, she saw a crowd of TV crews waiting for them just beyond the fence. Reporters shouted questions at them as they drove past, but Sydney kept her windows up.

Fifteen minutes later, they were sitting down with their coffees at the local Starbucks.

"So, you first," said Brian. "What did Babcock have to say to you?"

Sydney told him all about her interrogation.

"Funny," he said when she was done. "He tried to convince me that *you* might have been involved with bringing the Malor here."

"Are you serious? What the hell is he up to?"

"I'm not sure. I had a meeting with an agent from the NSA a few days ago and went over everything with her. So, the government already knew everything that happened with the Othali and the Malor, from our perspective, before Babcock contacted us. It would seem that he was just trying to sow distrust between the two of us."

"And he was trying to make me distrust Melissa and Bomani, too," Sydney observed. "But for what purpose? They're gone, and it's all over now. And Jaden and Malia left, so it's not like he can get control of them anymore. I don't understand what he wanted with us."

Brian shrugged.

"It's hard to know with him. But it doesn't make any difference at this point—the pardons put us out of his reach."

"Yeah, and about that—who pardoned us, exactly?"

"There's only one person who can issue pardons for federal crimes," he said. "The president," he added in response to her blank stare.

"The *president*? Like of the United States?"

"The one and only," he said with a chuckle. "The NSA agent who interviewed me must have relayed the information to her superiors. I am a little surprised at how quickly this happened, though. Under normal circumstances, this type of thing would take months to come to fruition."

"Well, the circumstances weren't exactly normal."

"Hardly," he agreed.

"Hey, what was with all those reporters back there?"

"You mean they haven't been camping outside your house yet?"

"What? No—why would they? Are they camping outside *your* house?"

"I doubt they've been able to find where I'm living right now…"

"Off the grid?" she asked knowingly.

"Not exactly. Well, the press is aware that you and I were both closely involved with the events surrounding the invasion. I'm sure it's only a matter of time before all the major outlets have people stationed at your residence."

"Lovely," she said, rolling her eyes. "So. Tell me what this new job of mine is going to entail."

"You're still on board?"

"I am. The hospital was destroyed in the attack, so I would have been looking for something else anyway."

"Ah, yes," he said with a frown. "Well, I think, for now, we've both earned a little vacation. I'll start paying you immediately, of course, but take some time off. I'm sure you could use the rest—I know I could."

"Okay, fair enough. But what will I be doing once the vacation's over?"

"I'm not exactly sure yet. I've spent much of my time in recent years investigating the power station. After recent events, that project has come to an end. But I'm sure something else interesting will come along."

"You don't plan on having me work for your security company?"

"Not directly, no," he said. "I still oversee that business but have not been involved in the day-to-day operations for quite some time. It pays the bills, don't get me wrong. But I prefer to spend my time on more interesting pursuits—the power station, for example. The history of Atlantis. I was thinking of having you work with me in those sorts of endeavors.

"But it's hard for me to say at this point precisely what you'll be doing until the next, ah, pursuit presents itself."

"Okay, then," said Sydney, her eyebrows raised in surprise. "It doesn't sound like I'll have much job security this way..."

"You do, trust me," he replied. "After the way you took care of my niece and nephew, and the danger you put yourself in—and the resourcefulness you showed through the whole affair... the job is yours as long as you want it. Don't worry; we'll find plenty of work for you to do.

"At this point, I suspect the job will involve Malor activity in some capacity."

"Oh? How so—they all went down in their ship, didn't they?"

"Most, but not all," he said. "The majority perished in the inferno, but thousands survived. The military has been transporting them to holding facilities in Guantanamo."

"Cuba?"

Brian nodded. "But they weren't the only survivors. They had scout ships doing reconnaissance in most heavily populated areas around the globe. Those ships—all their technology—have reportedly lost power since the destruction of the mother ship."

"Why is that?"

"I'm not exactly sure. But it seems they had some method of transferring power from the engines on the mother ship across great distances to the smaller vessels."

"How intriguing..."

"Indeed! We've got the tech to transfer power that way using microwave radiation or lasers, but in both cases, a direct line of sight is required. The Malor were transmitting power to locations around the globe, so no such direct beaming should have been possible."

"How, then?"

Brian shrugged, throwing his hands in the air.

"This may end up being one of our first pursuits," he said. "My first guess would be satellites, but who knows.

"In any event, governments around the world have been rounding up the Malor who have become stranded in their territories. But I've heard reports that some of them have found ways to generate their own power and are causing mischief for the local authorities."

"Ah," she said with a nod. "They're pretty resourceful, too."

"Yes," he agreed. "They certainly are."

They left Starbucks soon after and agreed to stay in touch. Sydney drove back to her house.

Her cat, Charlie, greeted her at the door when she went inside.

"Hey, buddy," she said, scratching under his chin. "Who's my good boy?"

She spent the rest of the afternoon doing housework but couldn't stop thinking about everything that had happened with the twins and the invasion. She had some leftovers for dinner and fed the cat.

Then she poured herself a glass of wine and went to sit outside on the front porch.

Sipping her wine, she watched the sun setting over the neighborhood. It was so peaceful here, so quiet, but she knew the devastation of the attack was only a few miles away.

She'd driven inside the beltway a couple of days after it happened. The road she was on just ended, and beyond lay a hellscape straight out of some apocalyptic nightmare. The smoldering ruins of the city spread out for miles, plumes of thick smoke rising to the sky.

The wood frame buildings in that area had been obliterated, and nothing but ash remained. Ruins of some brick and steel buildings remained in places, random stalagmites poking out from the barren landscape.

Most striking, in a way, was the lack of color—everything was black and gray. Sitting now on her front porch, remembering that destruction, the green of the trees seemed like a miracle. So much life surrounded her here when nothing but death and ruin remained in the city.

A news truck pulled up across the street, snapping her out of her thoughts.

"Aw, shit," she muttered, getting to her feet as a reporter emerged from the truck and hurried toward her.

"Ms. Hastings?" the woman said.

Sydney didn't answer, moving back inside her house and locking the door behind her. Thirty minutes later, several other news crews had joined the first; each came knocking at her door when they arrived.

She ignored them all and sat in her living room drinking her wine, with all the blinds closed and her curtains drawn tight. She had music playing on the sound system loud enough to drown out the noise coming from outside.

Well, at least Brian had warned her this was coming.

She peered out through the curtains periodically, and as the evening wore on, the trucks departed one by one, giving up on getting an interview with her. Finally, there was just one car sitting at the end of the street. She wasn't even sure it was from a news organization.

Sydney was feeling pretty tipsy by this point, having polished off most of the bottle of wine. She brushed her teeth, changed into her pajamas, and made her way to bed.

She drifted off to sleep in minutes. But suddenly, there was a noise, jarring her awake.

Sydney sat up in bed, listening intently. There it was again—someone was knocking on her door.

"Oh, come on," she said, getting out of bed. It was probably another reporter. "Just go away."

She made her way downstairs and peered out the front window, but there was nobody on the porch. Someone knocked again—it was coming from her back door.

Sydney went to the kitchen and peeked through the curtain. There was an older woman on her back porch—she did not look like a reporter. Her hair was disheveled, as if from the wind, though the night was calm.

"Yes?" Sydney called through the door.

"Sydney? Sydney Hastings?" the woman said.

"Who are you?"

"My name is Martha—I'm in trouble, and I need to speak with you. I don't know who else to turn to..."

Sydney looked through the window again. The woman appeared to be extremely distressed. Her facial expression was anxious, and she was practically cowering away from the porch light.

"What kind of trouble?" Sydney asked. "What's wrong?"

"I'm being followed—they're coming after me. I have information—people need help! I need help! Can I please come in?"

Letting a stranger into her house in the dead of night went against her better judgment, but Sydney felt compelled to find out how she could help this woman. Perhaps it was instinct from years of working as a nurse, but she couldn't just turn someone away who clearly needed help.

She unlocked the door and let the woman inside. Martha moved past her, a heavy satchel hanging from her shoulder. After looking around her backyard to see if anyone else was out there, Sydney locked the door again and led the woman into the kitchen. She offered her a seat at the kitchen table. Martha sat down, lowering her satchel to the floor. Sydney took the chair across from her.

"Thank you—thank you so much," said Martha, her voice full of relief. "I'm so sorry for disturbing you in the middle of the night like this. But I'm afraid they're going to kill me, and I had to tell someone what's going on before it's too late..."

"*Who's* going to kill you? What's going on?"

Martha let out a long sigh. Sydney could see now that she'd been crying.

"It's a long story, and it's not something that most people would believe," she said. She seemed panic-stricken—she was breathing heavily and had a look of fear in her eyes. "But I know you'll understand—after everything you went through with those—aliens... There's so much; I'm not sure where to start..."

"Take a deep breath," Sydney suggested, "and start at the beginning."

"Okay," Martha said. "I'll try. It started, for me at least, about thirty-five years ago. I was just out of college. This was back when I lived in Kansas before I moved here to Washington.

"Anyway, I was staying with friends in Topeka for a few days, and I was driving back home. It was late at night. There wasn't a cloud in the sky—it gets very dark out there at night. Without all the city lights, you can see the Milky Way very clearly.

"But all of a sudden, out of nowhere, these clouds moved in. And there were these lights inside of them—it wasn't lightning, though. It's hard to explain. It was like floodlights, a ring of them, but hidden in the clouds. And it was like they were coming right at me.

"I turned off the route, down a side road, but it followed me..."

"The clouds?"

"Yes, and the lights, all of it. And then my car died. In the middle of nowhere, nothing but cornfields as far as the eye can see. And the lights—they came down just over the road. Still shrouded in those dark clouds, so I couldn't properly see where the light was coming from."

Martha paused, taking a deep breath and letting it out again.

"And that's all I remember. The next thing I knew, I woke up in my bed in the morning, and my car was parked in my driveway."

"Wait, I don't get it," said Sydney. "What happened out there? What were the lights? How did you get home?"

"I don't know," she said with a shrug. "Well, I think I know now, after researching this kind of phenomenon for all these years. But I can't remember any of it myself.

"What I know for sure is that I lost an entire day. It was late on a Monday night when I was driving home. But when I woke up in my bed, it was Wednesday morning."

"What were you doing between those times?" asked Sydney.

"I don't know—I have no memory whatsoever of anything that happened during that time period. I think I was abducted."

"Abducted? By whom?"

"Not whom. What."

Sydney only stared at her in confusion.

"I believe it was aliens," Martha told her. "I'm almost certain of it."

Sydney had heard stories about alien abductions before but had never given the idea much thought. And she'd certainly not considered it in light of the recent events and revelations surrounding the invasion.

"Go on," she said.

"Well, I spent a lot of time trying to reconstruct what happened. I drove back to the road where it all started. But there was no sign of anything strange happening there. Nothing at all.

"I was afraid to talk to the authorities, for fear that they would think I was crazy. I did go to my doctor for a complete checkup. I didn't say anything about aliens, but I told him there was an entire day I couldn't remember. He was no help. Said I was totally healthy, and there was no sign of trauma or anything."

"And you hadn't been drinking or anything? Nothing that would cause you to black out?"

"No, I didn't drink back then.

"But I started looking into it, and I discovered that I'm not the only one who's had an experience like this. There are *thousands* of people who have reported incidents just like mine."

"Thousands?"

"The first widely documented case in the U.S. was Betty and Barney Hill, back in 1961," said Martha. "But there were cases going back as far as 1954. There have been thousands since then, all over the world.

"And mostly, they're just like mine. People out in the middle of nowhere at night report seeing strange lights in the sky. Sometimes they can remember a spacecraft of some kind landing on the road. But almost nobody remembers anything beyond that. They all report missing time—some as much as two weeks.

"And then they wake up at home, or somewhere they'd normally expect to be as if nothing had happened. Except that they're missing time that they can't account for."

"You said *almost* nobody remembers anything else," said Sydney. "Some people do?"

"A few. And those people say for certain it was aliens. They describe beings who look very much like the aliens from the invasion. But these incidents date back decades, so I don't know how that could be possible if these Malor didn't show up until now."

"Well," said Sydney with a sigh, "they have been here before. They've been sending scout ships here for centuries. Trying to determine if our planet was ready to be processed to replenish their resources."

"Hmm, that might explain it," said Martha. "The thing is, the number of abductions has *skyrocketed* since the invasion. I've had reports from people all over the world these last several days."

"That's strange," said Sydney. "I'm not sure I understand why the Malor would be abducting people. Especially now—with the destruction of the mother ship, their technology has stopped working.

"Is it the Malor who are following you?"

"No, it's a man," she said, suddenly sounding more anxious again. "A man in a black suit. He follows me wherever I go."

"Wait—a *man in black*—like in that Will Smith movie?"

"They based the movie on this man, yes," said Martha. "But unlike in the movie, there's only one. And he doesn't make you forget—the forgetting happens on its own."

"Okay, so what does he have to do with anything?"

"I don't know," she said. "But abduction lore has mentioned him since at least the early 1970s. Many abductees who have tried to look into the phenomenon have reported being accosted by this man. He threatens them, tells them to stop their research, or great harm will come to them."

"He doesn't turn up during the actual abductions?"

"Not as far as I know," said Martha. "At least, I've never heard of that happening. He only seems to show up when people start nosing around too much. Like he's trying to cover it up."

"Has he threatened you?"

"Not yet," she said. "I've never actually spoken to him. But I've seen him. He's watching me. I've run away every time, but after this week, I see him more. I think I'm in danger."

"We should call the police," Sydney suggested. "Tell them what's going on."

"I've tried talking to the authorities," she said, rolling her eyes. "They won't listen. They think I'm a crazy old lady. I won't waste my time with them anymore."

"Then what do you want to do?"

She lifted her satchel from the floor and set it on the kitchen table.

"I want to give this to you. It contains interviews I've conducted in the last few months. Something is going on—something more than before. Since the invasion, the abductions have increased. And they're getting bolder—it's not just in remote areas anymore. I don't know why, but something's changed. They seem more urgent, more desperate now for some reason.

"I think the man in black is coming for me. Someone has to look into this and find out what they're up to. And I don't think I've got much time left. I don't want this information to be lost—someone has to help these people."

"I'll talk to my boss," said Sydney. "I think he'll be very interested in exploring this."

"Thank you," Martha replied, smiling for the first time.

They exchanged phone numbers, and Martha said farewell before departing into the night. Sydney tried once more to suggest calling the authorities, but the woman wouldn't hear of it. Sydney watched her disappear into the shadows. She looked around her backyard once but saw no one else.

Sydney sat at her table again and looked through the files in the satchel. Each one had a short bio about the victim, a photo, and a page outlining the events of their suspected abductions. The cases were all remarkably similar to Martha's, except that many were not in remote areas. In each case, the person was driving or walking late at night when they saw strange lights shrouded in dark clouds. They tried to get away, but the lights always followed them. And then they woke up in their beds, with no memory of what else might have happened, only to discover that they'd lost significant amounts of time.

Out of the twenty cases in the satchel, only one person recalled events after the initial encounter. He had described meeting aliens who looked very much like the Malor.

Sydney went back to bed, but it took her a while to get back to sleep. She couldn't stop thinking about the alien abductions. And one question bugged her the most: why were the Malor doing this?

Chapter Three: The Phone Call

Sydney woke up in the morning to find the news crews parked out in front of her house again. She made coffee and called Brian. He invited her to stop by his office in Bethesda so they could review what she'd learned from Martha. Sydney arrived later that morning.

"It's good to see you again so soon," he said with a grin, holding the door open for her. "Come in, have a seat."

The "office" could barely be called that—there was a table, not even a desk, with two chairs. Otherwise, the small room was completely empty.

"Kind of a minimalist approach for you, huh?" Sydney commented.

"Ah, yes, well, it had to do on short notice. I needed to be near Washington with everything that's happened. This was the best I could come up with. I'm staying at a hotel up the street."

"Oh—why didn't you tell me? You could stay at my place if you want—I've got a spare bedroom."

"Oh, no—I wouldn't want to impose."

"You wouldn't be, trust me. I could use the company—it's just my cat and me, and he's not much of a conversationalist."

"You are too kind, but I'll be alright. It shouldn't be too much longer now."

"Well, the offer stands, so let me know if you change your mind."

"Agreed," he said with a nod. "So, tell me—what have you got?"

Sydney told him all about her conversation with Martha and showed him the files she'd left her. He spent several minutes looking through each case.

"Hmm," he said finally, sitting back in his chair. "This is fascinating. I think you're right; any abductions that took place before the invasion could well have been their scout ships. But how can abductions possibly be spiking now that their tech has stopped working? Perhaps one or two rogue cells have figured out how to get things working again, but I daresay they'd be focused on their own survival now, rather than kidnapping the locals."

"I was wondering the same thing," Sydney agreed.

Brian thrummed his fingers against the table for a moment.

"This also begs the question, what is the point of the abductions? What are they doing with these people?"

"I've been wondering the same thing. Carl told us the scout ships have been coming here for centuries. Still, it was my impression they were evaluating our civilization's progress, waiting to see when we'd develop sufficiently to make our resources easy pickings for them. I didn't think they were interested in the *people* here for any reason."

"No, neither did I," said Brian, his brow furrowed. "That one man, who recalled parts of his abduction," he said, tapping on the files, "his description of the aliens he saw does match the Malor. But other than a physical exam, he doesn't recount much of what happened to him. I wonder if perhaps he remembers anything else that's not contained in this record—even small details could prove useful."

"She did say there are others who had memories of their experiences, too," Sydney pointed out. "He was the only one in this batch, but there were more."

"I believe this is worth investigating. Do you think you could arrange for me to meet this woman?"

"I think she'd be thrilled," Sydney replied. "She seemed desperate for someone to help. I've got her number; do you want me to call her now?"

"Yes, sure."

Sydney pulled out her phone and tapped Martha's number in her contacts. It went straight to voicemail. Sydney left her a message, asking her to call her back, and closed her phone.

"Keep me posted," said Brian. "We could meet here if that works for her, or I could drive out to Marlton—or wherever she lives, if that's easier."

Sydney drove home. The news crews accosted her on her way to the front door, but she ignored them. She went for a run—thankfully, the reporters didn't try to follow her—and then had some breakfast. Once she'd showered, she tried calling Martha again, but it went straight to voicemail.

She sat down at her desk and flipped open her laptop. She searched for information about alien abductions. Pages and pages of websites showed up.

Sydney found a page about Betty and Barney Hill—the couple Martha had told her about. Their abduction took place in New Hampshire in 1961. They'd been driving home from a vacation in Niagara Falls when a flying saucer followed them along a highway through the area around Franconia Notch. They'd reported seeing aliens in the craft's windows. Finally, the ship landed in the road in front of their car.

The Hills heard buzzing sounds and then entered an "altered state of consciousness." A period of time passed, and then they found themselves driving along a section of road dozens of miles from where they'd started, hours later, with no memory of what had happened or how they'd gotten there.

She found stories of other abductions going back to the mid-1950s. One man in Brazil was able to recall his time on the alien spacecraft. He reported a physical exam and a female alien having intercourse with him. Sydney rolled her eyes at this one—it sounded more like an erotic fantasy.

Nearly all of the stories she could find shared a few common elements. They all occurred at night, in remote areas. And in almost every instance, the abductees reported large amounts of missing time—hours or even days—and then waking up far away from where the encounter began.

She even found links to support groups for people who had been abducted. There was one that held monthly meetings only a few miles from her house.

Very few abductees could remember seeing the aliens. But they all described beings who looked remarkably similar to the aliens found at the 1947 Roswell crash in New Mexico—short and slender, with large, elongated heads, and protuberant black eyes: the Malor.

She read more about the man in black, too. From what Sydney could find on the internet, he'd been an element in the UFO stories for nearly as long as the abductions themselves. He only seemed to play a role, however, when someone tried to investigate the abductions. The garden variety abductee never seemed to report any kind of encounter with him.

Sydney tried calling Martha a few more times throughout the day but couldn't reach her, and she wasn't returning her calls. She sat up late reading about more alien abductions online but finally went to bed a little before midnight.

Only minutes later, her phone rang. It was Martha.

"Hello?"

At first, she could hear only heavy breathing. "Hello? Martha?"

She heard a scream.

"Martha? What's wrong? Are you there?"

"Sydney?"

"Yes, I'm here. Can you hear me?"

"I'm in trouble—it's the man in black..." she was panting—it sounded like she was running. "He's going to kill me! I'm so scared..."

"Where are you?" Sydney asked, getting out of bed.

Martha screamed again. It sounded like she'd dropped the phone.

"Martha?!"

"I can't get away—he's too fast!"

"Where are you?" she asked again.

"Alexandria... Harbor Park..."

"I'm going to call the police."

"NO! They won't help. I called them already—they said they're sending an officer, but they won't—"

The line went dead.

"Martha?!" It was no use—the connection was terminated.

Sydney tried calling her back, but it went to voicemail.

"Shit!"

Sydney threw on some clothes and ran out the door. She started her Explorer, tapped "Harbor Park, Alexandria VA" into her GPS, and sped off into the night.

It took her nearly a half hour to get there. It was a small park on the Potomac, just inside the Beltway, and within view of the destruction zone.

Sydney parked her truck and got out to have a look around. There was fog rolling in off the river, making it difficult to see very far. It was quiet here.

"Martha?" she called out, walking into the park. She made it to the river without seeing or hearing any sign of the woman. She tried calling her again, but she didn't pick up.

Suddenly, Sydney heard a scream. It was far off—to the north. She ran along the river toward the sound. The fog was so thick that she couldn't go too fast—she could see only a few yards in front of her.

Beyond the park, there were docks and warehouse buildings. She stopped short when she got to the first building and listened intently.

At first, she could hear nothing but the gentle lapping of waves on the shore. But suddenly she heard footsteps echoing off the buildings. It sounded like someone was running. Sydney ran toward the sound.

She stopped between two metal warehouse buildings and listened again. The footsteps had faded. But now she heard a scream.

"Martha?" she called out. She heard scuffling—it sounded like it was coming from around the corner.

Sydney dashed to the far edge of the building. Peering around the corner, she could see nothing through the dense fog. She moved to the end of the building and called out Martha's name again.

"Sydney?"

It was Martha. Her voice sounded weak. It echoed off the buildings, making it hard to tell where it was coming from.

"I'm here," yelled Sydney. "I can't see you—where are you?"

She heard only whimpering in response. She followed the sound, around another corner, and closer to the river.

But suddenly, she heard footsteps again, heels clacking loudly against the pavement. They were coming up behind her—and getting faster.

Sydney crouched down behind a large box truck and waited. The footsteps grew louder. Suddenly a man moved into her field of vision and stopped by the front of the box truck.

He was tall and thin, dressed in a black suit. And he was wearing dark sunglasses, despite it being a foggy night.

Sydney held her breath. This had to be the man in black. He looked around for a moment, then moved closer to the river.

Sydney peered out from behind the box truck. She couldn't see a thing.

But then she heard Martha scream again, much louder than before. The sound was cut off abruptly, and then she heard a whimper.

"Martha!" Sydney shouted.

She ran to the waterfront. Arriving at a dock, she stopped short. She could just make out a dark form at the end of the pier. She heard another whimper coming from that direction.

Sydney walked cautiously toward the end of the dock. As she got closer, it became apparent someone was lying there, face down.

She squatted down next to the form—it was Martha. Her eyes were closed. There was blood dripping down her face from a cut on her forehead.

"Martha?" said Sydney, gently grasping her shoulder.

Martha's eyes opened, and she sat up.

"Sydney? You found me?"

She sounded groggy as if she'd been asleep.

"Can you stand?" Sydney asked. "We need to get out of here."

Suddenly, Martha became much more alert. Her eyes went wide, and she looked around frantically.

"Where is he? Where did he go?"

"I don't know," said Sydney. "Can you get up?"

"Yes, I think so."

With Sydney's help, Martha got to her feet.

"Let's go!" said Sydney. They moved back to land, Sydney keeping one hand on Martha's arm to keep her steady.

Moving off the dock, Sydney heard footsteps again.

"Oh, no," she hissed. "Come on!"

She pulled Martha toward the nearest warehouse building. They crept along the wall, Sydney searching for somewhere to hide. There was a door midway down the wall. Sydney tried it, but it was locked.

They moved to the far end of the building and found another locked door. The footsteps pursued them relentlessly.

Sydney led Martha across an alley. There was an older brick building here. They moved around the far corner and found a rickety wooden door; it was locked.

"Screw it," said Sydney. She kicked the door as hard as she could. The wood cracked. She kicked again, and the door snapped open. Sydney led Martha inside.

It was dark inside, but not completely. This building looked like it had been abandoned for quite some time. They were in a large, open room that seemed to span most of the ground floor. Sydney could make out debris strewn about on the ground. She did her best to close the broken door, and then they moved to the far side of the room.

They found a staircase and climbed to the upper level. There was a long hallway, doors lining each side. Martha seemed to be gaining strength—Sydney suspected the adrenaline in her system was overcoming her grogginess.

Running to the end of the hall, they found an open door. They went inside, and Sydney closed the door. There were a desk and chair here—she took the chair and propped it under the door handle.

They hid behind the desk and listened.

Moments later, Sydney thought she could discern footsteps coming up the stairs.

"Crap."

Now she heard someone coming down the hall, a few steps at a time. The footsteps grew closer until they stopped right outside the door.

Sydney knew the chair wouldn't keep the man in black out for very long. They needed to get out of here.

She tried the door at the far end of the small room, but it was just a closet. Looking out the window, she saw there was a fire escape. She opened the latch, but the window wouldn't budge. By the looks of the place, the window probably hadn't been opened in years.

"Help me with this," she said.

Martha joined her, and together they were able to open the window enough for them to climb outside. Sydney followed Martha out onto the fire escape.

With the sound of the man in black banging against the door in the background, they made their way down the ladder. Dropping to the ground from the bottom rung, they dashed around the corner.

Sydney stopped and looked back around the edge of the building. She saw the man in black staring down at her from the window, still wearing his sunglasses.

"We need to move," she said. "If we can get back to my truck, we should be free and clear. Follow me!"

The fog was thinning now; this made running easier.

But once they'd reached the river and turned back toward the park where Sydney had left the truck, they stopped dead in their tracks. Standing in their path, a couple of blocks away, was the man in black.

"How the hell did he get in front of us so fast?" Sydney asked.

"I don't know," said Martha. "But we can't go that way!"

They ran back the way they'd come, Sydney leading the way. She zigzagged between buildings, running up one alley and down the next, hoping to lose their pursuer. But suddenly, they turned a corner and realized they could go no farther. They'd reached the destruction zone.

Sydney inhaled sharply, gazing out in terror at the sight before them: desolation as far as the eye could see.

"Let's move into Alexandria," she suggested. "There's nobody down here at night. But there are bound to be people out and about if we can get downtown."

Martha nodded in agreement, and they set out at a run.

But by the time they'd moved a couple of blocks, Sydney heard footsteps approaching at a run. They froze—the footsteps were coming from out in front of them.

"What the hell?!" Sydney yelled.

They turned down an alley and headed back toward the river again. But after rounding a corner, they found they'd reached a dead end.

"Crap!" said Sydney.

Martha was breathing hard. She seemed woozy and had to lean

against a building to steady herself. Footsteps echoed ominously off the façade.

"Are you alright?" asked Sydney. "We have to keep going!"

"I'll make it," Martha told her. "Just winded."

The door to the building was locked, but there was a window nearby. It slid open easily, and they climbed through. This was another warehouse building. They ran across the floor to the opposite side, opened a door, and emerged in another alley.

Sydney had lost her sense of direction. She led them along a route that she thought would take them back to the river, but she wasn't sure anymore.

But moments later, she saw a sight that sent a chill down her spine. The man in black was climbing down the face of a building on the next corner. There was no fire escape; he was moving down the brick wall like a spider.

"Oh, my God," she uttered, her eyes wide.

They turned to run the other way. But within moments, the man in black dropped out of the sky, landing in the road in front of them.

"Ladies," he said with a grin.

Chapter Four: Investigation

Sydney froze, staring at this man in shock.

"What are you?" she asked, using her own body as a shield to protect Martha from him.

The man in black only smiled in response.

Suddenly Sydney heard a buzzing sound. She felt herself growing woozy—her head was swimming, as if she'd had too much to drink.

Pinpricks of light started flashing around the man in black—she couldn't tell if she was imagining it or not. But the next moment, her vision went black, and she lost consciousness.

Sydney woke up. She was lying on the ground. It took her a few moments to remember where she was and what she was doing here.

But then she jumped to her feet, looking around frantically.

"Martha?!" she yelled.

She felt a sudden head rush—she'd risen too quickly. She had to drop to one knee for a minute.

Martha was nowhere to be seen or heard—and neither was the man in black. Sydney was alone.

She took a moment to get her bearings, then headed back toward her truck. As she was approaching the park, she heard a whimpering sound coming from one of the docks.

Running to the source of the sound, she found Martha, lying flat on her back on the boardwalk.

"Martha!" she yelled, dropping to her knees beside the woman.

She seemed to be only semi-conscious, muttering to herself, her words unintelligible. Sydney took in her appearance—she had cuts on her face and arms. Something had cut through her blouse and pants and opened numerous gashes on her torso and legs. She was bleeding everywhere, but not nearly as much as Sydney would have expected.

Her lips looked faintly blue, and her skin was cold to the touch. The blood loss didn't seem severe, but Sydney was worried.

"Martha, can you hear me?" she pleaded. "What happened to you? Where is the man in black?"

Martha's eyes fluttered open. Her pupils were dilated.

"Sydney..."

"I'm going to call 911," Sydney told her. "We need to get you to the hospital."

"No! Please, don't call them... useless, won't help." Her breathing was fast and shallow.

"I think you've gone into shock," said Sydney. "We need to get you to a doctor."

Martha didn't seem to hear her.

"You have to find... go there," she said. "San Juan... find him..."

"Find who?" asked Sydney. "Martha?"

But Martha had faded out of consciousness again.

Sydney pulled out her phone and dialed 911. She explained the situation and gave them her location.

"Hold tight, ma'am," said the person on the phone. "Help is on the way."

Sydney held Martha's hand. She was breathing, but erratically. Sydney felt her pulse—it was fast. She became more confident by the minute that it was shock.

Only a few minutes later, she heard a siren approaching. A police car pulled up, and the officer got out and approached her.

Sydney explained what had happened. She told him about the man in black chasing them, and her blacking out, omitting only the part about his ability to climb walls; she thought she'd sound crazy if she told him *that*.

"Alright," he said when she was done. "The ambulance is on its way."

"Hey, do you have a blanket?" she asked. "I think she's gone into shock. It would be best to try to warm her up. I'm a nurse," she added when he gave her a dubious look.

"Yeah, I've got one in the cruiser," he said. "Hang on."

He returned a minute later with a blanket. They covered Martha with it and waited for the ambulance.

It took only minutes. When the paramedics arrived, Sydney explained what had happened. They examined her and then moved her into the ambulance. Once they had her strapped in, Sydney climbed in the back with Martha, and they sped off.

When they arrived at the hospital, they took her straight into the emergency room. Sydney spoke to the woman at the front desk. She explained that she'd only met Martha recently and didn't have any information about her.

"I don't even know her last name," Sydney said apologetically. "Her first name is Martha, and I have her phone number. That's all I know."

Now, there was nothing to do but wait. Sydney took a seat in the waiting area and texted Brian to tell him what had happened.

"Which hospital?" he asked.

"Mount Vernon. It was the closest one not destroyed in the attack."

"I'll be right there."

Brian arrived twenty minutes later. Sydney gave him a rundown of the night in greater detail.

"Brian, this man in black, I don't think he's a *normal* man."

"But he's not Malor," he pointed out.

"No, definitely not, that's not what I meant. But how was he able to climb that wall? Jaden and Malia have telepathy and telekinesis—is it possible this man has similar powers?"

"I don't think so. I've seen the white paper about a device the military has experimented with that would give a soldier the ability to climb a wall in the way you described," he explained. "It's a kind of glove that uses thousands of hair-like filaments that exert an attractive force to the molecules in the brick wall. A soldier using these gloves can climb a wall—like a gecko."

"He wasn't wearing any gloves," said Sydney.

"Perhaps not by the time he got to you," Brian observed. "But my point is, there is tech that can give someone the ability to do the things you saw."

Sydney wasn't so sure. There was something about the man that seemed almost supernatural.

"What's his involvement?" asked Sydney. "Martha said he shows up when someone starts poking around these alien abductions. Intimidates them to try and stop them from investigating."

"Could be a government agent of some kind," Brian suggested.

"Working for the Malor?"

"With them, perhaps," he said. "Or it could be that the government is simply trying to keep people away from the Malor."

"But we didn't know about the Malor until very recently," she replied, "and stories about the man in black go back to the 1950s."

Brian nodded. "My guess is that some covert government agency has known about the Malor scouts at least since the Roswell crash. There have been stories about the government covering up evidence of UFOs. They certainly did that with the Roswell incident. This man in black could well be a government agent, aiding that cover-up. I'm sure it hasn't been the same man since the 1950s, of course. And despite the UFO lore, there are probably many of them."

The doctor came out then.

"Ms. Hastings?"

"Yes," she said, getting to her feet.

"I'm very sorry," he said. "We weren't able to save her."

"Wait—what? You mean... she's *dead*?"

"Yes, I'm sorry," he repeated. "Her wounds were too severe. The attack was remarkably precise—small puncture wounds in numerous areas, placed perfectly to damage internal organs."

"But there wasn't much blood," Sydney said in disbelief. "I thought the wounds were superficial."

"The attacker didn't hit any major veins or arteries," the doctor said with a shrug. "But the injuries were extensive."

Sydney turned to Brian and felt tears welling up in her eyes. She hadn't realized how badly Martha was hurt. Although she barely knew her, this loss felt devastating. She'd wanted to help, but in the end, had failed.

Brian saw the look in her eyes and pulled her into a hug.

They went to the front desk on their way out.

"She had no identification on her," the woman there told them. "Only her phone. But that's locked, and she didn't have any emergency contacts set up."

Brian handed her his card.

"I'll take care of the bill," he told her. "You can send me the invoice. And we'll find out who she was and notify her next of kin."

The woman thanked them, and they headed out of the hospital.

Brian offered to give Sydney a ride back to her truck.

"Oh, yeah, that would be great," she said.

"This man she wanted you to find—you don't know who he is?" he asked her as they pulled out of the parking lot. "The one in San Juan?"

"No idea. She hadn't mentioned him before."

"Alright," he said. "We've got some investigating to do. Why don't you meet me at my office in the morning, and we'll get to work."

"Your *office*?" she chided him. "You mean that empty box?"

"Yeah, yeah," he said with a grin.

He dropped her off at her truck, and Sydney drove home.

Once inside her house, she took extra care to make sure the doors were securely locked. She worried the man in black might show up *here*. Once she'd fed her cat, she went upstairs, stripped out of her clothes, and collapsed in her bed. It was already 3 a.m.—she wouldn't be getting much sleep this night.

Worse, she couldn't stop replaying the events of the night in her mind. She'd wanted so desperately to help Martha. It felt like the attacks on Miami and D.C. all over again—that feeling of powerlessness to stop people from dying.

It took a while, but Sydney did finally drift off to sleep. She woke up at dawn. Once she'd had some coffee and showered, she drove to Brian's office.

"Hey," he said by way of greeting as he opened his door. But then he added, with a look of concern, "you look awful."

"Aw, you sure do know how to charm a girl," she replied, taking a seat at his table.

"Did you sleep at all?" he asked, sitting across from her.

"A bit. I'll be alright."

"Okay," he said, opening his laptop. "I've found Martha. Her last name is McClure, and she lived in a house in the suburbs of Alexandria."

"You've got the address?"

He nodded.

"But before we proceed... we need to talk."

"About what?" she asked, her confusion showing on her face.

"I have felt terrible for putting you in so much danger to rescue Jaden and Malia," he began. "With the events of last night, it has become clear that I would be putting you in harm's way again if I were to ask you to pursue this. I have other people who can do the heavy lifting for us on this project."

"Not a chance," she said. "This is what you hired me for!"

"Yes, but I can't ask you to risk your life—"

"Listen. First of all, *you* didn't ask me to risk my life for the twins. I did that myself. I'm the one who thought to take them to your ranch in the first place. Nobody held a gun to my head, and I did everything I did of my own free will. Those kids were family to me—even though I'd had a falling out with Melissa, they were still family.

"And now this, with Martha—I *have* to do this. I felt so helpless on that Othali ship, standing by and watching while the Malor killed *hundreds of thousands* of people. This is different—I can *do something*. Martha's gone, but I can make sure she didn't die in vain. Something's going on here; somebody's abducting people against their will, for who knows what reason. And I can act to help stop it. This is what I signed up for—you're not putting me in any danger against my will; I'm taking this on freely."

Brian took a deep breath and opened his mouth to speak, but then stopped.

"Okay," is all he said.

"Good," she replied. "Now that that's settled... what do we do?"

"Ultimately, I believe our objective should be to determine *who* is abducting these people, and *why*. And to ascertain who the man in black might be and the nature of his role.

"It seems likely to me that the Malor are behind this. Reports from the abductees with some degree of recall seem to indicate this, and we know from our previous activities that the Malor have been visiting this planet for a very long time.

"It seems *unlikely*, however, that the Malor from the invasion are the ones behind the abductions. But I've begun to suspect that perhaps some of their scouts have been here all along, stationed here, maybe, on an ongoing basis, to monitor our progress, and do whatever it is they're doing with these abductions."

"Oh, that's interesting," said Sydney. "That would explain a lot!"

"Indeed," he agreed. "The trouble is that we have nothing to go on if we want to confirm this hypothesis. We have no information whatsoever.

"But Martha collected a *wealth* of information regarding the victims. And she wanted you to find someone in San Juan. There must be some significance to that—whom did she want you to find, and why? I am guessing that she interviewed an abductee from that city who provided some new and vital information.

"Therefore, I think the most logical starting point would be her house. Based on the files she gave you, it would seem she kept meticulous records. I'd like to get a look at whatever else she might have collected."

"Sounds like a plan," said Sydney, jumping up from her chair. "Let's go!"

Brian followed her out of the office with a chuckle.

"I was thinking we could have some breakfast first," he said.

"We can stop somewhere. You driving?"

They took Brian's Mercedes. After stopping at a Dunkin' Donuts drive-through for some food and coffee, they proceeded to Martha's house in Alexandria.

Brian parked on the street, and they walked up to the front door.

"Locked. Do we kick it in?" she asked uncertainly. Unlike when she'd done this in the warehouse district, it was a bright, sunny morning in a busy, residential neighborhood. Breaking and entering didn't seem like a great idea.

"No worries," Brian replied, pulling a key and a small mallet out of his pocket. He inserted the key in the lock, tapped it a few times with the mallet, and then unlocked the door.

"Uh... how in the hell did you do that?"

"Lock bumping," he said with a grin. "Ninety-five percent of all deadbolts in this country are susceptible to it. Let's go."

"Good to know," she murmured, thinking she'd be changing her locks as soon as possible. She followed him into the house.

"Someone beat us to it," Brian commented upon moving into the living room.

"Oh, my God," said Sydney, looking around the room.

Someone had ransacked the place. Dozens of cardboard boxes were lying around the area, their contents—hundreds of files—strewn about everywhere.

"What... a... disaster..." Sydney said, taking it all in.

They moved through the house and found more of the same throughout the first floor—in the dining room, the kitchen, and the hallway. Upstairs, they found a room Martha seemed to have been using as an office, and more files scattered about there.

Sydney picked up a file.

"Rachel from Sydney, Australia," she said, looking through the documents. "This was two years ago."

She picked up another.

"Anatoly from Moscow," she read. "Six months ago. Every one of these files represents an alien abductee she found and interviewed. There must be thousands here."

"I wonder if she had any of this stored electronically," said Brian. "Let's see if we can find a computer somewhere."

They searched the entire house but came up empty.

"Given the sheer volume of physical files we're looking at, I get the impression Martha was old-school when it comes to technology," Sydney suggested.

"Unfortunately, I would have to agree. And if she *did* have a computer, whoever got here before us has already taken it."

"Now what?"

"I'll have my people collect everything and compile it all in a database," he said. "That'll take a few weeks, I'm guessing, but it'll only need to be done once. Once it's stored electronically, we can sort through it much more easily."

"And in the meantime...?"

"Have you ever been to Puerto Rico?" he said with a grin.

"No, but I've always wanted to go!"

"Good. I'll make arrangements for you to fly there on my private jet."

"The only trouble is, what am I looking for? Where do I start?"

"Yes, we don't exactly have much to go on," Brian confirmed. "We could try to look through some of this, but finding a file for someone from San Juan is going to be like looking for a needle in a haystack. And there may very well be dozens of them from San Juan—were we lucky enough to find one, we'd have no idea if it were the right one."

"Yeah, screw that," said Sydney. Just the thought of having to go through this mess herself was giving her anxiety.

They left the house, locking the door behind them, and returned to Brian's car.

"Now we go from one haystack to another," said Sydney. "I've got to find someone in San Juan with critical information about the abductions. But I have no idea where to start."

"Exactly," he agreed. "And there are over 300,000 people in San Juan, last I knew."

"When I was researching abductions online, I found links to support groups," Sydney told him. "The ones I saw were around here, but I'm sure that's just because this is where I was when I ran the search. Maybe there's something similar down there."

"Good thinking," he said approvingly. "I'll arrange your flight for tomorrow morning! Let's meet at my office at nine, and go over some things, and then I'll drop you at the airport."

"Sounds like a plan!"

Chapter Five: San Juan

Back at her house, Sydney found the news crews waiting for her. She was getting used to this by now and studiously ignored them on her way inside. She spent a few hours researching UFO and abductee groups in San Juan. She found one Facebook group in particular that looked promising. It was a closed group, so she applied to become a member. She had to answer a couple of questions about her experience with UFOs and agree to their rules that prohibited ridiculing or judging people because of their stories.

What set this group apart was that the members met together monthly—in person. This was an excellent place for her to begin her hunt.

She started packing for the trip but abruptly realized that she had no idea how long she'd be gone. She texted Brian.

"As long as you need," came his reply.

"How helpful," she said out loud.

In the end, she packed enough for a week's stay. If she needed more than that, she was sure she could find a laundromat somewhere.

"And I'm definitely packing this," she said to herself, throwing her favorite bikini in the suitcase.

The next morning, she met Brian at his office.

"We should be good to go," he said as they sat at his table. "I've booked you a beachfront condo just outside the city."

"What, you mean you don't own any property in Puerto Rico?"

"Actually, I do…"

"Hah! I was *kidding*! How many houses do you have?"

"I've got this beautiful oceanfront villa down on the southeast shore… but it's a little far from San Juan."

"Well, the way I see it, you owe me a vacation, so once this job is done, you could always send me there!"

"Agreed," he said with a grin. "Now, check this out."

He turned his laptop so they could both see it, then opened a browser window with what appeared to be a satellite image.

"Google view of San Juan?" Sydney guessed.

"Oh, no," said Brian. He zoomed way in on a random street in the middle of the city, and Sydney could see people walking up and down the sidewalk.

"Wait—video? You have satellite *video*?"

"Yes, and unlike Google, this is live."

"Are you kidding me?"

"We did some work for a company that provides live satellite imagery to its clientele."

"Like who, exactly?" she asked. "Who would have the kind of money a service like this must cost? And what would they be doing with this?"

"Ah, well, that's part of their business model—no questions asked," he said, zooming back out. "Anyway, this is what I wanted to show you."

"What exactly am I supposed to be seeing?" she asked. He'd centered the image on Old San Juan, with the city's outskirts visible in all directions.

"It occurred to me that if our mystery man is from San Juan, then perhaps there might be some sort of alien camp there or something."

"Oh? Where is it—I don't see anything."

"Precisely," he said with a sigh. "I've analyzed the entire area—both in the visible and infrared wavelengths—and I cannot find anything that would be immediately identifiable as alien tech."

Sydney chuckled. "That's not exactly helpful."

"I know, but it does confirm that your idea of starting with the support groups is the best one," he said. "If there is something related to the Malor in San Juan, you're not going to find it with a ground search. Locating this man is, without question, your best path forward."

"Got it," she said with a sigh. "And here I was hoping you were about to tell me you'd found an alien base or something."

"Nothing so dramatic, unfortunately."

"Well, I'm off to a good start." She told him about the Facebook group she'd found. "I'm still waiting to be approved to join the group, but it seems like a good beginning."

"Yes, agreed," he said. "That's all I've got, but I also wanted to remind you to be careful. If this man in black shows up, we should pull you out of there."

"That's a good point," she observed. "He does show up when someone starts nosing around, and that's exactly what I'll be doing."

"Oh, before I forget," he said, reaching into his pocket and handing her a credit card. "It's in your name, but it goes to an expense account I've opened for you. Use it for everything—meals, drinks, whatever.

"The jet will remain stationed at the airport down there, so you can depart at any time. I'm sending you an e-mail that will include the address and phone number of the condo complex, as well as the pilot's name and number. And if you need anything while you're there, you have my number as well. Don't hesitate to use it."

"You got it, boss."

He drove her to the airport and introduced her to the pilot, Dave. Fifteen minutes later, they were in the air, headed to Puerto Rico.

Once they'd landed, and Dave had parked the plane in a private hangar, he accompanied her to the terminal.

"I'll be staying in the hotel here in the airport," he told her. "I'll have the plane gassed up and ready to go, so just call me when you're ready to leave. You have my number?"

"I do," she confirmed. "Thanks for the ride!"

Sydney called an Uber, and twenty minutes later, arrived at the condo. She checked in with the concierge and got her keys.

"You're on the ground floor, at the end of this hallway behind you," the woman told her.

"Great, thanks!"

Sydney found her unit, dropped her suitcase on the bed and went directly to the back patio.

"Yeah, I could get used to this," she said with a sigh.

The condo was right on the beach, affording her a sweeping view of the ocean. It was a public beach, but there were only a handful of people around.

Sydney was eager to get to work but decided it could wait a little while. She changed into her bikini, found a giant towel in the closet, and went out on the beach. After spending a few minutes diving into the ocean waves, she went back to sunbathe on her towel for a while.

She decided she needed to convince Brian to relocate his base of operations to the island.

"Okay," she said to herself once she'd returned to her room and showered. "Time to buckle down."

She grabbed her laptop and sat outside on the patio. Checking her Facebook account, she saw that she'd been approved for the private group.

They had a post about a meeting they were holding that same evening. It was to be held at a banquet hall in the city.

"Perfect," she said to herself.

She spent some time searching for more information about alien abductions in the area but widening her search to include the rest of the island.

This time, she found many accounts of UFO sightings and alien abductions throughout Puerto Rico. The place was a hotbed for this type of activity—she'd had no idea.

Sightings were particularly frequent in the El Yunque National Forest, and especially on the El Yunque mountain. There was no time today, but she decided she'd have to pay a visit to the forest and see if there was anything interesting there.

She shot Brian a text asking if he could get a look at that area with his satellite feed. He replied twenty minutes later that he couldn't see anything interesting there, either.

"But a visit may still be worthwhile—the foliage is so thick there that anything noteworthy on the ground wouldn't be visible to the satellite."

That evening, Sydney called an Uber and went into the city. She found the banquet hall without a problem. She was early, but there were about a dozen people here already.

A woman greeted her at the door, but in Spanish.

"I'm sorry," said Sydney. "I don't speak Spanish."

"It's your lucky night," the woman responded. "I speak English! My name is Sofia, and I'm hosting the event tonight. I don't think I've seen you before—is this your first time meeting our group?"

"It is," she said. "I'm Sydney, and I'm visiting from the mainland. I'm trying to find someone, but all I know about them is that they're in San Juan, and they've experienced an alien abduction."

"Well, you've come to the right place! Help yourself to some food, and we'll get started soon."

There was a buffet set up in the back of the room. Sydney filled a plate and sat down to eat. More people filed into the hall, and by the time they started, there were at least thirty people here.

They had chairs set up in a circle in the middle of the room.

Sofia announced that it was time to begin, and everyone took a seat. Sydney took the chair next to Sofia—she was hoping she'd be able to translate for her.

Sofia spoke to the group in Spanish; Sydney didn't understand a word. Thankfully, she repeated everything in English for Sydney's benefit.

"I reminded everyone that this is a safe space, that they can tell their stories with no risk of judgment or ridicule. And I let them know that we have a visitor from the mainland." Sydney felt herself blushing and gave a little wave to the group. "And I asked them who wants to go first," Sofia concluded.

A man across the circle raised his hand, and Sofia nodded to him. He spoke for a minute in Spanish.

"That is Felipe," Sofia whispered to Sydney. "He experienced an abduction three years ago. He was hiking in El Yunque. He'd gone in with a group, but he was separated and then got lost. The sun went down, and he tried to find the trail back out of the forest. But suddenly, there were bright lights on the path in front of him. He called out, but no one answered. He realized the lights were above the trees, a big circle of lights.

"Then he saw a figure silhouetted in the lights. It was short and thin, with a big head. That's the last thing he remembers. After that, he woke up at home, with no idea how he got there. Three days had gone by. His friends had searched for him in the forest every day but found no trace of him. He has no memory of where he went for those three days."

A woman spoke next.

"Her name is Alana," Sofia told Sydney. "She says that she has not had any experience herself with the aliens. But her family in Miami was killed in the invasion. She says that she was supposed to move there with her boyfriend and her baby daughter the week after the aliens destroyed the city. Now she has nobody left.

"She says she recognizes you—she's asking if you were the American woman who was on the friendly spaceship?"

"Oh," Sydney said with a start, her heart suddenly racing. "Y-yes, that was me. I was on the ship."

Alana spoke more rapidly now and seemed to be addressing Sydney directly.

"She is asking, isn't there anything you could have done to stop the attack?"

Sydney felt tears welling up in her eyes.

"We tried, oh my God, we tried, I begged them to fire on that ship... but they would have destroyed us, and then there wouldn't have been anyone to stop them... I'm so sorry..."

Sofia translated for her. Alana just shook her head and retook her seat, covering her face in her hands.

Another man spoke next, but Sydney noticed then that a man next to Alana was staring at her. He didn't seem like he was with Alana, and didn't look upset, but was very focused on her.

Sydney tried to turn her attention back to Sofia's translation of the next speaker, but she felt rattled now. Alana's plea had struck a nerve. She'd already felt guilty for being unable to stop the attack.

Meeting someone who had lost so much felt like having the wound torn open again.

The man who was staring at her spoke next. When he was finished, Sofia translated again.

"His name is Carlos. He says he also had an abduction experience that started in El Yunque. He went hiking there alone, at night, to go stargazing. He says the sky is very dark there, and it was a clear night. There was a light moving across the sky—he thought at first that it was a satellite. But then it grew brighter, and larger, and moved very rapidly toward him. When it came in close, dark clouds gathered around it, and he could see that there were multiple lights arranged in a circle. He ran, but it followed him. Suddenly, a beam of light came down from the center of the object, like a spotlight, and he found himself rising into the air. He passed inside what looked like a giant flying saucer. But he cannot remember anything after that. He says he woke up the next morning, on the top of the mountain. At first, he thought he must have been dreaming. But then he read about other people who had had similar experiences."

A few more people spoke, and then Sofia asked Sydney if she wanted to address the group.

"Yes," she said, trying to compose herself. "I am looking for someone, a man, who may have had an abduction experience. I don't know his name, but I know he's from San Juan. He would have spoken with an American woman named Martha McClure. She spent many years investigating alien abductions, but she was killed recently. Before she died, she told me I needed to find this man here in San Juan. Whoever he is, there's a good chance he has critical information about the abductions. There may be something about his experience that is different in some way from what most people have experienced, but I can't say for sure. I'm hoping one of you might be that man, or maybe could lead me to him if he's not here."

Sofia translated her words to the group. Carlos was still staring at Sydney.

Sofia finished, but nobody spoke up. Many people shook their heads or shrugged their shoulders, but not one person was able to help.

Sydney felt her heart sink. Somehow, she'd imagined that her mystery man would just show up here, but it would not be so easy.

"Why don't we exchange numbers," Sofia suggested. "Everyone here has my number—I'll let them know that they can contact me if they think of anyone who might be able to help you."

"Thank you, that would be great," she said. She pulled out her phone; Sofia gave Sydney her number, and Sydney sent her a text so she'd have hers.

Sofia told the group what she had suggested.

Several more people spoke, and then the group broke up for the night. Sydney caught an Uber back to the condo.

She went out for a walk on the beach to clear her head. Being confronted by Alana had shaken her up. It had stirred up all the emotions from the attack. She couldn't help but imagine all the other people out there who had been impacted by the invasion the same way Alana had.

Sydney decided she didn't want to be alone tonight. Walking a little farther up the shore, she found a beachside bar. It wasn't too crowded, but there were several people here.

"Perfect," she said to herself, taking a seat on one of the stools. She ordered a piña colada. The bartender set it in front of her a few minutes later—in a pineapple.

"Hah," Sydney said, "I love it!"

Taking a sip of her drink, she turned to look out at the ocean—and her heart almost stopped. Strolling up the beach toward her was Carlos, the man from the meeting who had been staring at her.

She turned back toward the bar, trying to decide what to do. But he took a seat right next to her and ordered a beer. Sydney stared pointedly away from him.

"I think I might know the person you're looking for," the man said.

Sydney turned slowly to face him.

"How did you find me here?"

Carlos paused for a moment but then said, "I followed you."

Sydney didn't know how to answer this. This man didn't *seem* threatening, but following a woman home like this wasn't precisely innocent behavior, either.

"Why would you do that?"

"As I said, I think I know who you're looking for. I think it might be my boss. But he's a very private man, and I do not think he would have appreciated it if I'd spoken about him in front of so many people."

"Sofia has my number. You could have asked her to contact me for you."

"True," he acknowledged. "But I guess I wanted to meet you, as well."

"Oh?"

The bartender served him his beer.

The man took a sip and turned back to Sydney.

"I'm Carlos, by the way," he said.

"I remember," she said. "Sydney."

"That woman who asked you about stopping the attack... that wasn't right. I saw what that ship did to the city. There's no way anybody could have stopped that. I'm no scientist or military genius, but it was obvious to anyone watching on television that those aliens were way more powerful than we are. Or those other aliens. I know you couldn't have done anything."

"Well, I certainly appreciate that," she replied, taking a long drink. "I guess I should have expected it, but I didn't think I'd ever meet someone like that. Someone who had lost loved ones in the attack, I mean."

"I'm surprised it hasn't happened before," he said. "You're all over the news these days. You and those two kids."

Sydney had been avoiding the news like the plague, but she figured she shouldn't have been too surprised. Those news crews were pretty much living on the street in front of her house now.

"Tell me about your boss," she said.

"Well, I cannot say much until he authorizes me to do so. He is wealthy and powerful, and while I know the story, tales of alien abductions carry a certain stigma, no? It is not the type of thing he would want to be associated with him in the public's mind."

"Oh, I get it," Sydney said with a knowing smile. "He's worried about his reputation. Well, since the invasion, it would seem to me that stories about aliens and UFOs are no longer regarded the way they once were."

"Perhaps," he conceded. "But it is not my place to make that decision for him. I will speak to him on your behalf and see if he would be willing to meet you. Then he can tell you his story himself."

"Fair enough," she said with a nod.

"So, tell me. What is *your* story? Why are you involved with this?"

"It's like I said at the meeting," Sydney said, taking a sip of her drink. "I met a woman who spent her life investigating these abductions. She came to me for help—she knew someone was after her. And her dying request was that I find this man in San Juan. So, here I am."

"And so that's it, you're doing this because of a stranger's dying wish?"

"No, I guess it's more than that. I mean, I was already involved, right? With everything that happened in the invasion. I mean, I know how powerful the Malor are. But to be standing there on the bridge of the Othali ship, forced to watch as they destroyed entire cities... I don't like feeling helpless."

"And so, taking on this investigation provides a way to take action."

"Yeah, exactly."

Carlos nodded his understanding.

"I will speak to my boss. I believe he will be very interested in meeting you—privately and discreetly. And in the meantime, could I interest you in a hike through El Yunque? I could show you where my abduction took place."

"Yes, I would be very interested in that," she replied, surprised by the invitation.

They exchanged phone numbers and agreed to meet the following morning.

"Good night, Carlos," she said with a smile before heading back to the condo.

"Good night," he replied. "I'll see you in the morning."

Chapter Six: The Boss

Sydney went back to her condo but was too wired to go to bed yet. She lay out on the beach for a while, gazing at the stars and listening to the ocean waves crashing onto the shore.

Carlos seemed like he was attracted to her romantically. And she had to admit that attraction was mutual. He was "tall, dark, and handsome"—definitely her type. She'd felt butterflies in her stomach when they were at the bar as if this were some high school crush.

Sydney hadn't been involved with anyone—seriously, at least—for a couple of years, and she preferred it this way. She cherished her independence and did not want to feel "tied down" to anyone. There was no way she was interested in a "relationship," but hell, she decided, a little fling in paradise couldn't hurt. She'd just have to make her intentions clear.

She slept well that night and woke up in time to take in a breathtaking sunrise over the ocean. After a little breakfast and coffee at a nearby café, she showered and got dressed for her outing with Carlos.

At nine o'clock, she met him out front.

"Good morning, sunshine," he said with a big grin.

"Hey!"

"I was thinking, how would you feel about a little, ah, adventure before our hike today?"

"I don't know; what have you got in mind?"

"It's a surprise—follow me!"

"Alright, then," she said, and they set off down the road.

"I sent my boss an e-mail, by the way," he told her.

"Oh?"

"He said he would think about it and let me know," he said. "But I think he'll go for it. I told him you've been investigating the abductions. He knows I had an experience, too, so we've discussed it before. My guess is that he'll agree to a meeting, as long as you're willing to share information with him, too. I know he's very curious about what happened to him."

"Of course," Sydney agreed. "I don't know very much yet, but I'm certainly willing to share the info I have so far."

"Excellent."

They walked only a few blocks from the condo and came up to a business located on the docks. Sydney's jaw dropped when she read the business sign.

"You're joking!"

"You're not scared, are you?" he chided.

"Hell no, I'm game—I've always wanted to go for a helicopter ride!"

They went inside, and Carlos purchased two tickets for a helicopter tour of El Yunque. Minutes later, a bus picked them up and took them to the airport. They met the pilot and boarded the aircraft with two other couples.

"I did this once a few years ago," Carlos told her. "You're in for a real treat!"

"This is awesome! I'm so excited!"

The pilot made sure everyone was strapped in, went over the safety guidelines, and a few minutes later, they were in the air.

They flew along the coast, past dozens of pristine beaches, on their way to the forest. When they turned inland, Sydney could make out El Yunque mountain looming ahead, in the middle of the trees.

The pilot narrated for them throughout the tour, pointing out all the various flora and fauna in the forest. Sydney learned that El Yunque was the only tropical rainforest in the United States. The chopper took them over the forest and came in close to a couple of dazzling waterfalls. They made a loop around the mountain peak before finally returning to San Juan.

"That was exhilarating!" Sydney told Carlos once they'd disembarked from the helicopter. "What an amazing way to see the rainforest!"

"I had a feeling you'd like it," he said.

They took the bus back to the dock and then caught another bus down to the forest entry. Setting out along the trail, Carlos pointed out some of the exotic birds as they hiked. They passed numerous other hikers going both ways on the path. It took about two hours to make it to the peak.

There was an observation tower, and they climbed to the top of that. Only a few other people were up here. Looking out, Sydney could see across the rainforest, all the way to the sea.

"This is beautiful," she said, beaming at Carlos.

"It is. I'll never come here again at night, though."

"I don't blame you! So where were you, exactly, when you spotted the UFO?"

"Right down there," he said, pointing to the ground. "I was lying on my blanket, gazing up at the sky. I first saw the light when I thought it was a satellite, over there," he added, pointing to the northwest. "When it came closer, I ran down that same path we just hiked to try to get away from it."

Sydney looked all around, but there was nothing here to indicate anything strange had ever taken place. She wasn't sure what she'd expected, but whatever it was did not exist here.

"I read online that this area—the forest, in particular, has had a tremendous amount of UFO sightings over the years," Sydney told him.

"I've heard that, too," he agreed. "But that one time was the only experience I've ever had."

They took in the panorama for a moment, and then Sydney found him standing much closer to her. She turned to face him and had to look up into his eyes because he was so much taller. Her butterflies kicked into high gear again.

"I was wondering," he began hesitantly, "if you have a boyfriend back home. I don't see a ring, so I presume you're not married?"

"No, definitely not married," she said, rolling her eyes. "And I'm an eligible bachelorette, to answer your first question."

Carlos sighed with relief, and his grin broadened. He moved in to kiss her, but Sydney pulled away.

"Listen, I'm only here for a short while, and I'm not too keen on the long-distance relationship thing..."

"Okay," he said, suddenly looking more serious but waiting for her to say more.

"Just wanted to throw that out there," she added, feeling awkward now.

"No, that's cool," he said, "I don't have any expectations."

"Good," she whispered and leaned in to kiss him.

Carlos held her in his arms and kissed her passionately. Sydney spared only a moment's thought for the other people at the top of the tower, throwing herself into the moment.

"I've wanted to kiss you since the moment I saw you at the hall that night," he said.

"Ah, so *that's* why you were staring at me," she chided.

"I was *not* staring!"

"Oh yes, you were—I was afraid you might be an ax murderer or something!"

They both chuckled at that, then kissed again.

Once they'd taken in the view for a few more minutes, they climbed back down the tower. They strolled around the peak, and Sydney again kept her eyes open for anything odd about the place. Nothing stood out, though—the view was beautiful, but there was nothing here to suggest any kind of unusual activity.

They hiked back down the trail—more quickly than they'd gone on the way up, and caught a bus back to San Juan. It had been a long day, and sunset was upon them. Carlos walked her back to her condo.

"So, uh... do you want to come in?" she asked with a smile.

"Ah, I'd love to, but unfortunately, I'm busy tonight," he replied apologetically.

"Going to see your other girlfriend?" she asked teasingly.

"No, no—nothing like that. I have to work tonight. But I *will* follow up with my boss and try to get you your meeting."

"Alright, sounds good," she said. "Call me tomorrow."

"I will," he replied.

They kissed, and then Carlos headed off into the city.

Sydney went inside. She changed into her bikini and went for a swim in the ocean, unable to stop thinking about Carlos. After that, she showered, ordered some take-out, and lay out on the patio until it was time to pick up her food. As she ate, she thought again that she might just have to convince Brian to relocate down here.

Sydney woke in the morning to the sound of her phone chiming. She had a message from Carlos.

"My boss has agreed to meet you!" it read. "Can you be ready in an hour?"

"Absolutely," she typed back.

She jumped out of bed, ran to the neighborhood café for a bagel and some coffee, and then got ready.

By the time Carlos arrived, she was already out front waiting for him. But this time, he'd come in a limousine.

"Well, this is a little more upscale than the city bus," she said, as he emerged from the back of the car.

But Carlos wasn't smiling.

"I'm so sorry about this," he said, worry marking his features.

"What...?" she asked.

But at that moment, two more men stepped out of the vehicle. They were huge—standing even taller than Carlos, they looked like bodybuilders. One of them grabbed her, pulling her arms behind her back.

"What the hell!" Sydney yelled, trying futilely to escape his viselike grip.

The second man bound her wrists with a zip tie and then threw a hood over her head.

Sydney screamed; it did no good. They stuffed her roughly into the car.

She heard the doors slam shut, and the tires screeched as the limousine drove away.

"What the hell are you doing?!"

One of the men shouted at her in Spanish.

"Hey—you don't talk to her like that," someone replied. It was Carlos. "I'm so sorry for this," he said again. "I didn't realize they were going to do this. My boss said he would meet you, but I guess he wants to keep his location a secret. I promise you'll be perfectly safe..."

"I was right—you are an ax murderer!" she screamed, struggling against the zip tie.

"No, I swear—my boss only wants to talk to you. I was right; he is very interested in learning anything you might know about these abductions. But you have to understand... he's not your normal kind of guy. He is very private. He cannot risk you disclosing the location of his compound to anyone—"

"Nobody I know would *give a shit*," she shouted. "If you'd asked nicely, I would have agreed to be blindfolded. But *Jesus*!"

One of the other men yelled loudly in Spanish again. Carlos hollered back at him, also in Spanish.

"What the hell was that about?"

"Nothing, listen, if you'll just settle down, I promise, nobody is going to hurt you."

Sydney took a deep breath, trying to calm down.

"I'll tell you what," she said. "Untie my damn arms, and I'll keep the hood on and come along quietly."

"You have to swear to it," he told her. "If you try to take the hood off, I don't know what these guys will do."

"Fine, I swear. I'll keep the stupid hood on—but untie me, *now*!"

"Okay, stay still."

She felt his hands on her, pulling her away from the seat. Suddenly, her hands were free. She immediately started punching any part of him she could find.

"Ow! Stop!"

He grabbed her wrists and stopped her from hitting him anymore.

"*Let go!*"

"Promise you'll stop punching me!"

"Fine."

He released her, but she punched him one more time before sitting back in the seat.

"I'll settle up with you later," she told him. "But you'd better realize you've destroyed your chances with me."

"I know. I'm sorry."

She sat quietly for the rest of the ride, wondering where they were taking her. But it did not seem like the men in the car with her, at least, intended her any direct harm. She had to wonder what awaited her at their boss's compound, however.

Sydney could feel the vehicle taking sweeping turns to the left and right. And her ears popped a few times as well—wherever they were going, it was up in the hills somewhere.

They rode in silence the rest of the way. Finally, the car came to a stop. She heard the doors open, and suddenly the man with the viselike grip was pulling her out through the door by one arm.

"Can I take the damn hood off now?" she demanded.

One of them removed it for her. Sydney found herself standing in front of an enormous mansion, with a dazzling view of the ocean. She was right; they were up in the mountains somewhere. The view was at least as picturesque as the one they'd enjoyed from El Yunque the other day.

"This way," said Carlos, leading her toward the mansion. The two henchmen followed close behind.

They walked into an open foyer, with floors of marble and columns flanking a grand staircase to the upper level. Carlos led them off to the left, down a hallway, and into what appeared to be a library. The room had cathedral ceilings, and bookshelves lined three of the four walls, with rolling ladders to provide access to the books on the upper shelves.

The far wall was made up entirely of glass walls and doors and boasted a fantastic ocean view.

"If you'll have a seat, my boss will be with you in a moment," said Carlos. He left the room, taking the henchmen with him, and closing the door behind him. She heard a click that she was pretty sure meant he'd locked it. She gave it a moment, then tried the door handle.

Sure enough, it was locked.

She crossed the room and tried one of the doors facing the ocean—that wouldn't open, either. They'd trapped her in here.

Sydney took a deep breath and let it out slowly.

"Probably the finest prison in the whole world," she muttered to herself.

She walked around the room, scanning some of the books on the shelves. There were works about history, archaeology, physics, astronomy, art—and hundreds of fiction titles. Some of the books looked very old. Whoever had amassed this collection clearly had a love of books—not just of reading, but of the physical books themselves.

Sydney was about to pull an ancient-looking tome from a shelf when she heard a door open across the room. A man walked in, closing the door again behind him.

He was about her height and older—she guessed he must be in his sixties, at least. His body was lean, and his head was balding. He wore white linen pants and a white button-down shirt of the same material. There was a vigor to him as he walked toward her.

"Greetings," he said without smiling. "Sydney, I presume?"

"Yes," she replied, staying where she was. He did not tell her his name.

"Come, join me," he said, taking a seat at a table in the middle of the room.

Sydney hesitated for a moment before sitting down adjacent to him at the table.

"I must apologize for the manner of your transit here," he said. "But I value my privacy very highly. I will not risk giving anyone the ability to violate my sanctuary.

"Tell me... for whom do you work? A government agency, perhaps? Law enforcement?"

"No, nothing like that," she said. "Private sector."

Sydney was no privacy nut but knew that telling him the nature of the work Brian's company did wouldn't win her any points here.

"I see. What industry?"

Sydney sighed.

"No industry, per se. My boss is quite wealthy, and independently so. He chooses to spend his time exploring things that interest him. I assist him in that capacity."

"Hmm. A kindred spirit, then."

Sydney highly doubted that but said, "It would seem so."

The man regarded her for a moment, then said, "I have seen you, have I not? On the television?"

"Ah, yes. I'm sure you probably have."

For the next few minutes, he asked her about her involvement in the events surrounding the invasion. Sydney held nothing back. She wanted to find out whatever this man could tell her, and it cost her nothing to give him the whole story.

"And what, now, is your involvement with these, ah, abductions?"

"That work is only in its beginning stages," she said. She told him about Martha showing up in the middle of the night, about the man in black, and Martha's dying request.

The man considered everything she'd told him for a minute.

"I have not encountered this man in black," he told her finally.

"What about Martha? Her full name was Martha McClure. Did you ever meet her or talk to her?"

"No. I have never heard of this woman before."

"Has anyone ever interviewed you about your experiences before?"

"Never. I have discussed it with Carlos, but only because he came to me and told me about something similar happening to him. But never have I spoken to anyone else about it."

"But you have been abducted?"

Again, a pause.

"Yes. Three times."

"*Three* separate times?"

He nodded.

"Where? How did it happen?"

"The first and third times took place on the way here, late at night."

Sydney thought about this for a moment.

"Did your driver see anything?"

"I do not always travel by limousine. Both times, I was driving myself. The third time was on the other side of the world. I was on holiday in Tahiti, walking along a beach, alone, in the middle of the night.

"In all three instances, it happened the same way. First, I saw a light in the sky that resembled a shooting star, except that it lasted much longer. And then the light stopped moving. It grew brighter and came in much closer to my location.

"The first time, I had no idea what was happening. I drove faster, trying to outpace the—whatever it was. I failed. Suddenly, my car simply died. It stopped; I could not start it again. The lights went out. And that is when they took me.

"When I encountered this phenomenon the second time, I knew precisely what was about to happen. And I understood that trying to run would be futile. So instead, I hid. There were rock formations along the beach on the island where I was staying. I crawled inside a hollow section of one of these formations—a cave, you might say. Yet that proved to be futile as well.

"And then the third time, knowing any attempt at escape to be entirely useless, I surrendered. I stopped my car, walked out on the road, and allowed the inevitable to transpire.

"On all three occasions, as the craft drew closer, dark clouds engulfed it. The light I had seen from far away turned out to be a ring of lights, seen up close only through those clouds.

"Once the vessel had positioned itself directly above me, a beam of light shot out from its center and lifted me into the air, and inside the ship."

"And do you remember anything that happened after that?" asked Sydney.

"Oh, yes. Not everything; when I first entered the vessel, I did lose consciousness for a time—I cannot say how long. This happened all three times. And when I woke, I found myself in some sort of lab. I was lying naked on a metal table. It was cold. I was not restrained by any bonds, yet I could not move."

"Did you see anyone—or any*thing*?"

"No. I am aware that some people who have experienced this phenomenon have reported seeing beings like the ones responsible for the attacks. However, I saw no such thing. I saw no one at all.

"They performed a physical examination each time, but there was no living being administering the exam—or, none that I could see. I believe they were examinations, anyway. There were metal probes that hovered into view—some remained above me—what it was they did, I could not tell. But others physically touched me. One here," he said, tapping his forehead. "Another here," he added, tapping his chest. "Others, well, I would prefer not to describe it in too much detail. Suffice it to say, others were rather more, ah, *invasive*."

"Oh, dear," said Sydney.

"Yes."

"And these exams, do you know how long they lasted?"

"Hours, I believe. It is hard to say for sure. Each time, I did eventually lose consciousness again, only to find myself back where

I had started, fully clothed. The first time, I woke up sitting in the driver's seat of my car. Someone or something had pulled the car off to the side of the road.

"The second time, I woke up on the beach, roughly a kilometer from where I had started, lying on my back on the sand.

"And the third time, I awoke in my bed. The car I had been driving was parked safely in my garage, though I cannot say how it might have arrived there."

"And when did these abductions take place?"

"The first was soon after I purchased this home, so let me see, perhaps twenty years ago. The second time was last winter. And the third only two nights ago."

"Two nights ago?! After the invasion."

"Yes, that is correct."

"And you saw nobody, no kind of life form during any of the abductions?"

"Certainly not."

"Do you know where you were during the abductions? Did they take you somewhere, or were you in the ship the entire time?"

He thought about this for a moment.

"I have assumed I was in the ship the whole time, but now that you ask this, I realize I do not know for sure. Each time, as I first entered the ship, I could see only metal walls around me, and I was in some sort of cavity or room. But I blacked out all three times at that moment.

"Each time I woke up in a chamber with metal walls, but this time there were other tables around me and instruments of some kind on the walls. I could not see the ceiling—it was only black. And there were no windows or doors that I could see.

"The metal walls looked identical to the ones surrounding me when I first entered the ship, so I guess that is why I have always assumed I was inside the vessel during the examinations as well. But I realize now that I cannot say so for sure."

Sydney found this fascinating—it was the first time she'd spoken with anyone who could recall any details of their ordeal beyond the initial contact.

"Can you remember anything else about your experiences?"

"No. Nothing. Only the exams. And then waking up again where I belonged."

"And you weren't missing any time on any of these occasions?"

"What do you mean by *missing time*?" he asked.

"For some of the abductees I've read about, when they wake up back home, they realize that days have passed for which they cannot account. Time has gone by, but they have no memory of what might have happened."

"I had no such experience. Each time, I woke up where and *when* I would have expected.

"I think, though, that we are done here. Unless you have any other questions?"

"Not that I can think of," said Sydney. "Could we exchange phone numbers—if anything else comes to mind, I could contact you..."

"No. That will not be possible. I wish never to see you or hear from you again. Have a pleasant day."

And with that, he got to his feet and strode from the room. Sydney understood her meeting to be over.

Chapter Seven: Ransacked

Sydney rode back to her condo in the limousine with Carlos and the two henchmen. This time, she wore the hood, but they did not attempt to bind her.

Carlos removed her hood when they arrived. Sydney opened the door and got out without saying a word. Carlos came after her.

"Will I see you again?" he asked.

She rounded on him, finally unleashing her pent-up fury.

"How can you even ask me that?! Like your boss said to me, I never want to see you again! You kidnapped me! My first impression of you was the right one—you *are* some sort of ax murderer—or rapist!"

"No, I'm not—I swear! This was not my decision—it wasn't up to me! I had no idea they would treat you like that! My boss agreed to meet you, and I thought—"

"Oh, give me a break! When the two goons got in the limo with you to come here, what did you think they were coming for? A little joyride?"

"Well, no, I mean by then I figured—"

"Yeah, by then, it was *obvious* what was about to happen, and you did nothing to warn me, nothing to try and stop them!"

"Sydney, I'm sorry—"

"Yeah, you *are* sorry. Because now you're never going to see me again, and that's *your* loss. Tell me, though, what exactly is it that your boss does? What is it that *you* do for that matter?"

"Oh, uh... you mean he didn't tell you?"

"Let's see—nope! He didn't even tell me his name, much less what he does. That place where he lives, that's gotta be worth what, three million, at least? Four million? What kind of business is he involved in that makes that kind of money? And sending his henchmen here—what kind of businessman has hitmen on the payroll, huh?"

"I could tell you, but you're not gonna like it..."

"Yeah, it's pretty obvious, isn't it? What is he, a drug dealer? Organized crime boss?"

Carlos's discomfort was growing by the moment—it seemed like he might squirm right out of his clothes.

"You might be on the right track..."

"Uh-huh. Okay, I figured. And what do *you* do for him, precisely?"

Carlos said nothing and would no longer look her in the eye.

"You know what, never mind. Forget it. I don't *want* to know. Go crawl back under whatever rock you came from. And don't ever try to contact me again."

She turned her back to him and headed toward her door.

"Aren't you overreacting, maybe just a little?"

Sydney rushed back over to him, stood on her tiptoes, and got right in his face.

"*Overreacting*?" she screamed. "I worked as a hospital nurse for most of my life. Do you have any idea the nightmares I've seen? The destruction I've witnessed firsthand that comes from people like you and your boss? You peddle your drugs and get rich off other people's misery and desperation. Kids—that shit you sell ends up in the hands of kids who get hooked young and then can't ever quit.

"Forget it, I'm not wasting another minute on scum like you," she said, backing away, looking at him in disgust. "I can't *believe* I was attracted to you. I was ready to *sleep* with you! Thank God that didn't happen."

"Sydney..."

"No, that's it. I'm done. Go away."

And with that, she went inside the condo and slammed the door behind her.

She kicked off her shoes and collapsed in her bed. Moments later, she heard the limousine diving away.

It was only lunchtime, but she decided she needed a drink—or three. She walked up the beach to the waterfront bar she'd found earlier in the trip.

"Hey," she said, recognizing the bartender from last time as she sat on one of the stools. "I'll have one of those piña-colada-in-a-pineapple deals you made me last time, please."

"You got it, senorita!" he said with a grin.

The guy at the other end of the bar tried to pick her up while she was waiting for her drink.

"Sorry, pal, but I'm in no mood."

He left the bar.

"Here you go," said the bartender, pushing the pineapple toward her.

"Awesome, thank you. I'll be wanting another in a few minutes, just to forewarn you."

"Coming right up," he said with a chuckle.

Sydney turned to face the water and took a long drink. What a day she was having.

It was clear Carlos's boss was *not* the person Martha wanted her to find. But he sure had given her some things to think about.

Every single report she'd found prior to this where the person had any recall of events beyond the initial abduction included a description of aliens who looked precisely like the Malor. But this man claimed there had been *no one* present.

His memory seemed clear enough—he recalled the probes they'd used in great detail. But no aliens. At least, none that he could see.

Sydney tried to figure out what to do next. This seemed like a dead end, though. Martha had given her virtually nothing to go on—a man in San Juan. That's all she knew for sure. She *assumed* it would be someone who had been abducted and someone whom Martha had interviewed. But she didn't truly know any of that for sure.

What the hell was she supposed to do next?

She finished her second drink and then called Brian.

"Hey, kid, what've you got?"

"*Kid?*"

"Oh, sorry, I didn't mean anything by it—I'm just, well, I'm *old*—"

Sydney laughed.

"You're what, ten years my senior? Forget it. You can call me 'kid.'"

"Okay, well... how are you?!"

Sydney told him everything that had happened with Carlos and his boss and about the boss's abductions.

"Sydney, do you remember when we talked about *not* putting you in danger?"

"I know, I know—but we got some really good info from this guy. He's not the one Martha wanted me to find, but I'd say we're net positive from this trip so far, right?

"I just have no idea what to do next."

"Hmm."

"I was kind of hoping you'd have some incredible insight into my next avenue of investigation..."

There was only silence on the line for a moment, then Brian chuckled.

"I'm sorry, but I don't. My team is plowing through all that data entry, and I've got them keeping their eyes peeled for anyone with some kind of connection to Puerto Rico, but so far, nothing."

"Damn. Well, I'm gonna have another piña colada," she said, looking pointedly at the bartender, "get good and hammered, and see if inspiration strikes."

"Alright," he said. "Have one for me. And let me know if you need anything."

"Will do, boss."

Sydney spent most of the day on the beach, swimming, sunbathing, and making frequent stops at the bar to keep her buzz going.

"I'm going to have a raging hangover after this," she said to herself. "But it's so worth it!"

Three different guys tried picking her up through the course of the day, but she turned them all away. It was too bad—one of them was very cute, but she had no interest in hooking up after the morning she'd had.

As evening approached, she found she was ravenously hungry. She'd seen signs for "food kiosks" a little farther up the beach—it didn't look like much in the photos but had rave reviews.

Sydney went inside to change and then headed out to find the place. It was a beautiful day, so she decided to walk. Twenty minutes later, she arrived to see more than sixty "stalls," each offering some type of local cuisine. Sydney sampled food from several of them and had a couple more piña coladas to wash it all down. She was sitting in a bar finishing her last drink when she noticed someone walk through the rear door and take a seat at one of the back tables.

It was a tall man, wearing a black suit—and dark sunglasses. He didn't look at her or give any sign that he'd seen her. Sydney wasn't sure this was *the* man in black, but she was taking no chances.

She paid her tab, and discreetly exited the bar, hailing an Uber on her way out the front door. There was one waiting nearby. She got in and looked back through the rear windshield as they drove away. She didn't see any sign of the man in the suit.

"Good," she thought. "Hopefully, that wasn't *him*."

It was still early when she returned to the condo, but she was wiped out and still buzzed. She went to bed and fell asleep the moment her head hit the pillow.

She woke in the morning with a splitting headache. Her stomach was rumbling, but she didn't want to risk eating anything for fear that she wouldn't be able to keep it down. She went out to grab a coffee and came back and showered.

She wanted to have a look around the city that day. There was a company offering Segway tours of Old San Juan, so she decided to try that.

She found the business in an old building by a pier in the city. Once she'd paid for the excursion, she joined six other people in a quick orientation lesson on how to operate the Segway. She'd used one before, so she had no trouble getting used to it again.

They had a guided tour of the historic district, visiting several old buildings, including a cathedral, and a military fort, both of which had been here since colonial times.

They stopped at a little pub for lunch. The bartender had the news playing on the television above the bar. Sydney recalled the news trucks stationed out in front of her house back home and suddenly had an idea.

She pulled out her phone and looked up the number for the local TV station. Calling the number, she reached a receptionist and asked about setting up an interview. Once she'd told the man who she was, he put her through to a reporter.

"Hello, this is Clarita Diaz. Can I help you?"

"Yes, I do believe you can," said Sydney.

She explained her idea. Clarita was very eager to help, and they arranged to meet back at the pier at the end of the Segway tour.

"Hah, perfect!" Sydney said out loud when she was done. The tour guide and the other tourists gave her a funny look, but she didn't care. She was about to find her mystery man.

The tour finished up, and they arrived back at the pier an hour later. Clarita Diaz was waiting for her there with a cameraman.

Sydney introduced herself, and they set up their interview with the harbor in the background. Clarita asked her questions about her involvement in the invasion, and Sydney recounted how events had gone down from her perspective.

"Ms. Hastings, I understand you are now involved with a new investigation. Can you tell us about that?"

Sydney told her about how she'd met Martha and all the alien abductions that were going on.

"And you believe our viewing audience may be able to help you with this endeavor?"

"I do," said Sydney. "Martha had a dying request for me. She asked me to find a man in San Juan. Now, I have no idea who this man might be, but I strongly suspect he is someone who has had an abduction experience—and perhaps one that was out of the ordinary in some way. And most likely, he met with Martha McClure at some point before her death. I believe this man may have information that will help with this investigation."

"And there you have it," said Clarita. "Now, there will be a phone number on your screen at the end of this segment. If you believe you may be the man in question or have information about that man, you can call that number, and we will forward your information to Ms. Hastings."

"Great, thank you so much," Sydney said once they'd finished filming.

"You're very welcome," said Clarita. "And thank you for the interview! I hope our audience can come through for you!"

"Do you know when the segment will air?"

"I believe tonight, during the six o'clock newscast."

"Awesome, thanks again!"

Sydney went back to her condo and called Brian to tell him about what she'd done. And then she lay out on the beach for the rest of the day waiting for the newscast.

She found the station on the TV a little before six. To her surprise, they led with her interview.

"Oh God, does my voice really sound that nasal?"

Sydney hated seeing or hearing herself on film. But she hoped it would be well worth it, especially with it being the lead story.

She went back into the city to find some dinner.

After eating the local food for several days, she found herself craving pizza. She found a pizzeria downtown in Old San Juan and ordered a small pie.

When she was done, she went for a walk through the city. There were quite a few people out and about, enjoying the pleasant evening.

She went by a couple of clubs that seemed very busy. After a while, she found herself back at the military fort she'd visited on the tour earlier. Thirty-foot-high walls surrounded the main gate. The walls followed the coast as far as she could see in either direction. She was leaning against the railing, looking down the wall when she saw someone staring back up at her.

Her heart jumped into her throat—it was the man in black. She was sure of it.

Her knee-jerk reaction was to run, but she hesitated just long enough to see him start scaling the wall. Then she ran.

It wasn't that late, and the city was still busy—she couldn't believe the man would attack her with so many people around. But she wasn't taking any chances.

Sydney headed in the direction of her condo but kept to busier streets to make sure she wasn't alone.

After a few blocks, she slowed down and looked back the way she'd come. She didn't see him anywhere. But when she started moving again, she spotted him sitting at a table on the front patio of a restaurant on the next corner. He waved to her.

"Shit!"

Sydney turned back and ran the other way. She turned up another road with plenty of foot traffic and kept heading in the general direction of the condo.

As she was running, she pulled out her phone and found the contact for Brian's pilot.

"Hello?" he answered after the third ring.

"Dave! It's me, Sydney. Listen... I gotta get outta here... like right away! How soon... can you have the plane ready?"

"Is everything okay? You sound winded."

"I'm running... and everything is NOT okay!"

"Alright, yeah—I'll have her ready in ten minutes!"

She opened the Uber app next. There was a driver nearby. She hailed him and kept running to his location.

Once she'd found the car, she got in, and they zoomed off into the night. Sydney looked back through the rear window and saw the man in black standing in the middle of the street, feet from where she'd found the car.

"Jesus Christ!"

She wasn't going to stay on this island a minute longer than she had to. There was no more reason to remain here—the news station would forward her any messages that came in, and she could call her mystery man from home if need be.

After what she'd seen the man in black do to Martha, there was no way she was going to risk getting caught by him.

It took only a few minutes to get to the condo.

"Hey, can you wait here just a minute?" she asked the driver when they pulled up in front of her building. "I gotta get to the airport right away, but I need to grab my stuff."

"Si," he said. "I be right here."

Sydney got out of the car and hurried inside her condo. And the moment she crossed the threshold, she stopped dead in her tracks.

Someone had been here and strewn the contents of her suitcase all over the room.

As quickly as she could, she stuffed everything back in and ran outside. She got in the back seat, and the driver sped off the moment she'd closed the door. But he slammed the brakes only seconds later.

"What is it?" Sydney yelled, peering out the front window. The man in black was standing directly in front of the car.

"Shit! Back up! Back up!"

The driver didn't need to be told twice. He threw the car in reverse, backed up a hundred feet, and made a tire-screeching K-turn. As they sped off, Sydney looked out the back window in time to see the man in black launch himself straight up into the air and out of sight.

"Crap! Drive faster—I need to get to the airport *now*!"

"Si, senorita!"

He sounded terrified.

"I'm sorry, I didn't mean to yell at you. I'm just afraid of what might happen if that man catches up to us."

"No need to say sorry," he said. "I am afraid, too!"

"Once you drop me off, you won't have anything to worry about—he's only after me."

Sydney pulled out her phone and called Brian.

"Hey! Are you okay? Dave called me—what's going on?"

"It's him," she said. "The man in black. He's following me—he ransacked my condo. Well, I assume it was him—my crap was all over the place. I'm getting out of here!"

"Yeah, good call! Dave's filed the flight plan; he'll be waiting for you at the terminal."

"Perfect, thanks. I gotta go—we're here!"

"Text me the moment you're airborne!"

"You got it!"

Sydney gave the driver a huge tip, then grabbed her bag and hurried off toward the terminal entry.

She ran into Dave before she got there.

"This way," he said. "No need to go inside."

The two of them set off at a run toward the private hangar where he'd parked the jet. Sydney kept looking over her shoulder but didn't see the man in black anywhere.

They boarded the plane. Sydney sat down and buckled her seatbelt, and Dave started the engines. As they taxied out of the hangar, she kept her face glued to the window, looking for any sign of their pursuer.

Sydney didn't see him anywhere. The plane moved toward the runway.

"We're third in line," Dave told her. "I'll have us out of here in no time."

She kept her gaze fixed out the window. Every few seconds, she leaned across the seat to look out the other side of the plane.

"Second in line," said Dave.

Suddenly, off in the distance, she spotted something falling out of the sky and landing on the tarmac.

"Oh, shit!"

It was too far away to see clearly, but whatever it might have been, it was moving toward them. Within seconds, she could see that it was a man. He was walking directly toward the plane.

"Dave, get us out of here! He's coming!"

"We're next—hang on!"

For whatever reason, the man in black didn't seem like he was in any hurry. He was walking at a brisk pace but not running.

"Go, go!" Sydney yelled.

She was suddenly pushed back into her seat as the plane built up speed to take off. The man in black broke into a run, parallel to their course. He shot straight into the air as they lifted off into the night sky.

Chapter Eight: Safehouse

"Holy shit—where the hell did he go?!" Dave yelled back to her.
"I don't know!"

She sent Brian a text: "We're in the air, but so is the man in black!"

They'd be above the range of the cell towers soon, so she didn't expect a reply.

As they climbed higher, Sydney kept her eyes out the windows. Several tense minutes went by. She half-expected to hear the man in black landing on the roof of the plane or see him out on the wings at any moment. But by the time they'd reached their cruising altitude of 40,000 feet, there had been no more sign of him.

Sydney relaxed a little. Maybe he couldn't actually *fly*.

They landed at the airport just south of D.C. and found Brian waiting for them by the hangar.

"You made it," he said with a big grin. "No more sightings of our friend, I presume?"

"No, nothing," Sydney told him. "We didn't see him again once we took off."

They said farewell to Dave and got into Brian's Mercedes—he'd parked it next to the hangar.

He drove her to her house.

"Hey, you wanna just wait here a minute while I go inside?" Sydney asked. "You know, just to make sure..."

"No problem," he said. "Go ahead."

Sydney grabbed her suitcase from the trunk and went into her house. She froze, only steps into her living room.

"You've *got* to be kidding me!"

Someone had ransacked her house. Bookshelves were knocked over, their contents scattered throughout the room, furniture was overturned, and sofa cushions were torn open, their stuffing thrown all over the place.

Sydney dropped her suitcase and ran back out to Brian's car. He rolled down his window.

"Good?" he asked.

"No! Come here!"

She ran back into the house. Brian turned off the car and followed her inside.

"Oh, no," he said with a gasp.

Sydney moved cautiously into the kitchen—what if someone was still here?

The kitchen was worse than the living room. Someone had emptied the contents of the cabinets and the refrigerator all over the floor.

Brian picked up a milk carton—most of its contents were on the floor, but there was still some in the container.

"This is still cold—whoever was here did this very recently."

Sydney felt a chill go down her spine.

"Where's the cat?" she asked, suddenly panic-stricken. "Charlie? *Charlie*?!"

She ran around the first floor, but couldn't find him anywhere.

"He *always* greets me at the door! Where could he be?! Charlie?"

She was about to dash up the stairs, but Brian grabbed her by one arm.

"Careful—they might still be here," he whispered.

She nodded and continued more slowly.

Her office and bedroom were torn apart. Clothes were scattered everywhere; the bed was ripped open.

"Charlie?" she called out.

Suddenly, she heard a noise. She froze, listening intently. There it was again.

"That was a meow!" she said. "Charlie, where are you?"

She went from room to room, checking the bathroom, her office, and her bedroom. There were more meows—they sounded muffled.

Finally, she found him in her closet, stuffed inside an old hatbox under a pile of clothes.

"*Charlie*!" she said, lifting him out of the box and holding him tight to her chest, kissing him on the top of his head. Tears welled up in her eyes. "I was *so worried*! What did they do to you?"

"I hate to interrupt the happy reunion," said Brian, "but we should get out of here."

"Yes, right you are!"

She carried the cat back downstairs, fetched the cat carrier she kept in the basement and coaxed him inside. Running back upstairs, she grabbed a larger suitcase and threw every item of clothing she could find that wasn't torn to shreds haphazardly inside.

Hurrying back down to meet Brian, she said, "That should do it; I'm ready."

They ran out the door. Sydney almost left without locking the door but then thought better of it. She set her things down, locked the door, then took the cat carrier and suitcase out to Brian's car, dropping them in the backseat.

As they were moving to climb into the front, there was an explosion. Sydney felt the shock and heat of it knock her back.

"Oh, my God!"

Her attached garage had gone up in flames.

"Let's go," Brian yelled. "We can call 911 from the road!"

"Yeah..."

They got in, and he fired up the engine. He slammed the gas, and the tires screeched, launching them up the road.

Sydney looked back and watched flames growing higher. She was crying freely now.

Brian called 911 by voice command and reported the fire, all the while speeding toward the highway.

"Don't worry," he said when he was done. "They'll take care of it."

"I know," said Sydney, taking a deep breath. "Hopefully, the insurance will cover the repairs."

"If they don't, I will. Consider it hazard pay," he said.

"Thanks," she replied. "Well, where are we going now?" she asked as they accelerated onto the highway.

"My ranch," he told her.

"In North Carolina?"

"Believe it or not, that's the only ranch I own."

"Aw, poor baby only has one ranch."

Brian chuckled.

"How long will it take to get there?"

"Five hours or so," he said. "But the place is a fortress. If we can make it there, we'll be safe."

"I don't know," she replied. "If I recall correctly, the door was left wide open last time I was there."

"Yes, because I *left* it open for you," he said with an exasperated tone. "Trust me; they can't touch us there."

"I hope you're right."

They rode in silence after that, each lost in thought. Brian had classical music playing quietly in the background. He drove quite fast, and it ended up taking only a little over four hours to get to his ranch.

The iron gates opened of their own accord as they pulled up to the driveway.

"Uh... how did the gates know you were here?" Sydney asked.

"My phone," he said. "It's a geofence—they open when I come within fifty feet or so."

"Ah, well, that's convenient."

They pulled up in front of the ranch. Sydney grabbed her suitcase and the cat carrier from the back seat, and they went inside.

"Here, put your stuff down, and come over here for a second,"

Brian said from the door. She dropped her things on the couch and joined him at the door.

"See this?" he asked, turning the latch on the lock with the door still open. Half a dozen steel bars extended from inside the door. "Hardened steel throw bolts. They each extend three inches into the solid steel door frame when the door is locked. See the keyway here on the outside? This cannot be bumped like that crappy lock Martha had on her door. It's manufactured by a company in Sweden—there's no pin and tumbler in there—it's got eleven rotating discs, much like the locks they use for bank vaults."

"You know I have no idea what you're talking about right now, yeah?"

"Just making the point that nobody will be able to break through this door the way we did at Martha's," he said. "These walls are all steel-reinforced concrete block. The windows are quarter-inch polycarbonate—which means they're bulletproof, with hardened steel window bars over them.

"Add to that the cameras and proximity sensors all over the property. If anyone *does* try to get to us here, we'll know about it the moment they set foot on my land. And then I wish them luck trying to get inside this place.

"As I said, we're safe here. I promise."

"Thank you," she said. "I appreciate it. But I just realized..."

"Yes?"

"Unlike me, you didn't pack anything."

"Oh—this is my primary residence, so most of my wardrobe is here."

Sydney yawned and checked her watch.

"It's nearly dawn, I know," he said. "Let's do one more thing, and then get whatever sleep we can."

He closed and locked the door, and she followed him into his office. He went to a cabinet in the corner and removed a small box. Opening it, he pulled out a cell phone. It looked like a regular iPhone, but Sydney knew better.

"Use this, and only this from now on," he said. He powered it on and handed it to her. "All radio communication over this is fully encrypted, whether using cellular or Wi-Fi. Nobody can track you or intercept your communications. It's also got full access to the cameras and alarm system here. So, you can lock and unlock the doors, open the gates, and check in on the cameras from anywhere on the planet."

"Cool! As long as it's got Instagram so I can post photos of Charlie in his new home, I'm good to go!"

He gave her an exasperated look.

"Kidding. I got it, thank you."

"Well, let's get some sleep, and in the morning—well, later in the morning, we'll figure out what we do from here.

"Sounds good," she said.

He showed her to one of the bedrooms. Sydney closed the door, let Charlie out of his carrier, and collapsed on the king-sized bed. She kicked off her shoes and went to sleep without even bothering to undress.

She slept soundly for a few hours. When she woke, she went straight to the window and gazed outside. She was half-expecting to see the man in black out there, but there was nothing to see but the surrounding trees.

Sydney wandered into the attached bathroom, finally stripping out of her clothes, and took a long, hot shower. Once she'd dried off, she put on a thick, fluffy bathrobe she found hanging from the back of the bathroom door and wandered out to the kitchen.

"Good morning," said Brian, looking much more awake and refreshed than she felt. "Coffee's brewed and breakfast is almost ready."

"Mm, it smells delicious," she said, pouring herself a cup of coffee.

"Sleep well?" he asked as she sat at the table.

"Well, but not nearly enough."

"Yes, agreed."

"So, what, you have someone around here who keeps the place stocked for you? You've been in D.C. for weeks," she said, recalling the arrangements he had for his log cabin out west.

"That's correct," he said. "There's a local service that comes out weekly. I have an attached storage area on the back of the house—it's got a cooler and freezer. They have a key for that area that doesn't work anywhere else on the building."

Sydney shook her head.

"I know, I know," he said. "Everyone thinks I'm paranoid, but it's times like this when it pays off."

"Oh, I can't disagree," she said. "This isn't the first time I've found myself feeling grateful for your paranoia."

Minutes later, he set down platters of scrambled eggs, French toast, and bacon. They discussed their situation while they ate.

"In all the chaos, do you know if you got any messages resulting from your interview?"

"Oh, no—I forgot all about that. I'll have to check my old phone."

"After breakfast, I'll show you how to set up your e-mail accounts and such on the new one."

"Perfect."

"My team has processed a little over half of the records from Martha's place," he said. "Nobody from San Juan yet, but they did find something interesting."

"Oh?"

"There's an area in Kansas that has seen an inordinately large number of abductions," he told her. "More than any other place she recorded, by an order of magnitude. On this one stretch of road, in particular, they've found records of over a hundred abductions."

"That's crazy!"

"My staff have started calling it *Alien Alley*."

"Like tornado alley, only different?"

"There's one couple there that had been abducted six times, as of Martha's last interview with them."

"Oh, my..."

"So, I was thinking..."

"That would be a good place to go next!"

"Precisely. But I think I'll be joining you this time."

"Safety in numbers?"

"That, and I can't let you have *all* the fun without me!"

"Oh, you mean like in Puerto Rico? Yes, so much fun. Let me see—I was kidnapped by a drug lord, hunted down by a secret agent on steroids..."

"I was thinking more about the beach and the piña coladas..."

"It's *Kansas*, Brian. How much fun do you think it's going to be?!"

After breakfast, Sydney got dressed, and then Brian helped her set up all of her accounts on her new phone.

She did indeed have messages from her interview in San Juan—well over a hundred of them. It took a couple of hours to get through them all.

More than half were presumably single men expressing a romantic interest in Sydney. A significant minority of the remainder were women expressing a similar interest. Only about ten percent had anything to do with the actual reason for her interview, and of those, not one came from anyone claiming to have spoken to Martha.

"I give up," she announced to Brian when she was done, dropping into the sofa.

"Nothing?"

"Well, if I want a different date every night for the next year, I'm pretty much set. But other than that, no. Not a thing."

"Ah. Well, I think my team has found something interesting."

"Yeah?"

"Come here, check this out."

Sydney joined him at the table across the room, sitting next to him to see what he had on his laptop.

"*Miguel* San Juan?" she asked. "Are you kidding me? San Juan was a *name*, not a location?"

"Possibly," he said. "Martha interviewed him about a year ago. Seems to be a garden variety abduction story out in Arizona."

"Nothing noteworthy, though?"

"Well, no, but I wonder if maybe she'd heard from him again, right before the man in black got to her. If something critical had happened with him before she sought you out, she probably would have included his file in the batch she gave you, right?"

"Yeah, I guess so."

"But what if he reached out to her with something new *after* her initial meeting with you, but *before* that night by the river?"

"Makes sense," she said. "Yeah, the way she said it... when she said *San Juan*, she could have been naming a man, not a city. Have you tried calling the number?"

"Not yet."

Sydney pulled out her phone and entered the digits. It went straight to voicemail.

"Hi, Mr. San Juan," she said. "My name is Sydney Hastings. I spoke to Martha McClure right before her death, and she asked me to contact you—well, I have reason to believe you're the one she wanted me to contact."

She left her phone number and asked him to call her back.

"That's a start, at least," she said to Brian.

He nodded in agreement.

"Why don't we lie low today," he suggested, "rest up a bit. And then tomorrow morning, we can head out to Kansas. We'll keep trying to reach this Miguel San Juan in the meantime, and if we do make contact, we can hit Arizona next."

"Yeah," she said. "That works."

"Dave is already on his way up here with the jet, so he'll arrive in plenty of time."

"Oh, nice—where's there an airport near here?"

"There's a small airfield about fifteen minutes away."

"Well, there we go!"

"I'm going to run into town," he said. "Is there anything you need?"

"Actually, yes—some cat food... and some litter and a litter box."

"Oh!"

"Yeah. I'm going to have a look around—there's a good chance Charlie's already found a spot to do his business. I'm sorry, I'll clean it up, I promise!"

"I've never had a cat; I didn't think of this."

"After that, you think it's safe if I go for a run? I need to get some exercise."

"I have over a hundred acres here," he said. "There are trails throughout."

Brian left, and Sydney began her hunt. She didn't have far to look—the cat had relieved himself on her bathmat.

Sydney took care of that and then headed out herself. She took only her phone and had no trouble using that to lock the door behind her. It was a little chilly out, but it was bright and sunny, and the brisk air was invigorating.

She started out heading down the same trail she'd driven with Jaden and Malia the last time she was here. Before long, she came to a creek and ran along a path that followed that for a couple of miles.

The run was exhilarating—and the landscape here was beautiful. But she felt constant anxiety that the man in black might show up and remained much more alert to her surroundings than usual. In the end, she did about seven miles, and it was completely uneventful.

Sydney showered and got dressed. Brian had returned by the time she was done. She fed Charlie and set up his litter box.

After that, she contacted her insurance company to file a claim for her house. They said they would send out an inspector and advised her to get an estimate for the repairs. She spent some time contacting a few contractors in her area and making arrangements to get quotes from each.

Brian cooked dinner for them that evening, and then they settled down in the living room. He'd started a fire in the giant fireplace.

"That must be gas," Sydney observed.

"Yes. The heating is geothermal, but I have an underground propane tank just for the fireplace."

"I could get used to this."

"Oh—I almost forgot. Stay put; I'll be right back!"

"Staying put!"

He returned a minute later carrying a decanter of a golden-colored liquid and two glasses, and a water bottle tucked under his arm.

"Uh oh," Sydney said with a chuckle.

"I think we've earned it," he said.

"What is it, exactly?"

"Scotch," he replied, setting the glasses down and pouring some into each. Next, he opened the water bottle and poured a bit into each glass. He handed one glass to Sydney and said, "Cheers!"

She tapped her glass to his, sniffed it, and then crinkled her nose.

"Remind me what Scotch is again?"

"Whiskey. Aged twenty-one years in this case."

"Uh-huh. And what's the water for?"

"Brings out the flavor."

Sydney took a sip and resisted the urge to spit it out all over the carpet.

"I think I like my piña coladas better."

"I will admit it is an acquired taste."

"You can say that again," she said, taking another sip.

They sipped their drinks in silence for a few minutes, enjoying the fire.

"I miss them," said Sydney. She could already feel the alcohol going to her head.

"Hmm?"

"Jaden and Malia. And Melissa."

"Oh, yes," he replied with a sigh. "I do, too."

"I wonder what it's like out there. They must be outside of our solar system by now, right?"

Brian nodded. "By quite a bit, I should think. Interstellar space would be very dark—the Sun would appear only as a point of light, like any other star in our night sky."

"It was hard, finally reconnecting with them—the kids, and Melissa, only to lose them again so quickly. Melissa was the best friend I ever had."

"I know what you mean. I regret I never had the chance to reconnect with my brother. It was wrong to let things come between us."

He poured them each another glass of Scotch.

"I mean, from what I remember, Stephen was the one who kind of separated from you, didn't he?"

"Sure, but I drove him to it," said Brian, taking a deep breath. "I spoke my mind, and I should have let it go after that. But he was my little brother, and I was worried about his safety. I should have known to let him find his own way. He did anyway, so driving him away like that served no purpose."

"For some reason, I always thought he was the older one."

"No, I was. Only by a year, though."

They sat quietly for a minute.

"Can I make a confession to you?" Brian asked.

"Of course," she said.

He let out a long sigh.

"I have never vocalized this to anyone before," he began. "And I feel like a horrible person to think this way. But... there is a part of me that wonders... if we should have left well enough alone."

"How do you mean?"

"Bringing the twins to life."

Sydney said nothing, waiting for him to continue.

"I will always love Malia and Jaden dearly, even though I'll never see them again. They are family, and they will remain forever dear to me.

"But we opened a Pandora's Box when we entered that hidden chamber in the Great Pyramid—bringing the twins to life and accessing the power station. Had we not done that, none of those people would have died in Miami or D.C."

Sydney nodded. Then knocked back the rest of her drink.

"Fill me up," she said, holding her glass out to Brian.

He finished his glass, too, and then poured them each more.

"You know, not a day goes by that I don't think about standing on the bridge of that Othali ship, watching the Malor fire their weapon," said Sydney. "Wondering maybe if I had fought harder to get them to *do* something... well, that perhaps then those lives could have been saved."

"Ah, but if you had, then the Malor would have destroyed *us*, and there would have been nobody left to stop them.

"In my case, having a hand in bringing the twins to life and investigating the power station—those actions are what brought the Malor here in the first place."

Sydney considered this for a minute. She took a sip of her whiskey.

"On the other hand," she began, "how many other civilizations out there in the Milky Way would the Malor have exterminated if your actions *hadn't* brought them here?"

Brian opened his mouth to speak, but no words came out. He sat back in his chair, considering her words. Then he downed the rest of his whiskey.

He covered his face in his hands, and Sydney realized he was crying.

"I think you and I have something in common," she said. "Something profound."

"And what is that?" he asked.

"We both need to learn to forgive ourselves."

They each had one more glass of whiskey after that but sipped it very slowly. Then they said goodnight, and Sydney retired to her bedroom. She got undressed and slipped into the king-sized bed. Within minutes, she fell into the deepest sleep she'd had in months.

Chapter Nine: Alien Alley

Sydney woke at the crack of dawn and somehow, blessedly, did not feel hungover. She went for a run, came back and showered, and found Brian in the kitchen preparing breakfast.

"How ya feeling this morning?" she asked.

"Me? Oh, I'm fine. A little groggy perhaps, but no worse for wear. How about you?"

"I feel great," she said, sitting at the table. "Which is surprising. I drank more this week than I have in a year—and I felt terrible the next morning in Puerto Rico."

He set down the food at the table, and they dug in.

"I was thinking," she said. "Even once the repairs are done, I'm not so sure I'd feel safe going back to my house after this trip..."

"You're welcome to stay here as long as you'd like," he replied.

"Perfect, thank you. So, we can probably leave Charlie here while we're gone, yeah? I can leave plenty of food and water out for him."

Brian nodded.

"I don't expect we'll be gone more than a few days."

Sydney set out way more than enough food and water for the cat, just to play it safe. They packed their things and went out the door. Sydney stopped short and screamed halfway to the car.

The man in black was standing in the driveway.

"Final warning," he drawled. "If you want to live, *mind your own business!*"

"Back inside, quick!" said Brian, pulling out his phone.

They dashed back into the house, slamming the door shut behind them. Brian locked it, and not a second later, the man in black tried the handle.

It was silent for a moment, then there was a crashing sound, and the entire wall shook from the impact.

"Come with me!" Brian yelled, taking off through the house.

Sydney followed. He led her to the far end of the building, into an attached garage, and closed and locked the door behind him.

"Get in!"

There was an old pickup truck in the garage. Sydney moved to the passenger side, tossed her suitcase behind the seat, and climbed in.

Brian got into the driver's seat and started the engine.

"Hang on," he said. He pulled out his phone and checked the exterior camera outside the garage. "We're clear," he said and tapped a button to open the door.

The man in black was standing there, wagging a finger at them.

"Oh shit!" Sydney shouted.

Brian threw the truck into gear and gunned it. A moment before impact, the man in black shot into the sky to avoid being run over.

"Okay, *that* I cannot explain," said Brian, accelerating down the same path Sydney had used to escape with the twins when the FBI was after them.

Brian drove while Sydney kept a lookout for the man in black. But they made it to the main road without seeing him again.

Brian called the pilot and told him to have the jet ready for takeoff right away.

It took only fifteen minutes to get to the airfield. They'd had no further contact with the man in black. Brian pulled right up next to the jet and slammed the brakes.

"Quickly," he yelled, jumping out of the vehicle.

Dave was waiting for them by the steps to the cabin.

"Hey, Dave," said Sydney.

"Here we go again, huh?"

"Yeah, this is getting old pretty fast..."

They boarded and took their seats. Dave started the engine, and they taxied toward the runway. Sydney kept staring out the windows, looking for the man in black. But she still hadn't seen him by the time they took off.

She sat back in her seat and breathed a sigh of relief.

"So, what do you think?" she asked Brian. "That flying thing he does makes me think he must have some sort of... powers, I guess, like the twins do."

"Anything is possible," he said, furrowing his brow. "I truly can't explain it."

"How did he find us? I thought your places were all completely off the grid?"

"Most are, but not the ranch. That's my legal place of residence, so the listing is public. It's a fortress, but not a hidden one."

"Ah…"

"We've been lucky so far," he said. "I think, at this point, he's only trying to scare us."

"He's succeeding. But he blew up my garage—doesn't that make you think he's trying to kill me…"

"Not yet," said Brian. "Seeing firsthand what he can do, I believe we'd already be dead if that's what he wanted.

"I am curious, however, how he made it so close to the house without setting off any alarms."

He pulled out his phone and tapped away at the screen.

"Uh… you have a connection up here?"

"Satellite," he said. "Provides an internet connection for the onboard Wi-Fi, but there's no cell service."

"Well, that would've been good to know," she muttered.

He stared intently at his phone for a few minutes, occasionally tapping on the display.

"This is decidedly strange," he said finally. "The man in black doesn't show up on any of the cameras until the moment he walked up on the front porch. The video footage shows him trying the latch and then slamming himself bodily into the door. After that, he walks off the porch and disappears again."

"Does it show him out back, by the garage?"

"Yes, but only starting as the garage door opened. And then, of course, he does his Superman move, and that's the end of it."

"How is he able to disappear from view like that?"

"Your guess is as good as mine," he said.

The flight took a little over four hours. They landed at a small airport in northwest Kansas. There was a small rental car agency next to the airport, so they rented a vehicle and drove to the motel where Brian had booked them adjacent rooms.

Sydney dropped her suitcase in her room, then sat down with Brian in his.

"So, what's first—contact the couple, or go visit Alien Alley?" she asked.

"Well, Martha's file mentions the route where the abductions have occurred, but not the specific stretch of road," he replied. "We'll need some local guidance."

"Couple first, it is!"

Brian opened the file on his laptop.

"Ted and Susan Johnson," Sydney read out loud.

She called the phone number in Martha's file—this was Ted's cell phone, but it went to voicemail. Sydney left a message, then tried calling Miguel San Juan again. She got his voicemail, too.

But as she was finishing her message to him, Ted Johnson called her back.

"Hello, Mr. Johnson?"

"Yes, who is this?"

Sydney explained the reason for her call. He was very eager to meet them and tell his story.

"Reckon you could come on over to the homestead now if you'd like," he said. "We're both here."

"Sure," Sydney replied. "We'll be right over!"

She closed the phone, and they went out to the car. The Johnson residence was only a few miles up Route 23 from the motel. They parked in the driveway, and Mr. Johnson greeted them on his front porch.

"Come on in," he said. They followed him into the house.

He introduced them to Mrs. Johnson, and the four of them sat down in their living room.

"Thank you for taking the time to meet with us," said Sydney, "especially on such short notice."

"It's no problem at all," Mr. Johnson said; Mrs. Johnson nodded in agreement.

"We've been in contact with Martha McClure," Sydney told them. "She amassed an enormous collection of interviews with abduction victims, like yourselves. But nobody else she met has been through as many abductions as you folks—six in total if I recall correctly?"

"Seven now," said Mr. Johnson. "It happened again just a few months after Martha came out last."

"How is Martha?" asked Mrs. Johnson. "We've called her a few times since the most recent incident, but we haven't heard back."

"I'm so sorry," said Sydney. "Martha was murdered recently..."

"Oh, no!" said Mr. Johnson. Mrs. Johnson let out a little scream and covered her mouth with one hand.

"Who did it?" asked Mr. Johnson. "How did it happen?"

Sydney told them about the man in black.

"Have either of you seen a man like that around here? Or do you know of anyone else who has?"

The two of them looked at each other, but both shook their heads.

"No, can't say that we have," said Mr. Johnson. "Do you have any idea who he might be?"

"We suspect he is probably a government agent," Brian told them. "But we don't know for sure."

"Martha told me he only seems to show up when people start looking into the abductions," Sydney added. "And that's been my experience as well."

"You mean he's come after you, too?" asked Mrs. Johnson.

Sydney recounted her interactions with him.

"You'd best be careful, dear," said Mrs. Johnson.

"Can you tell us about your abduction experiences?" asked Sydney.

"Sure," said Mr. Johnson, taking a deep breath. "It's happened pretty much the same way every time." Mrs. Johnson nodded in agreement. "Always happens at night, and it's been here on this same road every time."

"Route 23?" asked Brian.

Mr. Johnson nodded.

"At first, there's a light in the sky—looks like a bright satellite, moving slowly across the sky. But then it gets brighter and comes toward us."

"When it gets real close, it's surrounded by clouds," said Mrs. Johnson. "And there's a whole circle of bright lights. And the truck dies at that point, every time."

"We tried running away the first two times," said Mr. Johnson.

"But it don't do no good. Stay or go, they come in and hover directly above us, and then there's this beam of light comes down from the center, and sucks us up into their ship, or whatever it is."

"We've blacked out after that each time," said Mrs. Johnson.

"Can you recall anything that's happened once you've been on board the vessel?" asked Brian.

"Oh, yes," said Mrs. Johnson. "Vividly!"

"We always wake up after a time," said Mr. Johnson. "Couldn't say how long. But we find ourselves in this room with metal walls, each of us lying on these exam tables, almost right next to each other."

"And we're always naked by that time," said Mrs. Johnson with a little giggle.

"And we can't move," added Mr. Johnson. "It's the oddest feeling—you try to move your arms or your legs, but nothing happens."

"Have you ever seen anyone else while you're there?" asked Sydney.

"Yes," said Mr. Johnson. "These little gray folks—look just like them aliens that took out the cities back east."

"They're short and thin," said Mrs. Johnson, "with abnormally large heads and big, black eyes."

"How many were there?" asked Brian.

"Three," said Mrs. Johnson. "Always three. One for each of us, and a third who seemed to be supervising the other two."

"They've done examinations on us," said Mr. Johnson. "Same damn thing every time. They use these... probes, guess you could call them. Sometimes they just hold them above us, but sometimes they touch them to different places. Put one on our foreheads, and then one on our chests, over our hearts. And then…"

He turned red at that point and didn't finish his sentence.

Mrs. Johnson looked from him to Sydney and Brian, and then added in a whisper, "and then they examine our nether regions with their probes. It's mighty uncomfortable. And embarrassing."

"Yes, and well, I reckon that's the end of it," said Mr. Johnson. "We always seem to black out again after that and wake up back in our truck. No sign of anything unusual at that point—no lights in the sky, or nothing like that."

"That's interesting," Sydney observed. "Most abductees aren't able to recall anything beyond their initial entry inside the spacecraft. But I interviewed one man in Puerto Rico who remembered more— his experience was similar to yours, except that he couldn't see any aliens—he didn't see anyone at all. He described the same kind of exam, but for him, the probes seemed to move of their own accord."

"How bizarre," said Mrs. Johnson.

"If you don't mind my saying," said Sydney tentatively, "I'm struck by how casually you're able to talk about these experiences. It must have been traumatic for you, I'd imagine."

"Terrifying," said Mr. Johnson. "It was downright terrifying, I'd say. The first couple times, at least. Less so, I guess, each time it happens."

Mrs. Johnson nodded in agreement.

"I'll never forget that first time," she said. "I was scared we were going to die. But after so many times, now, they've never done us any real harm. I can't rightly say what it is they want, but they haven't hurt us in any way. Part of me always worries that they will, of course, but they haven't yet."

"When we found out so many others 'round these parts have been through the same thing, that helped too, I reckon," said Mr. Johnson. "Makes it seem like what happened to us ain't so out of the ordinary, after all."

"Martha's files indicate that there have been at least a hundred abductions in this area," said Brian. "Have the two of you been in contact with any other abductees?"

"Yes, all the time," said Mr. Johnson. "We have monthly meetings over at our barn. That's a few miles up the road, and nearly all of the abductions have taken place between here and our farm. That's why it's happened to us so many times—we drive home from the farm every night and take that same route."

"When's your next meeting?" asked Sydney.

"Day after next," said Mr. Johnson. "Friday evening. You're both welcome to attend if you'd like."

"We'd like that very much," she said. "Would it be possible to speak to the whole group?"

"I imagine it would," he replied with a nod.

"I'd love to go get a look at that section of road," said Brian, "where the abductions occur. Your farm is... north of here?"

"That's right," said Mr. Johnson. "Not much to see this time of day, though. You'll want to go at night. Tell you what, why don't the two of you stay for dinner, and I'll drive y'all up there after we eat?"

"We wouldn't want to impose," said Brian.

"Nonsense, dear," said Mrs. Johnson. "We'd love to share a meal with you. Make yourselves comfortable, and I'll start cooking. Can we get you anything to drink?"

Sydney and Brian chatted more with Mr. Johnson while Mrs. Johnson busied herself preparing dinner. Once they'd eaten, Sydney and Brian went outside with Mr. Johnson, and the three of them climbed into his pickup truck.

"This is way nicer than yours," Sydney said to Brian as she sat down behind him. "It's even got a backseat!"

Mr. Johnson drove them a couple of miles up the road, then pulled over and parked on the shoulder.

"Well, this is the place," he told them as they got out of the truck.

"Alien Alley," said Brian.

Mr. Johnson chuckled. "Yep, I reckon you could call it that."

Sydney could see nothing but cornfields in every direction. The sky was extremely dark, and she had no trouble making out the Milky Way.

"Always starts on a night like this," said Mr. Johnson as they gazed up at the sky.

Suddenly, there was a flash of light that streaked across the sky, then faded.

"*What* was that?" Sydney asked.

"Shooting star," said Mr. Johnson. "See them pretty regular on a clear night like this."

"It's actually a meteoroid," added Brian. "Typically, a fragment of an asteroid, or other rocky debris, burning up as it races through the atmosphere."

"I prefer Ted's explanation," said Sydney. "What about that up there—that little point of light, moving past the other stars? That's a lot slower."

"That's a satellite," said Brian.

"We've seen both types of lights—ones that looked like shooting stars, and ones that looked like satellites, turn into UFOs out here," Mr. Johnson told them. "Always starts as one or the other."

They watched the sky quietly for a few minutes. Sydney kept her eye on that satellite, curious to see if it would get any brighter, but it passed out of view without changing in any way.

Several more satellites went by, and they saw a few more shooting stars, but nothing eventful happened. After an hour, Mr. Johnson drove them back to his place. Sydney and Brian said goodnight and went back to their motel.

The two of them came back the next morning to get a look around in the daylight. But there was nothing noteworthy to see here—no evidence that anything unusual happened, especially with such frequency.

On Friday, they met the Johnsons at their farm. They'd set up several rows of chairs inside their barn. By the time the meeting started, there were over fifty people here. Mr. Johnson introduced Sydney and Brian to the group, and then Sydney got up to speak.

She started by telling them about the way she'd first met Martha. Several people expressed shock and sorrow to learn that Martha had been killed. She then told them about her encounters with the man in black and the information they'd been able to gather so far about typical abduction experiences.

"And so, I'm wondering, how many of you all have been abducted?"

Every single person raised a hand.

"How many of you have been abducted more than once?"

Roughly half of the people kept their hands up.

"And how many of you can recall anything about the experience once you'd entered the spacecraft?"

Most of the hands went down, but a few stayed up.

"And for those of you who do remember something, how many saw aliens there?"

Every hand stayed up. Each of them told their story—they'd all seen aliens who sounded precisely like the Malor.

"I'm curious," Sydney said when they were done, addressing the whole group, "how many of you have had only a single abduction experience?"

Half the hands went up again.

"And how many of *you* folks can remember anything that happened after initially moving inside the vessel?"

Every hand went down. Sydney found this interesting.

She told them about the drug lord she'd interviewed in Puerto Rico and how he hadn't seen anyone at all.

They had an open discussion after that, and several more people recounted their experiences. Roughly half of the abductees reported having lost time during their experiences—one woman an entire week. Many had more questions for Sydney about the man in black—nobody in this group had heard of him before.

Once the meeting was done, Sydney and Brian headed back toward the motel. But Brian pulled over on the shoulder when they got to Alien Alley.

"We're heading out in the morning, so I figured we might as well have one more look while we're here."

They both got out and sat on the hood, gazing up at the sky.

"It's remarkable how homogenous their stories are," Brian observed.

"I know, right? That drug lord is the only one who had a significantly different experience."

"That is very curious," said Brian.

"And he was adamant about it, too," Sydney replied. "He was one hundred percent certain there were no aliens present, or visible at least, during his experience."

"It's also intriguing that only people who have had more than one abduction experience can recall anything from inside the spacecraft."

"Yeah, definitely," said Sydney. "It makes me wonder if it's simply a coincidence, or if there's a causal relationship there."

"Hmm."

They sat for a few minutes, watching the sky. A few satellites went by, and they saw some shooting stars, as well as several airplanes. But no UFOs.

Finally, they went back to the motel.

Chapter Ten: The Real San Juan

Sydney and Brian went out to a little diner for breakfast the next morning. They grabbed a booth in the back corner, and the waiter took their order.

"I think we've done what we can here," said Brian, taking a sip of coffee. "You haven't heard back from San Juan?"

"I haven't," Sydney replied. "I did leave another voicemail last night, and I tried texting him, too. No reply."

Brian nodded.

"I think we'll head down to Arizona today regardless. There's an address for him in Martha's file."

"So, what, we just show up on his doorstep?"

"Why not?"

Their food arrived.

"There's something I don't understand," said Sydney. "What the hell do you think the Malor are after? I mean, what's the point—why are they abducting all these people?"

"I've been wondering the same thing," Brian replied. "And I can't think of any purpose it might serve. They do seem to be very systematic. The exams they're conducting sound like they're identical for every abductee.

"But the truth is, we don't know for sure *what* they're doing in the exams. They're using probes to measure something, vital signs, perhaps, but we don't have any way to know for sure. Their tech is surely far more advanced than ours. They could be taking genetic samples—or they could be injecting these people with some sort of chemical or biological agent."

"Hmm. I hadn't thought of that."

"It would be interesting to have one of them undergo a full medical workup with a doctor and see if they can detect anything abnormal that might have resulted from the Malor exam."

Sydney nodded. "Definitely."

"Whatever they're up to, it must require vast amounts of data," Brian suggested. "It sounds like they've been doing this since the 1960s, at least. Martha knew of thousands of abductees—but in all those decades, there could be *tens* of thousands, or perhaps *hundreds* of thousands."

"Well, hopefully, this Miguel San Juan's got something earthshattering, and we can start cracking this thing!"

"Let's hope so!"

They flew down to northeastern Arizona later that morning. Bidding Dave farewell, they rented a car and found a motel in the town of Kayenta. Once they'd dropped their bags in their rooms, they set out to find San Juan.

Sydney drove, and Brian navigated.

"We're going to go north on 163," he said. "Shouldn't take long."

They drove north for fifteen minutes and then found the little side road listed in Martha's file. A quarter-mile down that, they located San Juan's address.

"There's nothing here," said Sydney, pulling over to the side of the road.

"How strange," Brian replied, getting out of the car.

They had a look around the site. A little sign confirmed the address, but there was nothing here. There were several other properties nearby, and they all hosted mobile homes, or in some cases, RV trailers.

Sydney headed to the mobile home on the next lot and knocked on the door. An older woman answered.

"Hi, sorry to disturb you," said Sydney. "We're trying to find Miguel San Juan, and the address we had for him is this lot next to you here."

"You're a little late," the woman said. "He picked up and moved a few days ago."

"Oh, do you know where he went?"

"I'm afraid I don't," she said. "I didn't know he was planning to leave. Woke up one morning, and his trailer was gone. Sorry I couldn't be more help."

"Now what," Sydney asked, heading back to the car with Brian.

They sat down in the car but didn't bother starting it or even closing the doors. Brian pulled out his phone.

"I'm going to call the office," he told her. He tapped a contact on the display. "Hey, Andre—I need you to run a cell phone number for me." Brian gave him San Juan's number, then waited for a moment.

"Oh, today? Okay... great. Alright... Yeah, run the GPS and let me know. Thanks."

He closed the phone.

"The number we've got is still active. He's used it today—in the last hour, in fact."

"Which means he's just ignoring us?"

"So it would seem. Andre's going to pull his GPS data, so we should be able to determine his new location. This might take a few minutes; why don't we head back to town and stop somewhere for some coffee."

They found a little café and headed inside. As the barista handed them their orders, Brian's phone rang.

"Hey, what've you got? Perfect... yes, text me the coordinates, please."

"Got him?" asked Sydney.

"Sure do. There's an address nearby that's seen significant activity from that phone number."

They went outside and got back in the car.

"We're heading east on 160 this time," Brian told her.

They drove for ten minutes, and he had her turn north onto a little dirt road. Within minutes, they arrived at another mobile home community.

"This is it—the trailer there on the right."

Sydney pulled over, and they got out of the car.

There was a white RV trailer on the lot, and separate from that, a black pickup truck. They went up to the trailer, and Sydney knocked on the door. There was no answer, and she couldn't hear anything inside. She knocked again.

"Mr. San Juan," she called out, "my name is Sydney. Martha McClure asked me to find you. Do you have a moment? I just have a few questions for you?"

She turned to Brian; he shrugged.

Sydney tried the door—it was unlocked. She pulled it open a few inches and called out through the opening. "Hello? Mr. San Juan?"

She opened the door a little wider and peered inside.

"There's nobody here," she said to Brian.

Sydney moved into the trailer, Brian close behind.

"The place looks lived in," she observed. The bed at the rear end of the space had been left unmade, and there were a few dirty dishes in the sink.

She moved toward the table at the front end when they heard an engine starting outside. They ran out the door in time to see the black pickup truck taking off down the road.

"Let's go!" said Brian.

They got back into the rental car. Sydney started it and took off after the pickup truck. When they reached Route 160, the truck turned west, fishtailing around the corner. Sydney was right behind him, but the pickup started pulling away.

"He's headed into Kayenta," said Brian.

As they approached the town, San Juan blew through a red light. Sydney stopped first, checked both ways, then followed.

"In the movies, nobody ever stops for a red light," Brian chided her, grinning.

"Hey, you wanna drive?" she shouted.

"No, no—you're doing fine. But you might want to speed up—we're losing him."

"Jeez, back seat driver much?"

The pickup reached the main road and turned right. This was a four-lane road, and San Juan was weaving in and out of traffic to lose them.

"Shit!" Sydney yelled when a garbage truck cut in front of her.

She managed to get around the garbage truck on the right, but then Brian yelled, "He turned!"

Sydney looked back and saw that the pickup had taken off down a side road.

"Dammit!"

She turned into the next parking lot and headed back the other way.

"Here," said Brian. "Turn right."

Sydney took the corner at speed, tires screeching.

"There he is!"

San Juan was far ahead of them, turning left. Sydney gunned it. They reached the road where he'd turned, and she followed.

But this was a dead end.

"Crap! Where the hell did he go?"

They got out of the car and looked around.

"Over here," she said.

There was a narrow alley between two buildings. When they reached it and rounded the corner to check it out, they saw the pickup truck—and a man standing behind it, pointing a shotgun at them.

Sydney and Brian froze, putting their hands above their heads.

"What the hell do you want?" the man asked.

"Martha sent us," said Sydney.

"Yeah?" he asked. "Martha's dead. She contact you from beyond the grave?"

"No—I was with her when she died! Her dying request was literally to find *you*!"

A shadow of indecision crossed the man's features.

"Martha came to me in the middle of the night," Sydney told him. "She told me she was afraid someone was trying to kill her. She gave me a bunch of files and asked me to look into the abductions. I was going to let her know we were taking it on, but the man in black got to her."

"Man in black..." he muttered, staring hard at Sydney as if he were trying to figure something out. "You're the woman from the TV," he said finally. "You were involved with the invasion."

"Yes, that's right, we both were," she replied, indicating Brian.

"Y'all work for the government?"

"No, sir," said Brian. "Not in any capacity."

"You're not with the man in black?"

"*With* him? Ah, no. He hunted me down in Puerto Rico and blew up my house, so no—we're not *with* the man in black."

Slowly, San Juan lowered his gun.

"Alright then," he said. "What is it you want?"

They decided to go to the café Sydney and Brian had visited earlier to talk.

"How did you meet Martha?" Sydney asked once they'd sat down.

"I found her," Miguel said, "online. I was abducted, and you know, it freaked me out. At first, I thought I might have hallucinated the whole thing. But I kept having these nightmares about it, and I couldn't sleep. It changed my life. I've never been one to worry about things, or have anxiety or anything like that... but this messed me up big time.

"I looked around on the internet," Miguel continued, "and found I wasn't alone. A ton of people have had experiences just like mine. And I found Martha in this forum for UFO people. She asked if she could come out and interview me. I said, sure, why not, you know?

"So, she flew out here, and I showed her where it happened. And she asked me a bunch of questions about my experience."

"Do you remember what happened during your abduction?" Sydney asked.

"I do," he said. "I mean, it's fuzzy, like remembering a dream. That's partly why I thought at first I might have imagined the whole thing."

"Can you tell us about it?" asked Brian.

Miguel took a deep breath.

"Yeah, alright... I was driving up the road to my trailer one night. It was late; there was no one else around. Beautiful, clear night. But suddenly these clouds move in—dark clouds, like there's a storm coming, right? But they moved in so fast. And in the middle of that were these lights... and then I can see there's something up in them clouds—like a saucer—it was like that one that took out the cities, but smaller. Way smaller.

"Hell, when I saw that, I flew. Man, I must've been doing a hundred up 163. But that thing kept up, stayed right above me. And then my truck just dies... good thing there were no other cars on the road—the power steering and power brakes went once the engine cut.

"Anyway, I managed to pull over. I got outta the truck and I ran, straight into the desert... like that was gonna do any good. That thing kept up with me in the truck; I don't know what I was thinking, I was just scared, you know?

"And so, this beam of light shoots down, and suddenly I'm floating, right up to that flying saucer. It pulled me inside."

"Did you see anyone?" asked Sydney.

"Not at first—I was in this room—it was dark. But then these two—I don't know if they were girls or guys, not sure how you're supposed to tell. But two of them aliens showed up, and one of them grabbed me. There was this buzzing noise, and then I felt weird... it was like being high and drunk at the same time. That's when everything went fuzzy.

"And then I was... floating, I guess you could call it. I couldn't walk, but they just kind of pushed me, and I glided into this other room. There were these... pods along one wall—reminded me of coffins, except they were standing up and more rounded. They pushed me into one of them. I was standing, but my feet didn't seem to be touching the floor—felt like I was floating, still.

"I was there a while, can't rightly tell you how long. But then the two aliens come back, and then I'm floating back to that first room, and the floor disappeared. Then there was this light all around me, and I'm going down to the ground.

"It was dark still. We must not have gone too far because I could see Monument Valley in the background."

"Monument Valley?" asked Sydney.

"Yeah, it's this land formation 'round here. All these buttes and mesas and what not."

"Oh, yeah—I know what you're talking about—like in those old John Wayne westerns, right?" asked Sydney.

"Exactly," Miguel said with a nod.

"That's somewhere near here, isn't it?" asked Brian.

"Sure is," Miguel confirmed. "Like I said, I knew then they hadn't taken me very far. So, they took me inside a hole in the side of this butte, and then there was like an elevator, and we're going down into the ground.

"At the bottom there was this tunnel... we went down the tunnel a ways—mind you, I'm floating this whole time. I still can't move my body. And then they take me into this room with these metal walls. Looked pretty similar to the inside of the ship, to tell the truth.

"Somehow, they got my clothes off me, and I was lying there, naked, on this metal table."

"They did a physical exam?"

"Yeah, guess you could call it that. I couldn't tell what they were after, but yeah, it was like an exam.

"Anyway, that lasted a while, and then they managed to get my clothes back on me and took me back up to their ship. Put me back in that pod thing again, and before I know it, they took me back to my truck. Lay me down on the ground, and the ship zooms off, like a shooting star.

"I reckon I must've nodded off at some point, 'cuz then I woke up, lying by the side of the road, in broad daylight. It was only a little after dawn, so I don't think anyone had driven by yet.

"And that was it. I got in my truck and drove home."

"You recounted that whole story to Martha?" asked Brian.

"Yes, sir, I did."

"I'm surprised Martha didn't give me your file when I first met her," said Sydney. "You're the only person I've encountered so far who has any memory of leaving the ship and being taken underground. Everyone else blacked out when they first got to the ship and then woke up in the exam room."

"Well, it's like I said," he told them. "The whole thing was fuzzy. Honestly thought a lot of it could've been a dream—and I said that to Martha.

"Not only that, but I spent a couple months exploring this whole area, trying to find the place they brought me. Couldn't find jack squat. It was only after that when I finally talked to Martha, so I was kinda questioning the whole thing by then."

"But you contacted her again, more recently?" asked Brian.

"Hell yeah, I did," said Miguel. "See, couple months after I met Martha, I found them."

"I'm sorry, found whom, exactly?" asked Sydney.

"Them aliens," said Miguel. "I found the place they took me."

"Are you kidding?!" asked Sydney. "Where is it?"

"Like I said, I could see Monument Valley in the background. Knew the place had to be near that. Took months to find it, but figuring the configuration of the big mesas and how far away they looked, I could tell roughly the area where it had to be. It's pretty much due east of the monuments, a few miles out."

"Could you take us there?" asked Brian.

"Reckon I could," said Miguel. "But it ain't exactly easy to get to. Can't drive there, that's for sure—the place is nowhere near civilization. It's a pretty long hike from the road, through the desert and what not. But yeah, I can take ya there."

"And so, you called Martha again to tell her about this?" asked Sydney.

"Sure did. 'Course, she was very interested in that, said she wanted to come out again and have a look. But I could tell something was wrong. She didn't say nothing, but man, she sounded terrible. Worried, like, and distracted. I asked her if she was alright, and she was a little vague; just said she was going through some things. So, I didn't think too much of it. Said she'd call me back the next day to arrange a visit.

"But that was the last I heard from her. She never called back and stopped answering my calls."

"That must be when the man in black caught up with her," Sydney suggested.

"Must've been, 'cuz a couple days later, she showed up in this news story on the internet. Just said she'd died suddenly, didn't go into how."

"I was with her when she died," Sydney told him. "The man in black had been following her, and he finally killed her. I guess he shows up when someone goes digging into things too much. Before she passed, she told me to 'find him,' and she said your name—'San Juan.' I thought she was telling me to find a man *in* San Juan..."

"That the reason you were in Puerto Rico?" Miguel asked with a grin.

"Yeah," Sydney said with a sigh. "Of course, that turned out to be a dead end, but then we finally found you in her files."

"Well, that man in black turned up here, too," Miguel told them. "Showed up at my trailer one time, in the dead of night, right after I found the aliens. There was a knock on my door, and I answered it, and he was just standing there. Black suit, sunglasses. All he said was, 'Leave it be, or else.' And just like that, he's gone. Coulda swore he flew then, like Superman... but that's crazy, right? Same time, I can't say where he went. Just gone."

"That's why you didn't take our calls," said Brian.

"Damn right, it was," Miguel confirmed. "Guy like that shows up in the middle of the night and makes a threat; I don't need telling twice. I moved my trailer, and I haven't gone back out to the alien place since. And I wasn't too keen to go talkin' to anyone else about what I saw, neither."

"You're willing to take us there, though?" asked Sydney.

"I mean, we ain't gonna be knocking on their front door or anything, are we?" Sydney shook her head. "Then yeah, I'll get ya most of the way out there, close enough to see where they are and all."

"Can we go now?" asked Brian.

"Can't say I'd recommend it," said Miguel. "It's about a two-hour hike, one way, and if we go now, we're gonna be out in the desert during the hottest part of the day.

"No sir, I'd say it'd be best to set out first thing in the morning. We leave at dawn, I'll get ya out there and back again before the whole place turns into a furnace."

"Good thinking," said Sydney.

"How about if you two meet me at my trailer at first light, and we'll head out there?"

"Works for me," said Brian. Sydney nodded.

"Good deal," said Miguel. "You'll wanna wear some comfortable shoes, and make sure to take a good bit o' water. You're gonna need it."

They said farewell to Miguel, and Brian and Sydney headed back to the motel.

Sydney was thrilled—finally, they were getting somewhere. Now it made perfect sense why Martha had wanted them to find this man.

She was nervous and excited at the same time. This was a huge breakthrough, but she worried about getting caught. It took her longer than usual to fall asleep that night.

They met Miguel at his trailer early the next morning.

"We should probably take your car," he told them. "We ain't all gonna fit in my truck."

Sydney drove, and Miguel navigated from the back seat.

They drove north on Route 163 for almost a half hour. The road led through the desert, and they didn't see any towns or cities once they'd left Kayenta. Moments after crossing into Utah, Miguel told her to turn off the road toward Monument Valley park.

"We're gonna have to pay the entry fee to the park to get where we're going," he told them. "We'll be crossing back into Arizona, but this here's all Navajo Nation land, and there's no other way to get where we're going."

There was no line at this hour. Sydney pulled up to the kiosk and paid the fee.

"Most folks take one of the tours they got here, but the road's open to drive yourself," said Miguel. "We're gonna go up toward that hotel there and then turn left down that dirt road."

There was a giant hotel a little beyond the kiosk, but no other buildings as far as the eye could see. Sydney turned onto the dirt road.

"That hotel's got quite the view," Brian commented. "Right at the top of that cliff, looking out over the monuments like that?"

"Sure does," Miguel agreed.

For the next twenty minutes, they followed a winding dirt road, through the desert, and around the giant mesas and buttes of Monument Valley.

They came to a scenic overlook area, and Miguel told Sydney to park there.

"We'll be on foot the rest of the way," he told them.

"We're way out in the desert here," Brian observed. "Looks like there aren't any homes or towns for dozens of miles around."

"Yeah, at least," said Miguel.

"Makes it the ideal place for the Malor to set up shop," said Sydney. "It's unlikely anyone would see them out here."

"For sure," Miguel agreed.

They grabbed their water bottles, locked up the car, and followed Miguel out into the desert. There was a trail that led from the overlook area down into the valley below.

The first hour was reasonably easy going. It was somewhat winding and hilly, but they were able to walk the trail without any difficulty. After that, the path became more difficult. They had to climb in places, and Sydney felt sure they would have lost the trail at this point without Miguel. They were walking on bare stone here, with no dirt or vegetation to show any clear evidence of a well-trod path.

After another hour, they came to the top of a ridge. From their vantage point, they could see for miles in every direction. Sydney looked around but could see no signs of life anywhere nearby. She had a feeling very few people ever ventured out this far into the desert.

Miguel pointed to the east.

"You see that big mesa out there? With the smaller butte over to the right of it?"

"Yeah," said Sydney, squinting a bit and holding her hand out in front of her to block some of the glaring sunlight.

"Okay, now right between them, you see that thing gleaming in the sunlight?"

"Oh, yes!" said Brian.

"Yeah, I see it," Sydney agreed.

"That's it," Miguel told them. "That there's the alien camp."

"It's tough to make much out from this distance," said Brian. "I should have thought to stop and buy some binoculars somewhere."

"I can get us closer if ya want," said Miguel. "But it's gonna be tougher going from here."

There was a steep slope directly in front of them—Sydney thought it wouldn't have been too bad to descend, except that it was covered in what looked like gravel.

"We have to go down *this*?" she asked apprehensively.

"I wouldn't recommend it," Miguel replied. "Best way is to loop around through the hoodoos to the south of here. Makes the trip a little longer, but it's safer that way, I'd wager."

"Hoodoos?" asked Sydney.

"Yeah, they're these tall spires of rock, some no taller than you or me, some as high as a house. A lot of them have these big stones balancing on the top, not too sure how that happens. But anyway, there's a whole field of them over this way, and going through those, there's a trail that loops around. Saves us having to go down something like this here."

"Lead the way," said Brian.

They set out again.

The trail followed the top of the ridge for a while and became quite narrow in places.

"Careful through here," Miguel warned them. Sydney was right behind him, and Brian was bringing up the rear.

But suddenly, Sydney slipped on some loose gravel. She tried to catch her balance, but her foot slid out from underneath her, and she found herself sliding down the slope.

Sydney screamed.

"Sydney!" Brian yelled.

She came to rest several feet from the top.

"Don't move!" said Miguel. "Hold still, and I'll try to reach down to you."

Miguel dropped to the ground, flat on his stomach.

"Hold my ankles," he said to Brian.

Sydney saw Brian squat down by Miguel's feet. Miguel slid partially down the slope and held his hands out to her.

Sydney reached out with one hand, but in shifting her weight, loosened some of the gravel beneath her. She started sliding again, and this time couldn't stop. Picking up speed, she screamed at the top of her lungs.

Chapter Eleven: The Camp

Moments later, Sydney hit solid ground and rolled a few feet away from the slope. A bunch of loose gravel had landed with her, and she inhaled a mouthful of dirt, coughing it back out again.

"Sydney!" Brian yelled from the top of the slope.

"Are you okay?" That sounded like Miguel.

Sydney got to her feet. She had cuts and scrapes on her hands and legs, but nothing felt broken.

"I'm okay!" she yelled up to them. "But I'm kinda stuck down here!"

"Hold on; I'm coming down to you," Miguel shouted back.

"Miguel, no…"

It was too late. Miguel was on his way down, bringing another shower of gravel with him.

He tumbled to the ground moments later. Sydney helped him to his feet.

"Fancy meeting you here," she said with a grin.

"I don't think I'm going to try that," Brian yelled down to them. "Can I get to you going through the hoodoos?"

"You could," Miguel called back. "I'd be hard-pressed to give you directions, though. I know the way myself, but it'd be tough to explain."

"You two go on ahead, then," Brian said. "I'll watch your progress from here."

"We'll be fast," she called up to him. "Right?" she added more quietly to Miguel.

"I'd imagine so," he said with a chuckle.

They set out again, Miguel in the lead.

"Have to confess, I don't know the way from down here," he told her. "I went through the hoodoos before. But I know we gotta keep heading east, so I don't think I'll get us lost or anything."

"I have total confidence in you," she told him.

"Alright, then."

They wound their way through the rocky ground in silence for the next twenty minutes. This area was relatively flat, with a few rolling hills and boulders strewn about. She could see more mesas and buttes up ahead.

"Getting close now," Miguel said, finally. The terrain was growing more uneven again. They followed a dry stream bed for a few minutes and soon found themselves in something of a valley.

"I think if we climb that ridge on the far side of the stream bed, we'll probably be able to see the place," he said.

"Okay..." she replied, somewhat apprehensively.

"I know it looks a little steep from down here, but it won't be too bad," he reassured her. "There are plenty of footholds and little plateaus, and it's not too far up."

"If I go first, do you promise to catch me if I fall?"

"Well, sure," he said. "You look like you hardly weigh a thing. I'll catch you. But I'm pretty sure you ain't gonna fall in the first place."

Sydney started her climb. The first few feet were a little scary, looking up ahead of her, but sure enough, she found it wasn't too tough at all. Within a few minutes, they crested the top of the ridge.

Sydney gasped. Miguel was right: they had a clear view of the Malor encampment from here.

"Get down!" he whispered urgently when he joined her at the top. He'd dropped to his stomach.

Sydney lay down next to him, staring out at the plain before them.

Dead center in the camp was a metal obelisk—this was what they'd seen glittering from afar. It was some sort of tower, but Sydney could not tell what its purpose might be. There was a blue light glowing in the center of it that seemed to be pulsating with some regularity.

Next, three saucer-shaped craft drew her eye, off to the right from the tower. They seemed to be hovering there. To the left of the obelisk stood a large metal structure that looked like a large barn or garage of some sort.

The area was crawling with Malor. Dozens of them were scurrying about the camp; they appeared to be quite busy with whatever it was they were doing. Some were doing some sort of work on the tower, others moving objects between the saucers and the building.

"That's definitely the Malor," she whispered to Miguel. "This is where they brought you?"

"I'm pretty sure," he said. "You see that butte out beyond the tower there? Down by the base, there's like a shadow. I think that's the entry to that cave where they took me. But I haven't dared to get any closer to this, so I can't say for certain."

"Yeah, I can see it," said Sydney excitedly. "That does look like a cave!"

They watched for a few more minutes, then she said, "I think that's enough. We should probably head back. I've got to tell Brian about this and see what he wants to do next."

Sydney found the descent back down to the stream bed quite a bit more harrowing than the trip up had been. But they made it without any further mishaps.

They set a quick pace heading back the way they'd come. But as they rounded the next corner, Sydney froze: two Malor were standing there.

In the instant it took Sydney to register their presence, Miguel yelled "Duck!" and pulled her to the ground. A moment later, there was a metallic crackling sound, and something hit the stream bed beyond them, spraying debris everywhere.

"Run!" Miguel yelled.

Sydney didn't need to be told twice. They took off, farther down the stream bed.

"What the hell was that?!" Sydney yelled.

"Some sort of weapon!" he said.

She'd noticed something in their hands but hadn't realized what it was.

As they rounded the next bend in the path, bits of rock to her right went flying, shattered by some unseen force.

"We gotta get out of this stream bed," she yelled.

"If we climb the walls, we'll be sitting ducks!" he shouted back. "Let's hope for open terrain ahead!"

They ran another hundred feet, dodging invisible projectiles every time they heard that metallic crackling until suddenly they emerged onto an open plateau. And standing across from them were ten more Malor, each pointing a weapon at them.

"Well, shit," said Miguel, as they pulled up short.

The two Malor who had been chasing them caught up. One kept a weapon on them, while the other bound Miguel's hands behind his back with some sort of handcuffs. Sydney wasn't sure how they worked, but the Malor held them up to one of Miguel's arms, and a glowing beam of energy encircled first one of his wrists and then the other.

Sydney started backing away and would've run, but the Malor in front of her fired his weapon near her feet. The shot sprayed her with dirt and debris, and she stopped, while the second Malor bound her wrists, too.

The Malor marched them across the desert floor, and ten minutes later, they arrived at the Malor camp. They took Sydney and Miguel inside the building, into a small chamber, and closed the door behind them, leaving them in total darkness.

"Well, this sucks," Sydney observed.

"Yeah, no foolin'," said Miguel. "What do we do now?"

"We wait, I think," Sydney replied. "Brian was looking out for us. I don't know if he'll have seen everything that happened here, but it won't take him too long to figure out that something's wrong. He'll know what to do."

"So, what's your relationship with him, exactly?" asked Miguel.

"Oh, he's my boss. Well, I mean, he was an old family friend. But now he's my boss, too."

"And what is it the two of you do? Well, when you're not tracking down alien abductees?"

"I used to be a nurse, and Brian owns a computer security company."

"Uh-huh. And so, how do you think he'll know what to do?"

"Oh, well, his company's done a lot of work for the government, so he has contacts in the Defense Department and the military and what not. Don't worry; he'll find a way to get us out of this."

"I sure hope so," Miguel said. "'Cuz these here folks did some *sick* shit to me last time I was here, and I'd prefer to avoid going through that again if you take my meaning." Sydney thought he sounded almost hysterical.

"Relax, Miguel," she assured him. "It's going to be okay. Brian will get help. I'm sure of it. And besides, they're keeping us above ground. You said they took you to some sort of underground bunker for the exam, right?"

He was silent for a moment, then let out a sigh. "Yeah, that's true."

"See? If they were going to examine us, they'd probably be taking us down there."

"That's a good point," he conceded. "But I worry what they're planning to do with us up here."

Sydney wondered the same thing.

She didn't actually know what Brian would do, but she truly did feel confident he'd find a way to get them out of here. He'd found a way to free Jaden and Malia from Area 51, and that time he'd had no choice but to act alone—federal agents were the ones who'd abducted the twins, to begin with. But now, in this situation, she was pretty sure he'd be able to get help from someone in the federal government. She knew they'd been rounding up rogue Malor and didn't think they'd be too happy with them setting up an encampment like this.

"Hey, I'm sorry for freaking out like that," said Miguel.

"No need to apologize—I don't blame you," she replied. "I'm kind of freaked out right now myself."

"After my abduction, man, it was rough. I kept having these headaches and the nightmares... It helped a lot when I finally realized I hadn't hallucinated the whole thing. But I was in tough shape for a while there."

"I know what you mean," Sydney told him. "I've been having the same problem since the invasion. My dreams are terrible. It's hard to sleep."

Just then, the door opened, and a Malor came into the room. He grabbed Sydney by one arm. She got to her feet, and he led her out of the room.

"Hey! Where are you taking her?!" Miguel shouted. But the

Malor closed the door behind them. Sydney could hear him yelling from inside the chamber as the Malor led her across the building.

There was an open area at the far end. Several other Malor were waiting for them. Floodlights lit the place; it was so bright, Sydney had to squint to see anything. The Malor released her, and the group of them formed a circle around her.

"What do you want?" she demanded.

They said nothing but stared at her intently.

"What the hell," she said.

She didn't understand what was happening—they were just standing there, looking at her. It occurred to her that perhaps they were attempting to read her mind or something—she'd learned during the invasion that they communicated telepathically. But to the best of her knowledge, their telepathy didn't work with humans.

Several minutes went by, and then the group broke up. One of them grabbed her by the arm again and led her back to the small chamber at the front of the building. It was empty now—she didn't know where Miguel had gone.

But only a few minutes later, he returned, too.

"I don't know what the hell that was," he said.

"Did they stand around you in a circle and stare at you?"

"Yeah! You, too?"

"Mm-hmm. I have a feeling they were trying to communicate. They're telepathic, apparently, but I don't think it works with us."

"Oh, well, then I guess maybe I shouldn't have kept shouting at them like that..."

Sydney chuckled.

They sat in silence for a while. Sydney didn't know how much time had gone by, but it felt like hours. She felt famished, and she could've used a restroom.

Noises were coming from inside the building, and more from outside, but nothing unusual—Malor moving around, doing who knew what.

But suddenly there was an explosion.

"What the hell!" shouted Miguel.

There was a great commotion in the building that sounded like it had moved outside. Suddenly, Sydney heard gunfire.

"That's no alien weapon," said Miguel. "I think you're right—your boss called in the cavalry!"

There was more gunfire, and Sydney heard the metallic crackling of the Malor weapons again. Then there was another explosion—this one was closer, and she could feel the ground shake.

A minute later, footsteps approached their chamber. The door flew open and silhouetted in the light flooding through the opening stood a man—a human, wearing a camouflage uniform.

"I'm here with the U.S. military," he said to them. "This is a rescue operation. I need you to listen very carefully. My team and I are going to escort you out of this structure. But I need you *not to run*. When we get out the door, we need to stop and wait there until we're given clearance to proceed. Is that clear?"

"Yes," said Sydney.

"Loud and clear," added Miguel.

"Alright, let's move," the soldier said, helping them to their feet. Their arms were still handcuffed behind their backs, making it difficult to stand up on their own.

They followed him through the building and out the front door. There was a group of four other soldiers waiting here, heavily armed. The soldier who'd rescued them held out his arm in front of them to make sure they didn't go any farther.

Chaos had engulfed the camp. Sydney could see Malor running around, trying to get to their flying saucers. It looked like human snipers were firing at any of them who moved close to the craft.

Suddenly, there was another explosion.

"That's our cue," the soldier told them. "Move out!"

The soldiers set out at a run, in single file, keeping Sydney and Miguel in the middle of the group. They darted across the plateau and up the same dry stream bed Sydney and Miguel had used to get here earlier.

Sydney could hear more gunfire and explosions behind them. Minutes later, they came to an open area, and she saw there was a giant military helicopter waiting for them.

"Quickly now, get on board," the soldier told them.

Sydney and Miguel boarded the aircraft, along with the rest of the soldiers. Moments later, they took to the air and flew to the top of the same ridge Sydney had slid down hours before. There was a broad plateau to the north of where she'd had her mishap, and the helicopter set down there, near a group of military vehicles.

Brian came running over to them as they disembarked. He gave them both a big hug.

"I can't tell you how good it is to see the two of you again!"

"The feeling is mutual," said Sydney.

Another man joined them moments later—the very last person Sydney had expected to see here: Officer Babcock.

Chapter Twelve: Fireworks

"What the hell are *you* doing here?" Sydney demanded.

"Such a pleasure to see you again, too," he replied with a leer.

"I contacted him," Brian told her. "I saw the Malor capture the two of you. I couldn't reach any of my military contacts, so I called Officer Babcock. He said he could get the military involved for a rescue operation, and so he did."

"Well, then thank you, I guess," said Sydney.

"You're very welcome," said Babcock. "If you'll both come this way, the sergeant in charge of this operation needs to speak with the two of you."

"Now hold on," said Miguel. "We're gonna need someone to get these laser handcuffs off of us first!"

"Wait here," said Brian. "I think I know someone who can take care of that."

He ran off and returned a minute later with one of the soldiers, who was holding a small black device in one hand.

"This is a short-range EMP generator," the soldier said, showing them the device.

"What does EMP stand for?" asked Miguel.

"Electromagnetic pulse," the soldier replied. "It'll fry the circuits on that alien tech binding your wrists, but we'll need to move away from our vehicles and equipment to make sure we don't take out any of our own stuff at the same time."

They followed the soldier away from the vehicles. Using the EMP generator, he removed Sydney's handcuffs first, and then Miguel's.

When they were done, they rejoined Babcock, who led them across the plateau, where they met another soldier.

"Step into my office," the man said, taking a cigar out of his mouth and indicating an area behind a Humvee.

Babcock left them with the sergeant. He went back and boarded the helicopter, which took off again moments later.

"So, tell me exactly how this went down, from the moment you encountered the hostiles until right now," said the sergeant.

They recounted the story for him.

"Now, did you see any other humans inside that building?" he asked once they had finished.

"None," said Sydney. "We didn't encounter any other humans anywhere in their compound."

Miguel nodded in agreement.

"If there are any abductees in there," he added, "they'd probably have them in the underground bunker I saw when they took me."

"Come again?" said the sergeant.

Miguel told him about his abduction experience.

"And you say the entrance to the elevator was inside of a butte somewhere over there?" the sergeant asked.

"Yeah, that's right," he said.

"Can you point it out to me?" asked the sergeant.

"Sure, you can see it from the ridge over there," said Miguel.

They walked over to the ridge, and he pointed it out to the sergeant.

"Very well," he said. "We'll take it from here."

"What are you going to do?" asked Miguel.

"Hopefully, we'll be rounding up the hostiles and getting them transported to a holding facility with the rest of their kind," the sergeant replied. "If that doesn't work out... well, you'll see. You've got front row seats up here."

He walked away.

Sydney and Miguel regrouped with Brian. They found a couple of rocks to sit down on and watch the military operation unfold.

"My understanding is that they've planned this operation in three phases," Brian told them. "First was your rescue. Next is going to be an air assault to take out their saucers and power station, and then they'll be going in with ground forces."

A few minutes went by, and then the sergeant came jogging over to them.

"Turns out that camp of theirs doesn't show up on our satellite imagery," he said. "I hear you might be able to help?" he added to Brian.

"I might," he replied and headed off to the command post with the sergeant.

A few minutes later, Sydney spotted an airplane flying in low over the area. It launched two sets of missiles—two toward the building, and the other two toward the power station and saucers.

All four exploded in the air, well before reaching their targets.

"Uh... I'm guessing that wasn't supposed to happen like that," Sydney observed.

"No, I imagine not," Miguel agreed.

Two fighter jets swooped out of the sky next, laying down gunfire on the Malor camp. Sydney couldn't tell if that had had any effect, but moments later, the three Malor saucers streaked off into the sky in pursuit of the jets.

"Uh-oh," said Sydney.

The aircraft had all moved out of range. Several minutes passed without their being able to see what was happening.

Suddenly one of the fighter jets came back into view—it was on fire. The pilot ejected moments before the plane crashed into a mesa in a fiery explosion.

One of the saucers shot by moments later and then disappeared behind the same mesa. It came back into view on the opposite side, shooting off into the sky.

"Oh, look!" said Miguel, pointing off to the south.

Sydney could make out a formation of six more fighter jets moving into the area.

For the next several minutes, they had a view of the jets engaging the three Malor saucers. It was chaotic and challenging to follow. Then, one of the saucers crashed to the desert floor. A whoop went up from a group of soldiers watching the action from their command post.

Two more fighter jets went down—the pilot was able to eject from one, but Sydney did not see anyone eject from the other.

They shot down a second saucer a few minutes after that. The remaining fighters took another twenty minutes to eliminate the third and final saucer.

"Well, that was quite the show," said Miguel.

"I hope the pilots who ejected are okay," said Sydney.

Several minutes went by, but they couldn't tell what was happening. The Malor were scurrying around their camp, but it was impossible to tell what they were up to.

"I wonder what they're waiting for," said Sydney. "Brian said there would be a ground assault."

"I don't know, but I can tell you this is the most excitement this area has probably ever seen," Miguel replied.

"Have you always lived here?"

"Nah," he said. "Lived up near Vegas for most of my life. Came down here about six years ago now."

"And the trailer is your... uh... primary residence? Like, you live there?"

"Sure do," he said with a chuckle. "I did the whole get married, buy a house thing. That didn't suit me, so after the divorce, I bought the trailer and moved down here. I love it, though—the freedom. I couldn't stand being tied down, ya know? This way, I go where I want, when I want. Don't gotta worry about being strapped down with mortgage payments or nothing like that. Feel like I want a different view out my front window, I pick up and move. Just like that," he said, snapping his fingers.

"I can see that," she said with a nod. "How long were you married for?"

"Oh, God, let's see... Eight years, I guess."

"What happened?" she asked, but then immediately added, "I'm sorry—that's way too personal, you don't have to answer that!"

"Oh, I don't mind. Thing was with Katie and me, we were high school sweethearts. Went to UCLA together and then got married right outta college. We'd been together so long, grew up together, really, that getting married was something of a foregone conclusion, right?

"But looking back, I think that was a mistake. I mean, we weren't ever a great match. She always liked structure, and following a plan, and that sort of thing. I've always been more of a free spirit.

"I ended up being a financial planner, and getting my masters in finance if you can believe it, but that was mostly because of her."

"You don't strike me as the financial planner type," Sydney said with a grin.

"Aw, it was hell. Couldn't stand it. I was good at it, made a ton of money. Socked a good bit of that away, and that's sure come in handy. But the work was pure tedium, and being cooped up in an office all day. Screw that."

"What did your wife do?"

"Katie's a mechanical engineer. She did physics in school but wasn't interested in academia or anything like that. That's what finally split us up—she had an affair with this guy at her company."

"Aw, I'm sorry," said Sydney.

"Don't be, worked out for the best. We'd had plenty of problems before that—never got along, not since high school," he said with a chuckle. "I think we're both way happier now. Know I am."

"What do you do now?" she asked. "I'm guessing you're not doing financial planning from your trailer?"

"Oh, hell no," he said. "I'm an author."

"Nice," she said. "What types of books do you write?"

"Westerns mainly, and crime thrillers. But I don't know, everything I've seen, might be switching to more of a sci-fi genre!"

"Hah, you've certainly got the life experience for that!"

"What about you?" he asked. "You're from somewhere out east, right? Near Washington?"

"Yeah, I've lived in Maryland my whole life. Just outside of D.C."

"So, your place wasn't hit in the attack, was it?"

"No, luckily not. But it's only a few miles from the destruction zone."

"Wow," he said. After a moment, he added, "You got a significant other waiting for you back home?"

"I do not," she said with a grin. "I'm kind of like you, I guess you could say. I mean, I'm still doing the bought a house thing, but I'm way too independent to settle down with a guy."

"You mean you've never been married?"

"I was engaged once," she said. "The guy I was with in college proposed about a year after we graduated. I went with it, only because I always thought that was just the way life was supposed to go. But man, the thought of spending my *whole life* with just that one person... I don't know—it was overwhelming. I mean, I loved him, but at the very least, I figured maybe we should live together for a few years first. You know, make sure it was right."

"He didn't like that idea, I'm guessing?"

"Ah, no. I called off the engagement and suggested we try living together for a while first. But he wasn't having it. So, that was the end of that."

"Hmm."

"*Hmm*, what?"

"Well, I'm just thinking he was a fool. It's not every day you meet such a beautiful woman, who's smart, *and* funny, *and* passionate..."

"Aw," said Sydney, feeling her cheeks flush. "That's sweet of you to say!"

Just then, she saw a commotion off to the north.

"Looks like the ground assault is starting," Miguel observed.

Two columns of soldiers moved into view to the north. Over the next thirty minutes, more and more poured into the valley, surrounding the Malor camp.

"Looks they've got at least four times as many troops as we saw aliens in that camp," said Miguel.

"More than that, I think," said Sydney. "They're certainly not screwing around down there."

They watched as the soldiers took up positions around the camp. Suddenly a group of Malor opened fire on the soldiers to their west—the ones positioned closest to Sydney's vantage point.

The soldiers returned fire. More Malor joined the fight. Before long, they overwhelmed the soldiers in that area. The Malor filed out of their camp in single file, hurrying along the dry stream bed. They had snipers stationed in key locations to lay down covering fire.

"Oh, shit," said Miguel. "They're headed this way!"

Sydney took a closer look and realized he was right.

"We should be safe here, though, right? I can't imagine they'd be able to climb that ridge..."

"I don't know about that," said Miguel. "They seem pretty nimble. We should probably get out of here!"

Just then, Brian joined them.

"The Malor are headed this way," he told them. "We need to leave—follow me!"

They ran back to the military vehicles. The sergeant they'd met earlier was there, and he ordered the three of them into one of the Humvees. He sat up front, and one of the other soldiers took the driver's seat.

Moments later, the vehicles took off through the desert. Sydney found herself bouncing around in her seat as the Humvee sped across the uneven terrain.

They drove for several minutes but then came to a stop. The driver got out of the vehicle.

"Stay inside the Humvee," the sergeant ordered them as he stepped out, slamming the door behind him.

"What the hell is going on?" asked Sydney, staring out the windows, trying to get a look behind them.

The soldiers had taken positions flanking the vehicles. They were armed, pointing their weapons back down the path they'd taken.

Only a few moments later, Sydney heard gunfire. The soldiers were firing, but she couldn't see their targets.

Then she heard the metallic crackling of the Malor weapons. Dozens of them crested a nearby hill, swarming toward their position.

The soldiers fired into the crowd. A couple of Malor went down; the rest pressed ahead.

"Holy shit!" yelled Miguel.

The Malor were on them. Sydney ducked down into the footwell, trying to keep her head below the windows. Brian and Miguel did the same. The gunfire outside their Humvee intensified, and she heard the sergeant shouting orders at the soldiers.

Things quieted down after a couple of minutes. Sydney poked her head up to get a look outside. The Malor had moved on.

The sergeant and the driver climbed back inside the Humvee.

"We're clear," he reported. "They rounded up about half of them back there by their camp. The half that got away just overran us."

"What now?" asked Brian.

"Calling in air support," said the sergeant. "We're gonna blow them away before they get to any populated areas."

"That didn't work back at their camp," said Miguel.

"They had some sort of energy weapon back there," said the sergeant. "But that thing ain't mobile. They've got nothing with them now that can take our missiles down like that. We're gonna stay put right here for a few minutes and stay out of the way while the planes do their job."

Minutes went by, and then Sydney heard and felt a series of three massive explosions. They could see the top of a large dust cloud rising above the nearby hills.

"That's it; we got 'em," the sergeant reported. "Let's move out," he added to the driver.

"You got them all?" asked Brian. "Half rounded up back at the camp, and the rest taken out with the missiles?"

"There are a few lone stragglers, I'm told, run off on their own," the sergeant replied. "But we'll have them taken care of in no time.

"Oh, and by the way, we checked out that butte you pointed out, where that cave entrance and elevator were supposed to be?"

"Yeah?" asked Miguel. "And what did you find?"

"Whole lotta nothing," said the sergeant. "The side of the butte was recessed—that was causing the shadow we could see from the ridge. But there was no opening—it was solid rock. Our boys had a good look around the whole area down there and found no sign of any kind of underground bunker or anything."

The convoy made its way back to the road. They went right by the parking area where Sydney had parked their rental car, so they let them out there.

"I don't know about you two," said Sydney, "but I'm starving!"

"After what we just went through, how can you possibly be thinking about food?" Miguel asked.

"What can I say? High-stress situations always make me hungry," Sydney replied. "And besides, we haven't eaten all day!"

They agreed to stop at a nearby diner to eat.

"I don't understand it," said Miguel once they'd sat down and ordered their food. "Everything else about that place matches what I remember from my abduction, but I don't see how there could not be an underground bunker there."

"You said your memories of the whole ordeal were fuzzy, like a dream, right?" asked Sydney.

"Yeah, it's all fuzzy," he confirmed.

"Maybe you saw the shadow on the side of the butte, and your brain filled in the rest," she suggested. "You were right about most of it. Did the inside of the building look anything like the exam room they took you to?"

Miguel considered it for a moment. "Yeah, more or less," he said, sounding uncertain. "The metal walls, and all."

"So maybe they performed the exams right there in that building," she said.

"I don't know. The elevator didn't seem any more or less real than the rest of it. Could there be another alien camp nearby?"

"I don't think so," said Brian. "I was able to help them with their satellite—the Malor had set up a kind of cloaking shield over their camp—it dampens light waves in the visible spectrum, effectively making the area invisible to satellites. But their shield doesn't block infrared, and the satellites could detect them in those wavelengths.

They did scan the surrounding area, out to a 100-mile radius, and found no other camps."

"This is it, then," said Sydney. "We shut down the camp, so that should be the end of the abductions, right?"

"I believe so," said Brian. "I'm guessing that that camp had been here for a very long time. Some rogue Malor probably joined them after the invasion, enabling them to increase the frequency of their abductions. But that's it. We shut down their entire operation."

They finished their meal, and Sydney dropped Miguel off at his trailer. She and Brian went back to their motel. They said goodnight, and she retired to her room.

But no sooner had she collapsed in her bed than Sydney got a text message from Miguel.

"Care to join me for a drink?" it said.

Sydney smiled.

"Sure, why not?" she replied.

Twenty minutes later, she met him at a local bar.

"Long time no see," she said, sitting across the table from him.

"Well, I figured I couldn't just let you walk out of my life like that, never to be heard from again."

"Fair enough," she said.

"I ordered us a couple of beers; I hope that's alright?"

"Yeah, sure!"

"So, I was thinking, now that the aliens are out of commission, you probably wouldn't be coming out west for anything anymore, would you?"

"Not for the job, no," she said. "But this area is beautiful; I'm sure I could be enticed to come out and visit again."

"I'd like that," he said with a smile. "I could show you around. You ever been to the Grand Canyon?"

"Not yet!"

"We'll definitely have to go there," he said. "The view from the south rim is amazing. But if you want to get the full experience, we'd have to hike down to the bottom."

"Yeah, I'm game!"

"It'd mean sleeping in tents—that ain't a hike you can get done in a single day. And going back *up*, well, that takes about twice as long as going down. Ya ever slept in a tent outdoors before?"

"Sure, but not since I was a kid," she replied. "But I would totally do that."

Their beers arrived.

Sydney took a sip and said, "I'll consider it a date then."

Miguel took a long drink of his beer and then suddenly looked more serious.

"I've been thinking about that alien camp," he said. "And I got a funny feeling. Like maybe that's not where they took me after all."

"Oh?"

"Yeah... I mean, I was damn sure they took me underground. But it's not only that. That place where we were today... it was just... *different*. There was a smell that I don't remember from my abduction."

"You're right—it kind of smelled like vomit in there," said Sydney.

"Yeah, exactly, and I don't remember smelling nothing like that where they took me. And while the walls were metal, that was different too. The place they took me... those walls were smooth and shiny, not a bunch of separate pieces like that building today.

"And that's the other thing—when they took me, and we got out of the saucer, I don't remember seeing no building there. I mean, I didn't exactly get a good look around—they took me straight from the spacecraft to the butte, but I figure I woulda noticed a big building like that."

"Okay, but you're *sure* you saw Monument Valley in the background?"

"Certain."

"So maybe if there's some other alien operation out there, it's *only* underground—that would explain why nothing else showed up on their satellite imagery anywhere near there."

"Exactly. And you wanna know another thing that's bugging me about this?"

"What?"

Miguel finished his beer.

"Why didn't the man in black show up?" he asked. "If this here was the base for the aliens doing the abductions, and he's trying to cover that up, you figure we woulda been dead before we ever got up close. But he don't even make an appearance? Doesn't that seem a little strange to you?"

Sydney drank some of her beer.

"You're right; I didn't think of that."

They had a couple of beers and talked long into the night. But then Sydney went back to the motel. Miguel had given her quite a lot to think about.

Chapter Thirteen: Recurrence

Sydney joined Brian for breakfast at the local diner the next morning. She outlined the reasons for Miguel's skepticism that the Malor were behind the abductions.

"The thing is, his memories of the entire experience are fuzzy," she pointed out. "The whole thing was like a dream for him. So, who knows—some parts of it could be dead accurate, but other aspects could be elements that his subconscious brain provided to fill in the blanks."

"Yes, I agree," said Brian. "He remembered being taken to the area near Monument Valley and then found a Malor camp precisely where he expected to find it, based on his experience. The United States military had not been able to find them—they've been hunting down rogue Malor since the invasion. And so, the notion that finding that camp at that exact location is only some sort of bizarre coincidence... well, I find that difficult to believe."

He seemed lost in thought for a moment, then added, "On the other hand..."

"What?"

"Now that I think about it, that camp did seem a little... thrown together. For the Malor, anyway. We do know that Malor around the world lost power when their mother ship went down. And this group found a way to generate their own power, which is what made me think they'd been here a long time.

"But at the same time, this group was much larger than any other we've heard about, and given their penchant for working collectively, this would have given them a competitive advantage. Perhaps this *was* purely a rogue group left over from the invasion, and they built their power station very recently.

"That structure they built didn't seem very old and looked like they could have constructed it from scrap metal. I'd expect to see something more permanent if they'd been operating from that location for decades.

"I don't know," he concluded. "I guess I'm torn."

"Hmm." Sydney took a bite of her hash browns. "The other thing that almost has me convinced that Miguel is right, and I recognize it's purely circumstantial, is the fact that the man in black did *not* show up, and has not shown up. Wouldn't he, if those Malor had truly been the ones abducting people?"

"Perhaps," he conceded. "But if he is some sort of secret government agent, it's possible he had orders not to interfere with an operation being conducted by another government agency—the military, to be specific."

"Yeah, maybe..."

"Well, look: Time will tell. If the abductions continue, then we'll know there's someone else behind it."

"That's true," she agreed. "I'll have to keep an eye on the forums online and see if there are any new reports."

They ate in silence for a few minutes.

"Oh, hey—I was thinking," said Sydney. "Do you think we can stop in Marlton so I can get a look at the damage to my house? Before we go back to the ranch?"

"Yes, of course. I'll text David now and ask him to adjust our flight plan."

They headed to the airport once they'd finished breakfast. When they landed, they called an Uber and went out to Marlton to check out Sydney's house.

"Oh, my," she said, stepping over the police tape and walking up the driveway.

The explosion had destroyed the attached garage. Only rubble remained. Pieces of her truck were strewn across the driveway and the backyard.

They went inside the house and found that part of the wall separating the kitchen from the breezeway was missing.

"Looks like the breezeway took the brunt of the force," said Brian. "The damage to the rest of the house doesn't seem too bad."

Sydney walked through the main level, then the second floor.

"It doesn't look like anyone's been here since we left," she reported as she came back down the stairs. "The mess is exactly how it was before."

"Have you heard back from the insurance company?" he asked.

"Oh, yeah—I did. They said to go ahead and schedule the repairs," she replied. "And I've got the quotes back from all three contractors. They're each very highly rated, and there wasn't much difference in their estimates. I'm going to call the one who came in the lowest and ask them to get started.

"I was thinking that maybe I'd come home and start cleaning up," she said, looking around her living room. "But... seeing it like this, and knowing it's going to be a few weeks to do the repairs... I don't know; this feels so overwhelming. Do you think I could stay with you at the ranch a little longer?"

"I was assuming you'd stay at least until the repairs were completed," he told her.

They took an Uber back to the airport and flew back to North Carolina. Brian drove them back to the ranch in his truck.

Sydney sat down with her laptop and checked the abduction forums she'd found online, but there were no reports of any new abductions.

The next few days passed in total peace and quiet. Brian kept busy doing whatever it was that he did, but Sydney found she had a lot of time on her hands. She went for a run every morning, then spent much of each day going through the data Brian's team had amassed from Martha's interviews. They'd finished the data entry, finally. Sydney kept an eye out for anything out of the ordinary but was struck mostly by how similar people's experiences were. Abductees from all walks of life and every corner of the country had gone through nearly an identical sequence of events. The aliens didn't seem to discriminate based on race, gender, or income—or any other factors that Sydney could identify.

Martha had collected interviews from some people in other

countries, as well—people outside the United States accounted for roughly twenty percent of her data. Yet still, the accounts were very similar to the rest.

Saturday morning, Sydney decided she needed a change of pace.

"I'd like to go into town today," she said to Brian at breakfast, "maybe do a little shopping. I've been rotating the same five outfits since I've been here—I should've grabbed some more clothes when we stopped at my place, but I didn't think of it."

"Sure," he said. "Take the Mercedes."

"Really?! I figured I could just take the truck..."

"Don't be silly," he said, handing her the keys to his car.

Sydney drove into town once they'd finished eating. It was a small community, but there were several stores and shops downtown.

She was in one of the shops, picking out a pair of jeans when she noticed a man in the back of the shop—a man in a black suit.

"Oh, no," she whispered to herself, her heart skipping a beat.

She put the jeans down and was about to bolt out the door when the man turned. His face was wrong, and he wasn't wearing sunglasses—this was not *the* man in black.

Sydney breathed a sigh of relief and went to try on the jeans.

She ended up buying three new outfits, then found a little café down the street. Once she'd ordered a coffee, she moved to the end of the counter to wait for her order.

And that's when she noticed another man in a black suit sitting in the back corner—and this one was wearing sunglasses. Sydney took a closer look. He moved his glasses up to his forehead and winked at her.

This was the man in black. And his eyes did not look human—the pupils weren't round—they were slits, like a cat's.

He put his glasses back on and smiled at her.

Sydney took off toward the exit.

"Ma'am, your coffee..." the barista called out.

Sydney ignored him and ran up the street to where she'd parked the Mercedes. She got in and started the engine, frantically looking around to see if the man in black was in pursuit. He was nowhere in sight.

She backed out of the parking space, threw it into gear, and took off back toward the ranch. Checking her rearview mirror the whole way back, she didn't see anyone following her.

Once she'd reached the house, she ran inside, slamming and locking the door behind her and dropping her shopping bags on the floor.

Brian came running from his office.

"What's wrong?"

She told him what had happened.

"Sit," he said.

He poured them both a Scotch, and they sat in the living room.

"If those Malor were the ones behind the abductions, then why is he here?" she said. "He shouldn't have any reason to bother with us anymore."

Brian said nothing, taking a sip of his drink instead.

"And what the *hell* is up with his eyes? Brian, I don't think he's human."

"Well, they do make contact lenses that can make your eyes look like a cat's. But I'm getting to the point that I'd have to agree with you," he said. "Between his eyes, and the unusual abilities... he may well be from a different world." He chuckled a bit and took another sip of Scotch. "Before the invasion, I would have insisted there had to be some other explanation. But now..."

"That's crazy, though, right?" said Sydney. "I mean, the Othali, and then the Malor, and now... *another* alien species? How many different intelligent life forms are there... *out there*?" she asked, waving one hand toward the sky.

"Have you ever heard of the Fermi Paradox?" he asked.

"No, what is it?"

"We've known for a long time that there are billions of stars in the galaxy and billions of galaxies in the universe. We know now that there are planets orbiting many, if not most, of the stars in our galaxy. And one team of scientists have confirmed a planet orbiting a star *in another galaxy*."

"Okay, and...?"

"With that many planets out there, how could we be the only intelligent life in the universe?" he asked. "It would seem incredibly unlikely. There is a mathematical formula called the Drake Equation that factors in the number of stars in the galaxy, the percentage with planets, how many of those have conditions hospitable to life—there are, if I recall correctly, seven variables it considers. And we're not able to provide precise values for every variable, but with modern exoplanetary astronomy, we have much more precise input values than we ever did before."

"Uh-huh..."

"Well, the equation predicts that, by now, after the billions of years that have passed since the formation of our galaxy, there should be at least *ten* advanced, intelligent species. The Fermi Paradox asks—or asked, prior to the invasion—why, then, if there *should* be so many advanced civilizations out there, have we never encountered any? After all this time?

"Many solutions had been postulated for the paradox over the years. Perhaps every advanced civilization has managed to destroy itself before achieving interstellar travel. Or maybe there *is* an advanced civilization out there, but humanity is not yet sufficiently advanced to be interesting to them."

"But now we *know* the answer," said Sydney. "There *are* other intelligent beings out there."

"Exactly," said Brian. "And based on the Drake Equation, now that we know about a couple for sure, we shouldn't be too surprised to discover a third.

"I always thought the equation yielded overly optimistic results, I'll confess. I tended to believe that any advanced civilization *would* find a way to annihilate itself before reaching other worlds. Our track record would seem to predict that. But I was wrong."

"Alright, then. So, our man in black could very well be yet another type of alien," she said, taking a drink of her Scotch. "What does he want? He said last time it was our 'final warning.' This time he didn't chase me, didn't try to kill me, nothing. Just smiled at me and showed me his eyes. It's like he's messing with us. He wanted to, what, remind us that he's still out there, and let us know that he's not human?"

Brian thought about it for a moment.

"This makes me think that Miguel might be right," he said finally. "Perhaps the Malor he found *weren't* behind the abductions. The man in black might not be alone—maybe there are more of his species here, and *they're* the ones responsible for the abductions."

Sydney finished her Scotch.

"Great."

"It is interesting, though, that so many abductees have reported seeing the Malor when they've been taken," Brian observed.

"Maybe the man in black aliens are working *with* some of the Malor?" Sydney suggested.

"That could be," said Brian. "But we've witnessed the man in black's ability to make himself invisible. I wonder if perhaps his species can disguise themselves to *look* like the Malor."

"But why?"

Brian downed the rest of his Scotch and put his glass on the table.

"I have no idea."

Over the next few days, she paid closer attention to the online forums. By the end of the weekend, she still had not found any new abduction stories. But Monday morning, she received a call from Ted Johnson out in Kansas.

"Hello, Sydney?" he said.

"Yes, hi! How are you!"

"Alright, I guess. I wanted to let you know Susan and I have been abducted again."

"You're kidding—when?"

"Last night," he said. "We were at the farm late doing some work, and it happened on the way home, on Route 23, just like always."

"That's incredible!"

"Don't know about that. Went down exactly like the other times."

Sydney told him about Miguel's story and the events that had taken place out by Monument Valley.

"Well, I'd venture to guess those particular aliens weren't the ones doing this," he said. "But we did see three of them gray ones, just like before."

Sydney thanked him for calling her and told him she'd stay in touch. She ran to Brian's office and told him the news. He had several windows open on his giant computer monitor, and Sydney recognized one of them as a satellite view of the ranch.

"What are you up to?" she asked.

"Oh, this?" he said, turning back toward the monitor. "I'm trying to figure out a way to adjust the cameras and proximity sensors to detect the man in black. I suspect he can probably camouflage himself in the visual wavelengths, so I'm recalibrating everything for infrared. Won't be able to test it unless he shows up again, of course..."

"Oh," said Sydney. "Well, listen, I'd like to go back to Kansas. This new abduction proves beyond the shadow of a doubt that Miguel was right! The Malor in Arizona *weren't* behind the abductions! There's been more activity in that area of Kansas than anywhere else. So, if we want to get to the bottom of this, I think that's the best place to continue with the investigation."

"I agree," he said, turning back to her again. "And see if you can talk them into getting a full medical work-up," he added. "Every abductee with any memory of their experience has reported that the aliens have done some sort of physical exam. I'd be very curious to see if they've done anything that might leave a trace—any sort of procedure, or injection, for example."

"Will do," said Sydney.

"Oh, and let them know we'll pay for it if need be. If they end up doing any sort of radiology, that could get quite expensive."

"Got it!"

They agreed she'd fly out there first thing in the morning.

Sydney called Miguel to give him the news, too.

"I'm heading back out to Kansas tomorrow," she said. "I'm going to meet with the Johnsons and see what else we can find out."

"I could meet you there if you think you might want some company," he suggested.

"Sure, but how far are you from there?"

"Well... it's probably a twelve-hour drive, more or less. But if I hit the road at dawn, I'll make there in time for supper."

"Oh, that's crazy," she said. "I can't ask you to come that far."

"Nah, it'd be my pleasure. Nothing tying me down here, remember?"

Brian dropped Sydney off at the airport the next morning. He gave her the login information for the onboard Wi-Fi. Sydney rechecked the UFO forums during the flight, and sure enough, there were two new abductions reports. The Johnsons weren't alone.

Once they'd landed, Sydney rented a car and drove out to the same motel where they'd stayed the last time. She called Mr. Johnson to let him know she was in town, and he invited her to come over for a visit.

She arrived there fifteen minutes later. The Johnsons greeted her at the door and invited her inside. They had a seat in their living room.

"So, Ted, you gave me the basic rundown over the phone," said Sydney. "But was there anything different about this abduction compared to your previous experiences?"

"No, not a thing," said Mrs. Johnson. "It was the gray aliens, as always. And they did their exam, and we ended up back in our truck when it was over."

"Fascinating," said Sydney. "I was talking to my boss, and we were wondering if the two of you would be willing to see a doctor for a full medical workup?"

"What for?" asked Mr. Johnson. "We feel fine."

"It would be interesting to find out what exactly it is that the aliens are doing during their exams. If they're performing any type of procedure, for example—if the probes they're using aren't only taking measurements but also doing something to your bodies—or injecting something—a full exam may be able to find some evidence of that. And don't worry about the cost—my boss is willing to cover the expense."

"Well, yes, I suppose we could do that," said Mrs. Johnson.

"Agreed," Mr. Johnson said with a nod. "If they *have* been doing something to us, I'd sure like to know about it."

"Great," said Sydney. "Here's what I'm thinking. Ask for a physical to start with. And a full-body MRI. If they've implanted anything, it would certainly show up that way. And blood work—have them do a full metabolic panel. That's a good place to start—if anything is off, they can do a follow-up."

Mrs. Johnson wrote down her suggestions.

"Very well," she said. "I'll call our doctor today and schedule the physicals. We'll have to find somewhere that does MRIs, but I'm sure our doctor will know where to go."

"Excellent," said Sydney. "Thank you. And keep me posted!"

Sydney drove back to the motel. She sent Miguel a text to find out when he expected to arrive but didn't get a reply. By six o'clock, her stomach was rumbling, and she started looking for a place to eat.

But finally, Miguel sent her a text.

"Hey, just rolled into town. You wanna get some grub?"

"Hell, yes," she replied. "What kind of GRUB do you feel like?"

They ended up meeting at a Chinese restaurant in the outskirts of town.

"Hello again," he said, pulling her into a hug.

"Good to see you," she said.

"Figure this must be the only Chinese joint in a hundred-mile radius," he said as they went inside. "But I'm starving, and I didn't see too many eateries on my way in."

"Where are you staying?"

"Oh, I parked the trailer at a campground nearby."

They ordered their food and sat down at one of the only two tables here. Sydney guessed it was probably mostly a take-out place, but it would do.

She told him about her encounter with the man in black.

"Well, that about proves my point, doesn't it?" he said. "Must be these cat-eyed aliens doing the abductions. Only they got some way to make themselves look like these other aliens."

"That could be," she agreed. "We also know they can make themselves invisible somehow. And the abductee I met down in San Juan said he couldn't see any aliens at all—the probes seemed to move around him of their own accord."

"How do you move forward here?" he asked. "You say I'm the only one who can recall being moved out of the UFO. And them military types couldn't find anything else down around Monument Valley. What next?"

"That's a good question," said Sydney. "We do know that this area right here has seen much more alien activity than anywhere else we know about. So, I figured it would be a good idea to investigate more around here.

"There's this one stretch of road where the abductions keep

happening. I'd like to head over there in the morning and have another look around. Maybe there's something that we missed last time."

"Why don't we meet up for breakfast in the morning, and I'll head over there with ya?" he suggested.

"Sounds like a plan!"

Their food arrived, and the conversation turned to Miguel's road trip to the area. When they were done, they headed outside.

"Alright then," said Miguel. "There's a little diner in town; you wanna meet there for breakfast?"

"Sure—we ate there last time I was here. It's pretty good. How's nine o'clock?"

"That works. I'll see you then!"

For a moment, she thought about inviting him back to her motel room. But she immediately thought better of it—she should probably get to know him more first and make sure he wasn't working for a drug lord or anything like that.

"Good night," she said with a smile.

Chapter Fourteen: Route 23

Sydney went to bed but could not fall asleep. For almost two hours, she tossed and turned.

She couldn't stop thinking about the abductions. *Was* the man in black from some kind of alien species? And was that species responsible for what was going on?

She finally gave up on getting any sleep. Rolling out of bed, she got dressed and went out to the car. She drove to the area of Route 23 where the Johnsons reported all of their abduction experiences taking place.

It was foggy here, making it difficult to see very far. She pulled over to the side of the road and turned the car off.

Getting out, she wandered up the road a bit. It was too dark and foggy to see anything very well—and she wasn't sure what she'd expect to find here, even in the daylight.

There were a couple of farmhouses nearby, barely visible through the fog, and a few barns. She saw a light turn on inside the front porch of one of the farmhouses, but there were no other signs of life here.

Was there something about this particular location that attracted the aliens' attention? The land was flat and open here—

fields stretched out as far as the eye could see in every direction. But that was true of vast areas of the Midwest. What was it about this stretch of road that set it apart?

Sydney could come up with no answers.

She walked a little farther up the road. Suddenly, she heard a faint buzzing noise coming from the field to her right. She stopped in her tracks, staring across the area to try and see the source of the noise, but it was impossible through the fog.

Sydney started moving back toward her car. Then, she noticed a light in the same area that the sound was coming from. She broke into a run.

She reached the car, got inside, and started the engine; the light kept coming closer. She threw the car into gear and took off down the road. The fog made it impossible to go very fast, but the light was converging on her position.

Sydney slammed the brakes, did a quick K-turn, and headed back in the direction of her motel. But the light tracked her progress, growing ever closer.

As she passed one of the farmhouses, the light overtook her, moving closer to the road. She hit the brakes again, watching in terror.

The light drew closer. Suddenly it dropped out of the sky, stopping directly in front of her windshield. Sydney screamed.

But then she got a closer look—this was a drone.

She sat back in her seat, letting out a huge sigh of relief.

Getting out of the car, she got a closer look at the thing. It was larger than other drones she'd seen and had six separate rotors. Suddenly, it took off toward the farmhouse.

Sydney followed it. Someone called out to her: "Sorry about that!"

As she drew closer to the house, she saw a teenage boy approaching her.

"Didn't mean to scare ya," he said sheepishly.

"And how do you know I was scared?"

"Well, I heard you scream, so…"

Sydney chuckled.

"We don't get people 'round here too often, so I was just curious to see who it was."

"Gotcha," she said. "Guess I'd be curious, too."

"Yeah… so, who are you?" he asked with an awkward laugh.

"Sydney," she said. "This might sound strange, but I'm out here looking into some, ah, alien abductions that keep happening in this area."

"Oh, that," he said. "Well, that ain't strange at all. We see UFOs quite a bit here—more than cars passing through, I'd say. I'm Owen, by the way."

"Nice to meet you, Owen. Have you seen UFOs yourself?"

"Many times," he said. "That's part of why I bought the drone. My mom never wanted to spend the money for one, but now I got my own job, I was able to save up and get one myself."

"Have you managed to capture a UFO on video?"

"Not yet, but I've only had the drone about a week now. Haven't seen any UFOs yet since I got it. But they come around at least a couple times a month, so I reckon it's only a matter of time."

"Have you ever seen one of the UFOs abduct someone?"

"Yeah, once," he said. "Last year. I was walking home from a friend's house, coming up this stretch of road right here. Saw this strange light in the sky—that's usually how it always starts when a UFO shows up. But it came down close to the road, over this pickup truck.

"Looked like the truck died, or at least the man driving it turned it off for some reason. He got outta the car, and this light came down from the UFO, and I saw him fly up right into the bottom of the thing.

"I wanted to get a closer look, but I ain't gonna lie, I was scared outta my mind. I hid in the cornfield when I saw the thing coming down over the road.

"But anyway, suddenly, the thing disappeared. I didn't see where it went; it was just gone. I went over to see about the man's truck, but that was gone, too."

"The truck was gone, too?" she asked. "Where did it go?"

"Couldn't tell ya," he said. "Didn't see it anywhere."

"Did it fly up into the UFO, too?"

"Not that I saw," he said. "I guess it might have, but it was hard to see from where I was hiding.

"Anyway, that was the only time I ever saw them take anyone. I've heard it happens quite a bit 'round here, but I don't know."

"Do you think you could stay in touch with me and let me know if you get anything on video with your drone?" she asked. "Anything at all—just a UFO, or an abduction, whatever?"

"Sure, I could," he said.

They exchanged phone numbers, and Sydney headed back to her car. She decided she'd had enough excitement for one night.

She headed back toward the motel. But before she'd gone more than a quarter of a mile, a bright light appeared in her rearview mirror. There was no car behind her—the light was in the sky.

"Oh, no..."

She stepped on the gas, but the light kept up with her. Looking in her side-view mirror, she realized it was a ring of lights.

There was a dirt road on the right—she hit the brakes and skidded sideways, turning onto that. She floored it and moved into the cornfields.

The object in the sky had followed her. She'd gone only a few hundred feet down the dirt road when her car died. She came to a stop and tried to start it again, but it was dead. The headlights had shut off, and not even the dome light would turn on.

"What the hell?" she said out loud.

She got out of the car. The ring of light was directly overhead.

"Oh, shit!"

She took off at a run, farther into the fields. Looking back, she could see the light was following her. It was dead quiet—she couldn't hear any engines or anything, which she found strange. She would have expected something that large moving through the air to be noisy.

She turned down an aisle of corn stalks and ran as fast as she could, hardly able to see where she was going. But it was futile—the UFO stayed directly above her.

Suddenly, a spotlight shot down from the center of the craft, directly on her. She stopped and looked up, and a moment later found herself rising into the air.

In one instant, she found herself inside some sort of chamber with metal walls; in the next, there was a buzzing noise, and everything went black, and she knew no more.

Miguel woke up and stretched. He glanced over at the clock—seven-thirty. Plenty of time.

He stepped out of the trailer and took a deep breath of the chill morning air. The campground was in an open field off the main road. There were about a dozen other trailers parked here. At least a few of them looked like they'd been here a very long time.

It was only ten minutes to the diner, so he got dressed and went for a quick run. He went only a couple of miles up the road and then turned around.

The land here was flat for miles around, and he could see nothing but cornfields, broken up by the occasional farmhouse or barn. He couldn't imagine living here long-term. Over the years, he'd fallen in love with Arizona—there was beauty in the desert, unrivaled by anywhere else he'd ever traveled.

Back at his trailer, he showered and got dressed, then headed into town to meet Sydney. He arrived a few minutes before nine. Going inside, he grabbed them a booth in the far corner.

The waitress came by to take his order.

"Oh, I'm waiting for someone," he told her. "She should be here soon."

"Coffee in the meantime?"

"Yeah, that'd be good."

She came back with the coffee a minute later.

Miguel finished the cup, and there was still no sign of Sydney. It was about ten minutes after nine, now.

He sent her a text. But several more minutes went by with no reply. He tried calling her, but it went straight to voicemail.

"Weird," he said out loud. "She didn't seem like the type to stand a fella up."

He paid for his coffee and then went out to his truck. She hadn't told him the name of the motel where she was staying. But he checked on his phone, and there was only one place anywhere close by. He headed out and arrived there ten minutes later.

The place was pretty rundown. There were a dozen rooms, all with direct access from the parking lot. Only a few cars were parked here, none of them Sydney's rental car.

He checked with the office, but the woman there didn't know anything.

"Very strange," he said out loud.

He tried texting and calling again, to no avail.

"I don't get it," he muttered.

Sydney had told him the name of the couple who had been abducted—the Johnsons. A pretty common name, unfortunately.

He looked them up online. There were only two Johnsons in the area and only one on Route 23. He put their address into his GPS and headed out to their house.

He knocked on the door when he arrived, and Mr. Johnson answered.

"Good morning, sir," he said. "My name is Miguel San Juan—I'm a friend of Sydney Hastings. I was supposed to meet her at the diner for breakfast this morning, but she didn't show up. I've tried calling her and what not, but I can't reach her, and well, I'm getting a little worried. I don't suppose you folks have heard from her today?"

"No, can't say we have. She came out here yesterday during the day, but we haven't heard from her since then. When did you hear from her last?"

"Met up with her for dinner last night," he said, looking out across the fields. "I checked at the motel, but her car wasn't there."

"That is concerning," said Mr. Johnson. He gave Miguel his phone number and asked him to keep him updated.

"Will do," said Miguel. "Thank you."

He drove back to the diner to make sure she hadn't turned up there and then checked the motel one more time. But Sydney was nowhere to be found.

Miguel thought of contacting her boss, but other than his first name, Brian, he knew nothing about him—not his last name, nor his address or the name of his company.

He went back to his trailer and waited a couple more hours,

hoping that maybe she would call him back or answer his text. But by that afternoon, he still hadn't had any contact.

Checking online, he found the town was so small that it didn't have its own police department. The next town over had one, but he doubted they'd have jurisdiction here. It looked like the county sheriff would be his best bet. Their office was only about twenty minutes away, down Route 23, so Miguel headed there.

He spoke to the man at the desk and explained the situation.

"So, can I file a missing person's report, or do I have to wait till she's been gone 24 hours?"

"No, in fact, it's best to file the report as soon as possible," the man told him. "Chances are she'll turn up, and there'll be some simple explanation. But in case that doesn't happen, it's best to have the report on file."

Miguel gave him the information he needed.

"You should be all set," the man told him. "We've got your number, so the deputy will be in touch if there's anything else he needs. And in the meantime, if Ms. Hastings does turn up, please give us a call and let us know."

Miguel thanked him and went out to his truck. There was one more place he wanted to check for himself.

He drove back up Route 23 and found the stretch of road where Sydney had told him the UFO activity was occurring. Pulling over to the side of the road, he got out of his truck and had a look around. But there was nothing to see here.

As he was getting back into the truck, he noticed a little dirt road up ahead. Curious, he walked over to it. There were fresh tire tracks.

Knowing it would probably be a waste of time, he decided to have a look anyway, just to cover all the bases. He set out on foot, following the tire tracks a few hundred feet up the road. But they ended there, with no sign of a vehicle anywhere nearby.

"Stranger and stranger," he muttered to himself, heading back to his truck.

He got back to his trailer and tried texting and calling Sydney one more time. But there was no reply. Miguel didn't know what else he could do but wait and see if she contacted him.

Chapter Fifteen: Missing Time

Sydney opened her eyes. Her head felt foggy, and her vision was blurry. As she moved, she found she had a splitting headache.

It took her a minute to remember where she was—the motel in Kansas.

She felt like she had a bad hangover, yet she didn't drink the night before.

Looking at the clock, she said, "Oh crap!"

It was quarter to nine—she was supposed to be meeting Miguel for breakfast in fifteen minutes. She got out of bed as quickly as she could. There was no time for a shower, so she washed her face and went out to her car.

Ten minutes later, she pulled up at the diner. Miguel's truck wasn't here, but it was nine sharp, so she figured he'd arrive soon. She decided to wait for him in the car.

Checking her phone, she saw she had quite a few missed calls and text messages from him.

"What the hell..?"

The messages were all asking her where she was. And then she realized it was Thursday, not Wednesday.

Sydney felt confused. How could it be *Thursday*? She'd arrived here on Tuesday, of that she was sure. After checking in at the motel, she'd gone out to meet the Johnsons. And she'd gone out to eat at the Chinese restaurant with Miguel for dinner. That much she could remember clearly.

After dinner, she'd come back to the motel and gone to bed reasonably early.

"Wait a minute..."

She'd had trouble getting to sleep... and she'd gone out to Route 23!

Suddenly, she remembered meeting the teenager with the drone.

"What was his name..."

She checked her phone and found the contact she'd created for him.

"Right, Owen..."

And then she'd returned to the motel... hadn't she?

No... she had no memory of actually returning to her room.

"Wait..." There had been a light in the sky... she'd taken off in her car and ended up driving down a dirt road...

"Oh, shit!"

There was a UFO! She'd been abducted!

But beyond rising into the air and moving inside the flying saucer, she simply could not recall anything else.

She called Miguel.

"Hey! Where the hell have you been?! I've been worried sick!"

"I'm sorry... I... it's tough to remember anything. Miguel, I think I was abducted..."

"Oh, damn... where are you?"

"I'm at the diner. I thought it was Wednesday morning, so I came here to meet you for breakfast..."

"Alright, stay put. I'll be right there."

Sydney waited for him in her car. She was feeling a little woozy and thought staying seated would be best.

When he arrived, she got out of the car and met him at his truck.

"Mornin'!" he said, pulling her into a hug.

"Thanks for coming out," she said. "I'm sorry for standing you up yesterday."

"Wasn't your fault," he replied. "You alright?"

"I think so... I don't know. My head is foggy."

"You hungry? Wanna get some food?"

"Yes! I'm famished; I feel like I haven't eaten in days, and now that I think about it, that might be the case..."

They went in and sat down at a booth by the front windows. The waitress brought them coffee and took their order.

"I have to tell you," said Sydney, "I've never been so scared in my life."

"I know what you mean," he replied. "Shook me up pretty good when I had my experience, too. So, you feel up to telling me about it?"

She told him the whole story.

"You know, I had a feeling that maybe something like this had happened," he said when she was done. "I went out to that stretch of Route 23. I found these tire tracks on this dirt road, but they ended, and there was no car there."

"I think that was me," said Sydney. "But I have no idea how the car got back to the motel—or how *I* did, for that matter..."

"And you don't recall anything after going inside the UFO?"

"I don't. I'm trying to... it's the weirdest feeling. It's like trying to remember the name of a song, and it's on the tip of your tongue, but you can't quite think of it... I'm pretty sure the memories are there, ya know? But I can't seem to get them to surface."

"I've been thinkin' about my abduction a lot since that whole thing out at Monument Valley. The whole thing seems so dreamlike; I honestly can't say for sure what parts definitely happened or not. I don't know. There's some weird shit going on, that's for sure."

"I feel terrible, too," she said. "Kinda hungover, except I didn't have anything to drink."

"You think maybe that teenager you met mighta captured anything on camera with that drone of his?"

"That's a great question," she said. "Hang on; I'll shoot him a text."

Sydney sent Owen a message, asking if he'd seen anything that night or managed to get anything on video. There was no immediate reply, and their food arrived a minute later.

Miguel phoned Ted Johnson and the sheriff's office to let them know Sydney had returned.

"Wow, you filed a missing person's report for me?" asked Sydney.

"Had to do something," he said. "I didn't know what the hell happened to ya."

They still hadn't heard back from Owen by the time they

finished eating, so they dropped Sydney's car off at the motel, and Miguel drove them over to the farmhouse where Owen lived.

Sydney ran up to the front porch and knocked on the door. It took a minute, but a woman came to the door.

"Can I help you?" she asked.

"Hi, my name is Sydney Hastings. I was out on the road here the other night, and I met Owen..."

"Yes, I'm his mother, Sharon Driscoll," she said. "Is Owen in any kind of trouble?"

"No, not at all. I met him because he was flying his drone around here—I have to confess, it scared the daylights out of me..."

"I'm sorry about that—I've warned him not to fly that thing near other people."

"Oh, well, I had, ah, an experience right after that, over on that dirt road over there, and I wanted to see if he might have caught any of it on camera..."

"You weren't taken by one of those UFOs, were you?"

"I'm afraid I was..."

"Oh, my dear, I'm so sorry to hear that. Seems to be a problem around here—I've tried to sell my place because of it. Hoping to get out of here before anything happens to my boy or me!"

"Is he home?"

"No, he's at his job today. But he should be home this afternoon if you want to try again then."

"Thank you, I will!"

Sydney joined Miguel back at the truck.

"No luck?"

"Kid's not home—she said to check back this afternoon. I wanna go take a look down that dirt road."

They moved the truck down the road a bit and parked on the shoulder by the dirt road. The two of them walked out to where the tire tracks ended.

"So, this is it," said Sydney, looking around across the fields. "This is where they took me."

"Being here jogging any memories for ya?"

Sydney took a deep breath.

"No. I remember the car dying, running a short distance... and floating up to the ship, but that's it. The next thing I can recall is waking up back in the motel room."

Miguel dropped her off at the motel, and they agreed to meet up again later that day.

Sydney took a long, hot shower and then got dressed and went for a walk. The hot water and fresh air did her some good, and she found her head getting clearer. She stopped at the café and ordered a coffee.

A couple of hours later, she finally got a reply from Owen.

"Hey, did you see that UFO that came after me the other night? Did you get it on video?"

"You bet I did!"

"Are you home? Can I come over and see it?"

"Yeah, I'm here."

Sydney called Miguel. He picked her up at the café, and they drove back out to the farmhouse. Owen was waiting for them in the front yard.

"Wait till you see this!" he said, his phone in hand. "I pulled the footage from the drone."

He held out his phone, and they watched the video he'd captured.

It was tough to see much—the night had been dark and foggy. But Sydney could make out the ring of lights in the sky and her car turning onto the dirt road. From the drone's vantage point, the car was no longer visible after that, but she could see its headlights moving through the cornfield.

The vehicle's lights went out, and then a spotlight shone down from the middle of the ring of lights. Sydney could just make out an object rising in the spotlight's beam and moving inside the UFO.

"Oh, my God—that's me!"

After that, the spotlight turned off. The ring of lights in the sky shot off into the distance and disappeared. That was the end of the video.

"Do you think you could send me this?"

"Yeah, no problem."

He sent her the file.

"Thank you so much for this," she said.

"Any time!"

Sydney and Miguel got into his truck and headed back into town.

"Not much to see on that video," he observed.

"I know," she said. "I want to get it back to Brian and see if he can enhance it—maybe get us a better look at the UFO, at least."

"And what's next, do you reckon?"

"I don't know… I do need to check in with Brian anyway, not just for the video—he doesn't even know I was abducted yet. I'm gonna call him now."

Sydney tapped on his contact. He answered on the first ring.

"Hey, it's me!"

"Sydney! What's going on?"

She told him about her meeting with the Johnsons, her experience with the UFO, and the video she'd obtained.

"This is a serious development," he said. "Are you feeling okay?"

"Better now. I was pretty groggy this morning, had a big headache. But yeah, I'm alright."

"I think we should bring you home," he said. "I'd like to have you see a physician, and we can get that video enhanced and decide what we do next."

"Alright, boss," she said. "I can head out first thing in the morning."

"Great," said Brian. "I'll let Dave know. Send me that video when you get a chance!"

"Yes, I'll do that right now."

She hung up with him, and sent him the video, then closed her phone as they arrived at the motel.

"So, you're heading back east?" Miguel asked.

"Yeah, in the morning."

"Hmm. You think I could go with you?"

"You wanna fly out to North Carolina with me?"

"Yeah, why not?" he said with a grin. "Someone's gotta keep an eye on you!"

"Alright," said Sydney, feeling a few butterflies in her stomach. "Let me call Brian back real quick and make sure he's cool with it—I'm staying at his house till they finish up the work on my place."

She called him right back and asked about bringing a guest.

"Sure," he said. "The more, the merrier!"

Sydney and Miguel went out to eat that evening, and then he dropped her off at the motel. She wanted to get to bed early—she still wasn't feeling right. And her headache had returned.

It took her a long time to fall asleep. Once she had drifted off, she had a nightmare about being abducted again and awoke with a scream. She sat up in bed and found she'd broken out in a cold sweat. She slept only fitfully after that.

Sydney dropped off the rental car in the morning, and Miguel drove them to the airport. They met Dave there and flew back to North Carolina. Brian picked them up at the airport.

Back at the ranch, they sat down in the living room to catch up.

"I've taken the liberty of scheduling a physical for you," Brian told Sydney. "It's later this afternoon, with the doctor I see here in town. I hope that's okay?"

"Yeah, absolutely," she said. "I recommended that the Johnsons get full-body MRIs done, too—I'll look for somewhere around here that I can do the same thing."

"Good thinking," Brian agreed. "I had another thought, too.

Regarding your missing time. It would be helpful to retrieve any memories you may have that are being blocked for whatever reason."

"Yes!" said Sydney. "I've had this feeling that they're just under the surface, somehow, but I can't quite get them back."

"There's a hypnotist over in Roxboro. I think he might be able to help you access those memories."

"Oh, yeah, I'll try anything at this point," said Sydney.

"Great. I spoke to him briefly this morning and explained the general gist of the situation. He thinks he can help. I'll call him back and book you an appointment.

"Also, I've sent that video to my team, and they're working on enhancing it for us. I should have it back this evening."

"Perfect," said Sydney. "I'm very interested to see what else may be visible in that footage."

Her phone rang; it was Ted Johnson.

"Hello?"

"Hi, Sydney?"

"Yes! How are you?"

"We're good. Wanted to let you know we had our physicals. The doctor says we're in good health, didn't find anything strange in the blood work or anything..."

"But?"

"Well, he did find something. We each had a small scar on the back of our necks. He sent us for X-rays, and there was something inside there. For both of us."

"Any idea what it is?"

"They were only just below the skin and very small, so he was able to remove them right there in the office."

"Remove what, exactly?"

"Can't rightly say what they are," Ted told her. "The doctor had no idea, either. Little squares of some sort of metal, it looks like. Only a little bigger than a pinhead."

"That's very strange," said Sydney. "Could you send me a picture of them?"

"Sure, hang on." Moments later, she received a text message with the photo.

"Great, I've got it, thank you."

"We haven't had the MRIs yet, but we got 'em scheduled for next week. After this, I'm very curious to see what else they might've done to us!"

"Yes, me too," said Sydney. "Let's stay in touch, okay?"

"Will do," he said.

Sydney hung up with him and took a closer look at the photo. It showed two tiny black squares.

"What is it?" asked Brian.

"I don't know," said Sydney. She showed him the photo and told him everything Ted had said. "You wanna check the back of my neck for me?"

"Yes, turn around."

Sydney pulled her hair out of the way so he could get a look.

"There's a small red line," he told her. "Looks like an incision."

"Damn, I must have one, too!" she said. "What do you think it could be?"

"I'm not sure," said Brian. "Let's see if the doctor can remove it, and then we can run an analysis on it."

Sydney suddenly felt very anxious. What the hell had they implanted inside of her? She was eager to get to the bottom of this.

Chapter Sixteen: Total Recall

Sydney drove into town for her physical later that afternoon. The nurse took her vitals and then left her in the exam room to change into a medical gown. The doctor walked in a few minutes later and introduced himself.

"Hello, Ms. Hastings?" Sydney nodded. "I'm Dr. Lee."

"Nice to meet you," she said, shaking his hand.

He proceeded with the physical. After a few minutes, he had her lie on her back, and he examined her abdomen.

"This is strange," he said suddenly, looking closely at an area on her lower abdomen.

"What is it?"

"This looks like an incision," he said. "It's quite small."

"What could that be for?"

"I'm not sure... do you have any pain in this area?"

"No, not at all."

"Hmm."

The doctor finished his exam. She asked him to check the back of her neck.

"Yes, this does look like an incision, too," he confirmed.

She told him about the abductions and explained what had happened with the Johnsons.

"Hmm. If there is something just below the skin, I can remove it now, if you'd like."

"Yes, please," she said. "I'm willing to bet I've got the same thing they did."

"Okay, hang tight, and I'll be right back."

He left the exam room, then returned a minute later with the nurse. Sydney moved her hair out of the way. The nurse wiped down the back of her neck with alcohol.

"I'm going to re-open the same incision," he told her. "This will sting a bit."

Sydney felt him cutting open her skin.

"Yes, there's something in there, alright," he said. "Hold on... We'll get it out with the tweezers... I've got it."

The nurse applied a bandage to the back of her neck.

"I'm not sure what this is," said the doctor, placing the foreign object in a small Petri dish. "But it looks just like you described."

He handed her the dish. Sure enough, it was a small, flat wafer that looked identical to the ones in the photo from Mr. Johnson.

The doctor put a lid on the Petri dish for her.

"What about the incision in my abdomen," she asked. "Do you think there could be something there, too?"

"Well, that's a possibility, but... I suspect something else."

"What?"

"The incision is directly over one of your ovaries."

"My *ovaries*?! You don't think they removed one, do you?"

"No, the incision is much too small for that. But I suspect that they could have removed an egg. A *human* doctor would do that through an intravaginal procedure. But, of course, if it's aliens we're dealing with here, who knows what kind of tech they might be using."

"I was already planning on getting a full-body MRI," she told him. "If they did harvest my eggs, would they be able to tell that from an MRI?"

The doctor nodded.

"Possibly. It should certainly turn up any abnormalities. Depending on how they did the procedure, it may leave traces that would show up in an MRI scan. There's a place in Roxboro. I'll leave the information for you at the front desk so you can grab that on your way out.

"I'm going to have the nurse draw a blood sample, and we'll run a full metabolic panel. I'll call you if anything comes up there—no news is good news!"

He left the room. The nurse came back in a few minutes later and drew her blood. When she was done, Sydney checked out and headed back to the ranch. She told Brian and Miguel about her exam and showed them the object the doctor had removed from her neck.

"Very odd," said Brian. He moved into his office and pulled a magnifying glass out of his desk. Sitting down, he examined it more closely.

"I don't see any surface features," he told them. "It's smooth and black. I'm a little surprised—I expected to see some sort of circuitry."

"What, like a microchip or something?" asked Miguel.

"Precisely," said Brian. "I'm going to take this to my office and have them analyze it in the lab. We'll try to get some idea of what this is. Oh, and I was able to get you an appointment for Monday with the hypnotist. I gave him more details of what's been going on. Hopefully, he'll be able to help you achieve total recall."

"That would be fantastic," said Sydney.

"I'm going to head to the office now," Brian told them. "I want them to get started right away on this... well, whatever this is," he said, holding up the Petri dish. "Help yourselves to the pantry and the alcohol if you'd like."

"You're not going to eat before you go?"

"I'll grab something on the road," he said. "Don't worry about me!"

Brian left. Sydney sat down and called the MRI facility; she was able to schedule an appointment for Tuesday.

After that, she got to work making dinner.

"I'm not much of a cook," she said to Miguel. "So, I'm afraid it's going to be spaghetti and meatballs..."

"Sounds delicious!"

After dinner, Sydney started the fireplace and poured them each a glass of Scotch. They sat next to each other on the sofa.

"This whole thing is so... messed up," she said. "I feel so *violated*. Someone, we don't even know *who*, implanted some sort of device inside *my* body and might have taken eggs without my consent... And chances are whoever it is has been doing this to *thousands* of people. I mean, that's a crime. If this were a human being, they'd go to *jail* for shit like this."

Miguel nodded, taking a sip of his Scotch.

"No doubt," he said. "And we have no idea *why* they're doing it. This has been going on for decades, it would seem, but for what purpose?"

"We have no idea," said Sydney. She drank some of her Scotch. "I still don't feel right. It's like... I almost feel like I'm not *me* anymore. It's as if I'm watching myself doing things, instead of actually doing them..."

"I know what you mean," he said. "I had that feeling, too."

Sydney felt herself tearing up.

"It's not right, what they did to us," she said through a sniffle. "I don't feel safe anymore. I'm scared *all the time.*"

Miguel pulled her into a hug, and she found herself crying into his chest.

"It's okay," he said. "We're both safe here. They can't touch you."

Sydney took a deep breath.

"I feel so stupid," she said. "I'm not normally a crier."

"Nothing wrong with a good cry," he told her. "I cried more than a few times after my abduction."

"How long did it take before you felt like yourself again?"

"Oh, I don't know... took a while, I guess. I don't want to make you feel worse, but to tell you the truth, I still have nightmares sometimes. But it does get better, slowly."

They sat there quietly for a while. Miguel started stroking her hair and then kissed her on the top of the head.

Sydney turned to face him, looking deep into his eyes.

"I think I like you," he said, smiling at her.

"Oh, you *think* you like me?"

"I mean, well..."

She kissed him, and he kissed her back.

After a minute, she got up and said with a smile, "It's getting late. I think I'm going to bed... Care to join me?"

Sydney led him into her bedroom and closed the door behind them.

A few hours later, as she started drifting off to sleep in Miguel's arms, she heard the front door opening. She started awake.

"Who's that?" she whispered.

"Must be Brian," he said. "I'll check."

He got out of bed and got dressed, then went out to see who was there. Moments later, she heard his voice and Brian's. She got dressed and went out to join them.

"Hey," she said to Brian through a yawn. "How'd it go?"

"We don't know much yet," he said. "I was right; there are circuits on that thing. They're incredibly tiny, though—it appears they've been printed on an *atomic* level."

"Any idea what the thing does?" asked Miguel.

"Not yet," said Brian. "But my team's going to keep up their analysis through the weekend.

"Anyway, it's very late—Miguel, let me show you to your room."

"Ah, actually," said Sydney, feeling a little awkward now, "he'll be staying in my room..."

"Oh!" said Brian, surprised. "Okay! Well, goodnight!"

The three of them turned in for the night. Sydney and Miguel went for a run together in the morning. Brian had breakfast prepared for them by the time they'd returned.

Sunday night, Brian received a call from his office.

"Andre," he said into his phone. "What've you got? Uh-huh… fascinating… Did that have any effect? Hmm. Oh… Are you serious? What frequency? That's incredible. Alright, thank you—great work!"

He closed his phone.

"So, what is it?" asked Sydney.

"It's a microchip," Brian told them. "There's no question. But they tried applying an electric current to the thing, and nothing happened. On a hunch, Andre had them apply heat—98.6 degrees, to be precise."

"Human body temperature?" said Sydney.

"Indeed. And that turned the thing on!"

"What does it do?" asked Miguel.

"That's the most interesting part," Brian said. "When exposed to heat, it emitted a *radio* signal. Very low frequency."

"What does the low frequency mean?" asked Sydney.

"Lower frequency radio waves can travel over longer distances than higher frequency ones."

"So, what the hell was it transmitting over that frequency, exactly?" asked Miguel.

"That they were not able to determine," said Brian. "I suspect it may be a beacon of some kind."

"What, you mean they were using it to *track* me or something?" asked Sydney. "Like a GPS device?"

"That's exactly what I suspect," said Brian. "Which would be incredible for such a small chip. It would have to have some way of performing geolocation—determining its exact coordinates on the planet and then transmitting that information to... well, somewhere. To someone."

"And the Johnsons had them, too," said Sydney. "I wonder if they're implanting one into everyone they abduct."

"It would help explain how they're able to abduct some people repeatedly," Brian observed. "They'd be easy enough to track down."

"One of you wanna check my neck?" asked Miguel.

He turned around, and Sydney took a look.

"Yep, there's a tiny scar there," she confirmed.

"Well, I'll be damned," he said. "I think I'll get an appointment with that doc of yours and have mine removed, too."

"Oh, I almost forgot—I got the video of your abduction back. Check this out," Brian said, pulling out his phone. He played the video for them.

Sydney thought it didn't look much different from the original. But she could make out the bottom of the UFO more clearly. The upper section of the spacecraft, however, was still not visible at all.

"Don't look much different," Miguel observed.

"True," said Brian. "But it is a little odd that the entire upper section of the ship is invisible. Could be the fog and lack of light, but I would have expected to see at least a vague outline of that area."

"Well, this doesn't tell us anything we didn't already know," said Sydney. "I was hoping for more."

Monday morning, she drove over to Roxboro with Brian and Miguel to see the hypnotist. They arrived a little early and had to wait until he was ready for them.

Finally, the receptionist invited them into the office.

The room was only dimly lit. There were a couple of candles burning on the desk, and Sydney could smell incense. There were four chairs set up in front of the desk—one leather recliner and three office chairs.

"Greetings, I am Dr. Kumar," the hypnotist said, shaking their hands. "Please, have a seat—Ms. Hastings, the recliner is for you."

"Thank you," said Sydney, taking a seat.

"I have spoken with Mr. Kwan," he said. "My understanding is that we will be attempting to recover some memories of a traumatic event? An alien abduction, yes?"

"That's correct," said Sydney.

"It is not uncommon for one to experience some memory loss after trauma," Dr. Kumar told them. "It is a defense mechanism the brain sometimes uses when an event is too overwhelming to process. However, in this case, it may be different. Mr. Kwan has explained to me that there are *thousands* of people who have had these abduction experiences, and the vast majority are unable to recall much of what has happened to them.

"This would suggest to me that whoever is behind these abductions may by some means be intentionally blocking out the memories of their victims. If they are using some sort of biological or chemical agent to achieve this, it could make the memories more difficult to access.

"It is also possible that the victims are being kept unconscious throughout their encounter. However, it is also my understanding that some people do remember at least parts of their experience. This leads me to believe that the victims are conscious for much of the time and that the memories are intact but suppressed.

"And so, I will be helping you relax your mind and attempting to help you relive your experience, to see if perhaps we can gain access to those missing memories."

"Okay," said Sydney. "Sounds good."

"Now, you should know, I have also spoken with Mr. Kwan about the details of your abduction and the reports from other victims. Thus, I do already have familiarity with how these events have unfolded."

Sydney nodded.

"Very good, let us begin. Please, open the recliner, and make yourself comfortable."

Dr. Kumar went behind his desk and played some quiet music—it sounded like a flute, with the sound of soft ocean waves in the background.

He returned to his seat.

"Ms. Hastings, I would like you to close your eyes. I want you to concentrate on the crown of your head. Imagine the stress and tension in that area melting away and leaving your body. Now, this release slowly continues, encompassing the rest of your head, your forehead, your face, all the tension washing away, leaving your muscles relaxed.

"This process continues, down your neck, into your shoulders, and down your arms. Let your muscles relax, and allow every part of your body to sink into the chair beneath you.

"This extends now through your chest and your abdomen. Your back, and now down your legs. The tightness in your muscles washes away, and you are relaxed and light as a feather.

"Now, I want you to listen to the sound of the waves. Imagine that you are on a beach. It is nighttime, and you see the moon over the ocean. The air is warm. The waves are gently lapping against the shore, and you feel the sand beneath your feet. How do you feel?"

"Mm, peaceful," said Sydney. "Calm."

"Good. Now you are going to maintain that calm. You are safe, and you have the power to go anywhere you choose, at any time, do you understand?"

"Yes."

"I want you to think back to that night when you saw the UFO. You are in your car, driving. You see a bright light behind you. What do you do?"

"I drive faster."

"And the light follows you. What do you do now?"

"There's a dirt road... I turn onto it, trying to get away."

"But the UFO follows you?"

"Yes."

"What happens next?"

"The car dies. The lights go out. I get out of the car. I'm running... but the light is still following me. I look up, and there's a spotlight..."

"What next?"

"I'm flying up through the air.... I'm inside the UFO."

"Very good. What do you see?"

"It's darker here... the walls are metal..."

"What else do you see?"

"Nothing... there's nothing here..."

"What happens now?"

"The opening I came through is gone... now it's completely dark... I can't see anything..."

"Is there anyone else with you?"

"No... I don't' think so... I don't see anyone..."

"Do you hear anyone?"

"No. It's silent. There's no noise at all."

"Do you feel anything?"

"No... yes..."

"What do you feel?"

"Air, I think... there's a breeze... a faint breeze on my skin..."

"What happens now?"

"I don't know... everything is black... I don't remember anything else..."

"Do you see anyone when they move you into the pod?"

"No... There's nobody in the pods... The pods! There were pods in the wall! They moved me into a different area!"

"Is there anyone in the pods?"

"No—they're empty..."

"Now, what happens next?"

"Nothing... I can't move. I'm trying to get out of the pod. But I can't move my arms or my legs."

"How do you feel?"

"I'm scared. I don't know what they're going to do with me."

"Remember, you are in control now. You can leave at any time."

"Yes."

"What happens when you leave the pod?"

"I'm moving back to the room where I started."

"Do you see anyone here?"

"No."

"What do you see?"

"The metal walls. There's a hole in the floor again. I can see the ground below."

"Do you move down to the ground?"

"Yes. I'm floating again. Floating down."

"Are you on the ground now?"

"Yes."

"Do you see the UFO above you?"

"Yes."

"Do you know where you are?"

"Yes. I'm in the desert. I'm near Monument Valley."

"You can see Monument Valley?"

"Yes. It's far away, but I can see it."

"What do you see close by? Describe your immediate surroundings."

"I'm in the desert. There's nothing here. I see a mesa nearby. There's a butte closer to me."

"Do you see any buildings? Any manmade structures?"

"No. There is nothing here."

"Any other flying saucers?"

"No."

"I want you to look again toward Monument Valley. Do you see it?"

"Yes."

"Look very carefully. Are you certain you see the mesas?"

"Yes."

"Is there anyone with you?"

"Yes."

"Who is with you?"

"Aliens. There are three aliens."

"What do they look like?"

"They're Malor. Exactly like the aliens from the invasion."

"What happens next?"

"They're taking me to the butte. I still can't move. I'm floating somehow."

"What happens when you get to the butte?"

"There's an opening. We're going inside. There's a tunnel."

"What's at the end of the tunnel."

"There's an elevator."

"Do they take you inside the elevator?"

"Yes... we're going down. Fast. We're going down fast."

"When you get to the bottom, and the door opens, what do you see?"

"Another tunnel."

"They take you down the tunnel. Where do you go next?"

"A room. It's a big room. I see metal walls."

"What is in this room?"

"Tables. I think they're exam tables... like in a hospital..."

"Is there anyone on the tables?"

"Only on one."

"Who do you see on that one table?"

"I don't know. A man. An older man. He's naked. I don't know who he is."

"Is he awake?"

"I don't think so. His eyes are closed. He's not moving."

"What happens next?"

"I don't know... it's dark now... I can't remember..."

"You wake up again. Where are you?"

"I'm still in the room. I'm lying on one of the tables."

"Are you naked now?"

"Yes."

"Is there anyone else here?"

"No."

"Is the man still on the other table?"

"No... I can only see a couple of other tables... there's nobody on them now."

"Does anyone join you in the room?"

"Yes. The three aliens again. I think they're the same ones from before. It's hard to tell. They all look alike."

"What do they do?"

"One comes over to me. He has something in his hand. I don't know what it is. It's egg-shaped... he's holding it against my forehead."

"What happens next?"

"He moves the device to my chest. He touches it against me again, over my heart this time."

"What purpose does this serve? Why is he touching you with this device?"

"I don't know."

"Does it hurt?"

"No."

"What happens next?"

"He moves the device again. This time to my abdomen. He touches me where the doctor found the incision."

"Above your ovary?"

"Yes."

"Do you know what he's doing with it?"

"No."

"Does it hurt this time?"

"No... yes."

"What does it feel like?"

"It's a little prick... like a needle."

"How badly does it hurt?"

"Only a little."

"Are the other two aliens still here?"

"Yes."

"What are they doing?"

"Nothing. They're watching, I think."

"Now, I want you to concentrate. Look very closely at these aliens."

"Yes."

"Are you sure they are there?"

"Yes... wait..."

"Can you see them?"

"No... there's nobody there..."

"Did they leave?"

"No... I don't know..."

"Think back again to when the alien first touched you with the egg-shaped device. He is touching your forehead with it?"

"Yes."

"I want you to look at him very carefully. What do you see?"

"Nothing. There's nobody here. I must have imagined it..."

"Is the device still touching your forehead?"

"Yes."

"Who is holding it there?"

"Nobody. There is nobody here."

"Does it move to your heart?"

"Yes."

"Who moves it there?"

"Nobody. It moves on its own."

"And does it move to your abdomen?"

"Yes."

"Do you feel the pinprick?"

"Yes."

"Who is holding the device?"

"Nobody."

"Now, I want you to think very hard. Have you seen anyone here? Since you left the UFO, have you seen anyone else?"

"Yes."

"Who?"

"The old man in the other bed."

"He was definitely there?"

"Yes."

"Nobody else?"

"Nobody else."

"When you first arrived here and left the UFO, was there anyone on the ground with you?"

"No."

"No aliens?"

"No."

"Who moved you to the butte, into the elevator there?"

"I don't know. I moved by myself."

"Did you walk there, willingly?"

"No. I was floating. Something moved me, but I can't see what."

"Okay. We are back in the exam room. The egg-shaped device has pricked your abdomen. What happens next?"

"I can't see the device anymore."

"Where did it go?"

"I don't know. It's gone."

"What happens next?"

"Nothing. I'm lying there for a long time. I can't move. There's nobody else here."

"Eventually, does everything go black again?"

"Yes."

"What happens when you wake up?"

"I'm moving down the tunnel again. To the elevator."

"Do you go back outside to the desert?"

"Yes."

"Is the UFO there?"

"Yes. It's above me, in the air."

"Do you go back inside it?"

"Yes. I'm floating up to it. Then I'm back in the metal room again."

"Do they move you to the other area, with the pods?"

"Yes. They put me in a pod."

"Do you see anyone else here?"

"No. I'm alone."

"What happens now?"

"Nothing. I'm in the pod. But then I move back to the metal room again. The floor opens. I'm floating down to the ground."

"Where are you now?"

"On the dirt road."

"Is anyone else there?"

"No."

"What do you see?"

"It's dark out. I see my rental car."

"What happens next?"

"I get in the car. There's no room to turn around. I back up to the main road. I drive to the motel."

"What do you do when you get there?"

"I go inside. I go to bed. I fall asleep."

"Okay, Ms. Hastings. Now, we are back on the beach. Do you feel the sand between your toes?"

"Yes."

"Do you hear the waves?"

"Yes."

"Very good. Now, I am going to count to three. And then you are going to open your eyes, and we will be back in my office. Are you ready?"

"Yes."

"One... two... three..."

Chapter Seventeen: Caught in the Act

Sydney opened her eyes. She looked around at Dr. Kumar, Brian, and Miguel.

"Holy shit!"

"Yeah, you can say that again," said Miguel.

"That crime boss in Puerto Rico was right—there were *no aliens* there!"

"Dr. Kumar, why did she believe there were aliens there at first?" asked Brian.

"This is something fairly common in cases where we lose memories in a traumatic experience," he explained. "Remember, the initial memory loss is a defense mechanism for our brain. When the events are too overwhelming, when they cause too much stress, the brain can suppress those memories to diminish that stress.

"When we do finally begin to recover those memories, often the brain will supply details to help process or explain what has happened to us.

"The image of what an alien looks like has been embedded in our cultural consciousness, if you will, since the events in Roswell, many decades ago. And, of course, that image has been reinforced by the invasion because the aliens have turned out to look exactly as we expect."

"You're saying that my brain supplied a memory of the Malor because that was what I expected to see there?" asked Sydney.

"Yes, in part," said Dr. Kumar. "But also, it was difficult for your subconscious to accept that these things could have happened to you of their own accord—being moved from one place to another, the device examining you. One would normally expect to see a person, or a being of some kind, in this case, performing those actions. That makes more sense, perhaps than what actually happened, and so the brain fills in the missing pieces."

Sydney thanked Dr. Kumar for his time, and they headed out to the car. Her phone rang as they were pulling out of the parking lot.

"Hello, Ms. Hastings?"

"Yes," she replied.

"This is Dr. Lee. We've run the blood work, and I wanted to go over the results with you. Do you have a minute?"

"I do!"

"Great. The metabolic panel was mostly good, but there were a couple of numbers that were a little off—still in normal range but at the low end. Entirely out of an abundance of caution, we decided to dig a little deeper.

"We did find traces of a compound we can't definitively identify. I can tell you it is similar to a couple of other drugs we are familiar with—both of which suppress neural activity in various regions of the body."

"Suppress neural activity... how, exactly?"

"Well, it could have any number of effects, from numbing pain to blocking certain motor neurons—creating a partial paralysis, to interfering with memory formation."

"That is very interesting," she said. "Did you find anything else unusual?"

"No, that was it. Otherwise, you are in excellent health. And the levels of that one compound in your system are very low—I wouldn't expect you to have any lasting effects."

Sydney hung up with the doctor and told Brian and Miguel what she'd found out.

"It would seem we are increasing our understanding of the what and how of these abductions, but gaining very little knowledge of the *why*," Brian observed.

Sydney dropped them off back at the ranch and went into town for her MRI. She checked in and then met the technician a few minutes later. The technician had her remove her watch and earrings.

"Any other piercings?"

"No."

"Anything in your pockets?"

"Yoga pants," she said with a grin. "No pockets."

"No metal zippers or rivets on any clothing."

"Nope."

"Does your bra have a metal underwire?"

"Not wearing one."

"Okay, we should be good to go."

She had Sydney lie flat on her back in the bed.

"Have you ever had an MRI scan before?" the technician.

"I have not, but I worked as a nurse for many years, so I'm familiar with the process."

"Perfect. We're doing a full-body scan, so this will take roughly sixty to ninety minutes. Some people experience claustrophobia in there. If at any time you're feeling uncomfortable, let me know, and we can take a break and get you out of there for a little while. Any questions?"

"No, I'm ready."

This process ended up taking a little over an hour. Sydney found herself feeling grateful for her slight physique. She could imagine how someone taller or bulkier would feel claustrophobic in such a tight space.

When it was over, the technician brought her over to the monitor.

"It'll take a few days to fully process the results," she told her. "There's a huge amount of imagery to assess when doing a full-body scan. But, I did want to show you this."

She moved through the images, then stopped on one, and zoomed in.

"This is the femur in your right leg, up near your hip. Do you see that dark spot?"

Sydney looked closer, where the woman was pointing. There was a small circular patch that was darker than the surrounding area.

"Yeah, what is that?"

"I can't say for certain, but it looks like someone made a small hole in the bone."

"Why would that be done?"

"The only reason I can think of is to collect bone marrow," she said. "That's usually done with a hollow needle, which could leave a tiny hole like this."

Sydney went into the bathroom before leaving the facility. Pulling down her pants, she looked for a small incision on her thigh, like the one the doctor had found on her abdomen. Sure enough, she found one in the same area where the technician had found the hole in her femur.

"I'll be damned," she said, wondering now if there were others she simply hadn't noticed.

Sydney drove back to the ranch. She sat down in the living room with Brian and Miguel and told them about the MRI.

"We're getting a more complete picture of things as we go on," said Brian. "It would seem whoever is behind the abductions is using a neural inhibiter of some kind to induce paralysis and possibly block memories.

"They're taking scans or measurements of each victim, possibly monitoring brain waves and heart rhythms, and harvesting reproductive cells and bone marrow. And leaving a tracking device inside the body."

"Why?" asked Sydney. "What could they possibly be doing with reproductive cells and bone marrow?"

"If they're taking reproductive cells from the men, too, could it be some sort of human breeding program?" said Miguel.

"That's possible," said Brian. "That's how in vitro fertilization is done. As far as the bone marrow, that is typically an excellent source of stem cells in an adult."

"Stem cells... they're the ones that can be used to grow into any other kind of cell, aren't they?" asked Miguel.

"Yes," said Sydney. "They can be used to grow heart or lung tissue, or muscle tissue, or many other things. The technology is limited so far, for us at least, but whoever is doing this would seem to have more advanced tech. So, who knows what else they might be capable of."

"And at this point, who do we think 'they' might be?" asked Miguel. "Not them skinny gray aliens from the invasion?"

"No," said Brian. "I'm becoming more and more convinced that the Malor may not have anything to do with the abductions, after all."

"It's the man in black," said Sydney. "It's gotta be. We've only seen one of him, but there could be lots more."

"Do we know for sure he's not human?" asked Miguel.

"No, we don't," said Brian. "But the evidence seems to be pointing in that direction. I know of military tech that would give someone the ability to scale walls the way we've seen. But I have no explanation for his ability to fly, or jump, or whatever it is he's doing."

"And his eyes!" said Sydney. "Those cat eyes definitely aren't human!"

"But those could be contact lenses," Brian pointed out. "We simply don't have sufficient evidence to conclude, for sure, that the man in black is some sort of alien.

"We do know for certain that he can make himself invisible.

And unless we want to believe that the probes used onboard the UFO are moving of their own accord, it would seem likely that other individuals share that ability."

"So, there was *someone* there, doing the exams on us when we were abducted?" asked Miguel. "It was just that we couldn't *see* them, and so our brains convinced us it was the grays?"

"Again, we don't have enough evidence to draw any conclusions. But it does appear likely, I think," said Brian.

"Okay, so what do we do now?" asked Sydney. "It would seem both Miguel and I *definitely* saw Monument Valley out there in the background, wherever it was that they took us."

"But the military didn't see anything else in the area," said Miguel.

"True, but they were only looking above the ground," Sydney replied. "Neither one of us remembers seeing any surface structures. Only the elevator inside the butte. There may not be anything on the surface to see."

"Then how would we find the place they're taking people if it's underground?" asked Miguel.

"One would probably have to use ground-penetrating radar," said Brian. "But that has a limit of roughly one hundred feet, so if their compound is deeper than that, we'd never see it. Moreover, that type of detection would only be possible from the ground. To the best of my knowledge, no satellite provides that kind of functionality. I saw a proposal for such a system several years ago, but it never came to fruition."

"And trying to find the butte with the tunnel entrance in it would be like finding a needle in a haystack," said Sydney. "Are we at a dead end here?"

"Maybe we're going about this the wrong way," Brian suggested. "Maybe the way to find the compound is to follow the UFO there—or one of the UFOs, if there's more than one."

"But how do we do that?" asked Miguel. "We have no way of knowing when, or where, they're going to show up!"

"That's not true," said Sydney. "That teenager in Kansas—Owen—he said that they see a UFO go through there at least a couple of times *per month*."

"That's why we call it Alien Alley," Brian added. "I think you might be on to something."

"So, what, we start camping out on that road every night till they decide to show up?" said Miguel.

"Yeah," Sydney replied. "Why not?"

"I agree," said Brian. "If the two of you are on the ground there, and you let me know when the UFO shows up, I can access radar stations in the area and track the thing. It should lead us right to their compound."

"Perfect!" said Sydney. "That's it, then—let's do it!"

Sydney and Miguel took the jet back out to Kansas the next morning. When they landed, Sydney rented a car again, drove Miguel out to his trailer, and dropped off her things there.

"I'll be back in a little while," she said. "We can grab some food and head out to Alien Alley."

"See you then!"

Sydney went out to visit the Johnsons. She told them everything she'd learned from her medical exams, and they updated her about theirs.

"The MRI scans showed holes in our thigh bones, too," said Mr. Johnson. "But they didn't turn up anything else unusual."

Sydney told them about the tiny incisions in her abdomen and thigh.

"Our doctor didn't find anything like that," said Mrs. Johnson. "But we'll have to take a look ourselves and see what we can find."

Sydney shared her experience with the hypnotist, too, and told them about their plans to track a UFO from Route 23.

"We wish you luck, but be careful out there," said Mr. Johnson. "And please let us know what you find out!"

Sydney drove back to the trailer to pick up Miguel. They stopped to eat at the diner and then headed out to the Driscoll homestead.

"Hello again," said Sydney when Mrs. Driscoll came to the door. "We're back!"

"Oh hello, I'm sorry, what was your name again?"

"Sydney," she said.

"What is it I can do for you, Sydney?"

"Well, as you know, this area has seen quite a lot of UFO activity. We're hoping to track them, so we need a base of operations, I guess you could say. Now, we don't want to draw their attention in any way. So, I was wondering if we could park in your driveway?"

"Yes, sure," she said. "Feel free to camp out on the property if you'd like. We own the land on this side of the road for a thousand feet in either direction from the house—got about two hundred acres all told."

"That's wonderful, thank you!" said Sydney.

"Hang on; I'll let Owen know you're here," she said. "I'm sure he'd want to be involved if that's alright with you?"

"Yes, of course!"

Sydney went back to the car and pulled farther into the driveway. Owen came outside to meet them, his drone in hand.

"Hey there," said Miguel, getting out of the car.

Sydney told Owen what they were planning on doing.

"How'd your boss get access to the radar network?" he said.

"I've learned not to ask," said Sydney. "His company does computer and internet security, and he's done a lot of work for the government over the years..."

"Ah, so he probably left himself some back doors to get into their networks," Owen said knowingly.

"Yeah, it's something like that, I'm sure," Sydney agreed.

"My drone is fully charged, too, so we can try to get up close and get some footage with that," Owen told them.

"Yeah, that would be great," said Sydney. "My boss tried enhancing the video from the last time I was here, but it was so foggy, it was impossible to see much."

They set up a few lawn chairs in the far end of the yard, near the cornfields, where they hoped not to stand out. And they waited, all eyes focused on the sky.

Sydney noted a couple of satellites moving by, and they saw a few shooting stars. Every once in a while, a car would drive by on the road. But after a few hours, they had not seen anything that looked like it might be a UFO.

As midnight came and went, Sydney found herself growing drowsy.

"Couple of times per month you see something?" she asked Owen.

"Yeah, about like that. It's not so regular—I've seen them come through three nights in a row, and then not again for a month. But twice a month seems like the average."

By two o'clock, Sydney was having great difficulty keeping her eyes open.

"Why don't we call it a night," suggested Miguel. "We can come back out tomorrow night again. We'll have to get ourselves onto a third shift kind of schedule, I think."

"Yeah, you're probably right," she said.

They said goodnight to Owen and drove back to Miguel's trailer. The two of them went straight to bed, and Sydney fell asleep within minutes.

The next night, they returned to the Driscoll's place, and this time made it until half-past three in the morning, still without seeing anything interesting. The night after that, they stayed up until nearly six o'clock before calling it quits.

"Well, it's nearly dawn now," said Miguel, as they drove away. "We shouldn't have any trouble staying up all night going forward."

They kept it up for the next two nights, staying up the entire night without seeing more than a few satellites and some shooting stars.

On the sixth night after their arrival, a few minutes after midnight, Sydney pointed out a satellite to the other two.

"I don't see it," said Miguel.

"Oh, I do!" said Owen. "It's there, a little to the right of Rigel!"

"That might help if I knew which one was Rigel..."

"The bright one at the bottom of Orion," Sydney told him.

"Ah, yeah, there it is," said Miguel.

Sydney heard a motor and then saw headlights approaching.

"Whoa—what the hell was that?" Miguel yelled suddenly.

"What did I miss?" asked Sydney, looking skyward again and trying to locate the satellite they'd been watching.

"Get ready," Owen told them. "That's usually how it starts!"

"What's how it starts?" Sydney demanded.

"That satellite we were watching turned into something more like a shooting star," Miguel told her.

"Where is it now?"

"Look—see that bright star there in the west?" said Owen. "Brighter than Venus—that ain't no star. I'm pretty sure that's our UFO!"

Sydney searched the western sky and saw the light immediately.

"That's gotta be it," she said. "It's almost as bright as the moon!" She called Brian.

"We've got something out here," she said when he picked up.

"Okay, hang on," he said.

"It's getting closer," she said. "Hurry!"

"Okay, logging into the radar network... now," Brian told her. "Setting your location... Oh, my! There's something there, alright!"

"It's moving," said Miguel. "It's going for that car!"

Sydney watched the light grow closer; she was sure he was right. It was headed directly toward the vehicle she'd seen moments before.

"I'm putting the drone in the air," Owen said. He picked up the remote control. Moments later, the drone's rotors whirred into motion, and it took off from the yard.

Sydney watched as the UFO approached the car. Dark clouds had gathered around it, filling only a small area of the sky. It had moved much closer, and she could now make out a ring of lights on its underside.

"The driver's realized what's happening," said Miguel.

Sure enough, the car had accelerated, but as Sydney watched, it turned onto the same dirt road she'd used right before her abduction.

"This is it," she said. "It's gonna get whoever that is!"

They lost sight of the vehicle but could see its headlights moving through the cornfield for a few moments longer. But then the lights went out, and everything went silent.

The UFO came to rest, floating eerily in the sky.

"I can only see the underside of the thing," said Sydney.

"Me, too," said Miguel. "The top part is shrouded in them clouds!"

"I'm taking the drone in closer," Owen told them. "I'll see if I can get it up above the thing."

Suddenly a bright spotlight shone down from the center of the UFO. A moment later, they could see a figure rising inside the light and then disappearing inside the ship.

"They got 'em," Miguel said.

"Get ready," Sydney told Brain over the phone. "They've got their victim, so it's gonna start moving again soon."

"I'm ready," said Brian.

A moment later, the UFO took off, roughly to the southeast. It had moved faster than anything Sydney had ever seen, streaking across the night sky like a shooting star.

"Whoa!" said Owen.

"What the hell," Brian said in her ear. "Where did it go?"

"Southeast," Sydney told him.

"I can't find it. It just disappeared from the radar. I'm tracking wider now, out to three hundred miles, but I've got nothing."

Owen brought his drone back.

"Let's go check out the scene of the crime," said Miguel.

"I'll call you right back," said Sydney, closing her phone.

They went across the road and moved down the dirt road. But after going farther down the road than the vehicle had, they found nothing.

"Where the hell did the car go?" asked Owen.

Sydney used her phone to shine some light on the scene.

"No tire tracks here," said Miguel. "We've come too far."

They backtracked a bit and found where the tire tracks ended, but there was no vehicle in sight.

"This is very strange," Miguel observed. "I didn't find a car out here during your abduction, either," he added to Sydney.

"Check this out," said Owen. "I've got the drone footage on my phone."

They gathered around him and watched the display.

The video showed the ring of lights on the UFO's bottom and the dark clouds gathering around it. As the drone moved closer, its point of view moved higher until it was looking down on the UFO—or where the UFO should have been.

"I don't see anything through the clouds," said Sydney.

"Hang on a second," said Owen. "You're not gonna believe this."

Suddenly, there was a break in the clouds. The drone was looking down, and through the opening in the clouds, they could see a human form rising through the air and the vehicle down on the ground.

"Now, hold on," said Miguel. "Are we looking *right through* the UFO at this point?"

"Sure would seem so," said Owen.

"How the hell is that possible?" asked Sydney. "We were able to see the bottom of the thing!"

A few moments later, the UFO's spotlight went out, and everything went dark in the video. Then, they could make out the dirt road and surrounding cornfield.

"That's it," said Owen. "I stopped the video there."

Chapter Eighteen: Mystery Meeting

They drove back to the trailer. Sydney was exhausted but called Brian to update him before going to bed.

"I think we should try again," he said. "Not right away, though. Why don't you two take a few days off and get some R and R."

"What good would it do to try this again if the thing is moving too fast to track?" she asked.

"Well, based on your experience, and Miguel's, we have good reason to believe their bunker is somewhere near Monument Valley," he said. "And we know the UFO you saw tonight did move off in that direction. If I set myself up with some radar installations in that area, then next time, we may be able to pick the thing up again, even if we lose it as we did here."

"Makes sense," said Sydney.

"Get some sleep. It'll take me a while to get that set up."

Sydney hung up and told Miguel what they'd discussed.

"We'll want to make damn sure he's got those other radar stations ready to go before we try it again," he said. "Who knows how long it'll take to get another sighting. Don't want it to be a wasted effort."

"Agreed," said Sydney.

They went to bed, and Sydney was asleep the moment her head hit the pillow.

She woke up a little after two o'clock in the afternoon. Miguel was already up. After a quick shower, she got dressed, and they drove to the diner for a late breakfast.

"I'm getting fat eating so much greasy food all the time," said Sydney.

"I don't think so," he replied. "But truth be told, you could use a little meat on your bones."

Her phone chimed. She picked it up and saw that she'd received an e-mail. It was from a service called "Asfalis," that offered "end-to-end e-mail encryption" and indicated that she'd received a secure message from one of their users. But to receive the message, she had to register for an account.

Sydney thought this was probably spam, but she texted Brian a screenshot just to confirm.

"That's a legit e-mail service," he replied. "I'd suggest you register for an account and see what the message might be."

Sydney followed the link and set up an account. Next, she had to download their app on her phone and enter the login credentials she'd just created. Once she'd done that, she was finally able to access the encrypted message.

The user who had sent it was listed only as "C.B." It contained a set of coordinates, a time, and the message, "Come alone."

Sydney plugged the coordinates into her maps app. It was a point in Colorado, just west of Colorado Springs. She called Brian and told him about the message.

"Who is C.B.?" he asked.

"No idea."

"Those coordinates are in Colorado..."

"Yes."

"Hmm."

"What's with this mail service?" Sydney asked. "I thought this phone was totally secure?"

"Oh, it is," Brian confirmed. "But that just means your connection to the cell tower or Wi-Fi hotspot is fully encrypted and that you cannot be tracked. But, if you're using a normal e-mail service, it would still be possible for someone to intercept a message between your e-mail account and the other party's. That service guarantees that the message is secure and encrypted from your device all the way to the other party's, and cannot be deciphered at any point in between."

"Okay..."

"This tells us that whoever sent you this message wanted to be extremely cautious to make sure that nobody but you could read the message."

"Whoever it is wants me at those coordinates at two in the morning, two days from now. Should I go?"

He paused for a moment.

"Yes, I think so. But you should *not* go alone. See if Miguel is willing to accompany you. Perhaps he won't go all the way, but I would have him standing by somewhere close, just in case."

Sydney hung up.

"What was *that* all about?" Miguel asked.

Sydney explained.

"I don't like it," he said, shaking his head. "We have no way of knowing who this is. What if it's that man in black, or someone working with him?"

"That doesn't seem likely, does it? I mean, it's not his style. He just shows up and climbs buildings and shit. I don't see him setting up a clandestine meeting like this."

"That's a fair point," he conceded. "But I still don't like it. This could be dangerous."

"As opposed to chasing UFOs, which is completely risk-free?"

"Yeah, yeah. Well, those coordinates are about four hours away. And they're a bit of a hike from the nearest road. So, we're gonna have to set out plenty early."

"Does that mean you're going with me?" she asked with a grin.

"*Obviously,* I'm going with you!"

Two days later, they hit the road in Miguel's truck after dinner. They took Interstate 70 most of the way and then a state road through Colorado Springs. Once through the city, their route took them up into the mountains. Finally, Miguel pulled into the parking lot for a scenic overlook. They got out and took in the vista before them, awash in the light of a nearly full moon.

"This is as close as we can get by road," he said. "Them coordinates are out yonder," he added, pointing out toward the mountains.

"There's a path at the end of the lot," said Sydney, looking at the maps app on her phone. "It looks like that's going to be the best way over there."

"Alright, I'll stay here and keep an eye out for ya," he said, pulling her into a hug.

"This says it's a twenty-minute hike," she told him. "Maybe if you don't see me coming back in forty minutes, come and see if you can find me?"

"Of course."

Sydney set out down the trail. Now that they were here, she felt anxious about this and wondered if it was such a good idea after all. But she forged ahead.

The path led her down into the valley at first, before climbing again. It wasn't too steep, and she made good time. But before long, she realized she no longer had cell service. The maps app had cached her route, and the GPS was still working, but she would be unable to call for help. This only increased her anxiety.

As the path went around a curve, it seemed to end at the entrance to a cave. This hadn't been visible from their vantage point in the parking lot.

Sydney looked around for a way to keep going forward without moving underground—a trail that led up and over the entrance, perhaps. But the rock walls on each side of the path were nearly sheer, and there was no way to climb over. She would have to backtrack and then leave the trail to find a way up there.

In the end, she decided to try going inside the cave first. She figured that meeting underground matched this mystery person's M.O. perfectly.

Sydney moved into the cave.

The moonlight penetrated only a few feet inside. She needed the flashlight on her phone to see beyond that. After about a hundred feet, the cave opened into a vast subterranean cavern, at least a few hundred feet across, and more than three times her height. She found the coordinates from the message were located roughly in the center of this area. Once she'd arrived there, she turned slowly, taking in her surroundings. Stalactites and stalagmites filled much of the space, and many were more than wide enough to conceal a person.

"Hello?" she called out and shivered when she heard her voice echoing off the rock.

There was nobody here.

She was about fifteen minutes early, so she decided to wait. But the time went by, and still, nobody showed up. After another fifteen minutes, her anxiety had transformed into outright fear, and she decided to head back.

Moving back across the cavern, she kept looking out for someone to step out from the shadows, but no one appeared. She made it back to the path and headed down into the valley.

As she reached the bottom, she ran into Miguel.

"Thank God," he said. "I didn't see you come out, so I was heading in to find you. Who was there?"

"Nobody," she said with a sigh.

"*Nobody?*"

"The path led to an underground cavern, and the coordinates were right in the middle of that. But there was nobody there. I wanted to try finding a way to the same spot above the ground, but I think I'll have Brian check his live satellite feed instead. I want to get out of here."

Sydney still had no cell service, but once they returned to the parking lot, she made the call. She told Brian what had happened.

"Got it," he said. "Hang on a moment. Okay, I've got the coordinates on my screen now. I don't see anyone. Not on infrared, either."

Sydney's phone chimed. She had a notification that there was a message waiting for her on the encrypted e-mail service. Opening the app, she found one message from C.B. again.

"I said *alone*. You have one more chance. I'll be in touch."

She read the message to Miguel and Brian.

"C.B. must be nearby *somewhere*," said Miguel. "He knew I was here!"

"Or he has satellite access like Brian," Sydney pointed out. "Either way, we're done here. Let's go."

She hung up with Brian, and they drove back to Kansas. In the morning, she found she had another message from C.B. It was another set of coordinates in Colorado, and the time indicated was two in the morning again, in two days.

"Alone this time. Last chance."

Sydney entered the new coordinates into the maps app on her phone. It was a three-story brick building in downtown Colorado

Springs. Dropping into street-view, it looked like an office building. There was a bank on the ground level—or, at least, there had been when the street-view photos had been taken.

She called Brian to relay the new information.

"I feel much less comfortable with this knowing that there won't be anyone nearby to back you up," said Brian.

Sydney replied the same way she had to Miguel. "If this C.B. person wanted to hurt me, they could do it at any time. This motel isn't exactly like the ranch when it comes to security."

"Point taken, but I still don't like it."

Two days later, Sydney made the drive over to Colorado alone. She arrived at the coordinates and drove past the building she'd seen from her phone. It was still about twenty minutes before two o'clock, and the streets were empty. She turned at the next intersection and parked on the road.

Once she'd locked the car, she texted Miguel and Brian to let them know she had arrived and walked around the corner to the office building. She had no idea *where* in the building she was supposed to go or how she'd be able to get inside. It looked like the bank had taken up the entire ground floor but had closed since the street-view photos were taken. She found the entrance for the upper levels and tried the door. It was locked. She circled the building and found a couple of other entries in the back—these were locked, too.

Returning to the front, she tried the main entry for the bank area—it was open. Looking up and down the street to make sure there was nobody around, she slipped inside.

It was dark here; the street lights shining through the windows provide the only light. She walked around the lobby and behind the counter but found nobody here. Moving into the back room, she saw a light coming from somewhere farther inside. She made her way over to it and found the basement steps—that was where the light was coming from.

Sydney proceeded slowly down the steps.

"Here we go again," she muttered to herself.

At the bottom, she saw the light was coming from the front corner of the building. She made her way across the basement. Near the light, she found the vault, which was also lit. But there was nobody here.

"Hello," she called out, turning about to scan the area.

"Good evening, Ms. Hastings," said a voice behind her.

She turned quickly. Someone stepped out from the shadows.

"*Babcock*!" she said, immediately recognizing the CIA agent. "What the hell do you want with me? What's with all this cloak and dagger bullshit?"

"That mouth of yours is going to get you in trouble one day," he said with a smirk.

"Go to hell. What do you want?"

"Into the vault," he said.

"Yeah, right. What, are you going to lock me in there?"

He rolled his eyes and moved inside the vault himself. Sydney followed him.

"Pull the door shut," he said.

"That won't lock us in here...?" she asked.

He said nothing.

Sydney pulled the door closed.

"What is the point of coming in here?"

"We can't be tracked in here, and there's no chance of electronic surveillance."

"What?"

"These walls provide a very effective shield against electromagnetic radiation."

Sydney pulled out her phone. She had no signal.

"Okay. Now, what is this all about?"

"I want to warn you to stop sticking your nose where it doesn't belong."

"And what is that supposed to mean?"

"You know very well what it means," he said. "The UFOs. The abductions. Your investigation has not gone unnoticed. There are players on the board here, forces at work, about which you have *no idea*. You're getting in way over your head."

"So, what? They're going to kill me? That's what they do, right? The man in black? Tell me, does he work for the CIA, too?"

Babcock stared at her for a moment, saying nothing. Sydney turned to leave.

"Thanks for wasting my time," she said.

"They *won't* kill you," he said. "Not anymore. It will be far worse than that."

She rounded on him, about to scream in his face, but stopped when she saw his expression—one of genuine concern. And his voice was different now—gone was his usual sardonic tone.

"What?"

"The man in black does *not* work for the CIA."

"Then who does he work for?"

He shook his head.

"I was like you, once upon a time. The man in black showed up, trying to dig up information about our, ah, project. He got away, but I couldn't just let him go. I *should* have dropped it, but I stayed on him. I went deeper and deeper down that rabbit hole. And one day, I found I could no longer get out."

"Wait a minute," she said. "Hold on. You're telling me the man in black knew about Jaden and Malia? What did he want with them?"

Babcock said nothing.

"He wanted them for the same reason you did, right? For their powers? To make them into weapons?"

"They *are* weapons."

"Who is the man in black working for? If it's not the CIA, is it another government agency?"

"He's working for the same people that I am."

"*What...*"

"Don't you see it yet?" Sydney said nothing, not understanding what he was driving at. "I'm a double agent, Ms. Hastings. I have been for more years than I'd care to admit. I still work for the CIA, but I've been *compromised*."

"By whom?"

"They threatened my son," he said, ignoring her question. "He works in the Defense Department. When I refused to give up tracking down the man in black, despite the warnings, they made me an offer I couldn't refuse. I could provide them with the information they wanted and continue providing it to them, or they would kill my son and his family."

Sydney felt her heart sink as a wave of dread overcame her.

"Now you understand?" he said, correctly interpreting the look on her face.

"But I don't know anything," she said. "I don't work for the CIA or anything—there's nothing I do that they could possibly care about, whoever these people are. The only thing I'm doing is investigating the abductions."

"I've told you everything I can," he said.

"But there's more?"

"I've risked my life to tell you this much. If they found out I was talking to you..."

"So that's the reason for the cloak and dagger," she said.

"*Please*, let it go. Don't pursue your investigation any further before it's too late. Walk away. Go back to nursing. Do whatever you want, but *let this be*."

"Why are you telling me this? We're sworn enemies, aren't we?"

"You became my adversary when you took the project away from me," he said. "But I never considered you an enemy. I was doing my job. I'd do it again. But I wouldn't wish my predicament on anyone.

"Please, heed my warning."

"But who..."

"I can say nothing else. And I need to get back to where I'm supposed to be before my absence is noted. Be on your way now."

Sydney decided there was no point trying to get anything else out of him—he'd told her everything he'd come to tell her.

She opened the vault door, made her way back up the stairs, and out of the building. Back at her car, she called Brian and told him about her meeting.

"This is... remarkable," he said. "I'm having a little trouble processing this. What do you think?"

"I believe him," she said. "You should have heard him—he dropped his guard with me, at least to a point. His usual acerbic manner was gone. When he told me about his son... Brian, I thought he was going to cry for a second there. Whoever these people are that he's working for, they've got him by the balls."

"And so, what do we do now?"

"We keep going," she said. "I don't think this changes a thing. They wanted Babcock because of his connection to Jaden and Malia. Who knows how they found out about them, but Babcock was clearly the one who could give them whatever information they wanted.

"But the twins are gone, and the government—Babcock in particular, knows everything that I do about what went down with them."

"It could be something else, though," said Brian. "They could have some other use for you that we're not realizing. That certainly seems to be what Babcock believes."

"I don't see what it could be," she said. "I think we should keep doing what we were doing. Speaking of which, how's it looking for your new radar stations?"

"I'm ready to go," he said. "We can pick up our UFO watch whenever you and Miguel are ready."

Chapter Nineteen: Plan B

Sydney drove back to Kansas. The next night, she and Miguel went out to the Driscoll homestead to start waiting for a UFO again. Owen came out to join them, drone in hand.

"Not to be rude, or nothin'," he said, "but what makes y'all think this is gonna end any differently than last time? As far as tracking the UFO, I mean to say?"

"We're pretty sure we know the general area they're taking the abductees," said Sydney. "My boss will have access to radar stations in that area this time, on top of the ones around here."

"Oh, I gotcha," Owen replied. "That's smart."

They stayed out till dawn, but there was no activity. Three more nights went by uneventfully. But finally, on the fifth night, a shooting star stopped and suddenly grew significantly brighter.

"I think we've got our first customer," said Miguel.

"There aren't any cars or anything nearby," Owen observed. "I hope they ain't coming for us!"

But at that moment, Sydney noticed headlights coming up the road.

"Look, there," she said, pointing it out to the other two.

"He's seen them," said Miguel. "He's accelerating."

The pickup truck came into view, moving at very high speeds. Looking to the sky, they could see dark clouds gathering around the UFO as it gave chase.

Sydney called Brian.

"Hello?"

"We've got one," she told him.

"I'm on it..." he replied. "I've got it on radar."

As expected, the pickup truck suddenly died. The driver managed to pull over to the side of the road. He got out of the vehicle and pointed something at the UFO. Sydney heard what sounded like gunfire.

"I don't believe it," Miguel said with a chuckle. "He's firing at them with a shotgun!"

"Don't reckon that's gonna do him any good," said Owen.

The driver seemed to realize this himself because he dropped the gun and ran up the road. Seconds later, he turned, taking off into the cornfield.

The flying saucer continued its pursuit. Moments later, the bright spotlight appeared from the bottom of the craft. They saw the figure of the driver rising into the sky and disappearing into the UFO.

"Get ready," Sydney said to Brian over the phone. "They've got their victim."

The UFO streaked off into the sky, blindingly fast.

"They're gone!" Sydney reported.

"Damn! I lost them again," said Brian. "But hang on—I'm monitoring the stations in Arizona."

They waited a few minutes, but nothing turned up in Arizona, either.

"Why don't you guys call it a night," Brian suggested. "There's no way to know how long it would take them to get back to base, so I'll keep monitoring from here."

"Okay, boss," said Sydney. "Keep us posted."

They said goodnight to Owen and headed back to Miguel's trailer to get some sleep. The moment Sydney woke up that afternoon, she called Brian.

"Did you get anything?"

Brian let out a long sigh.

"No. I don't understand it. There was no unusual activity anywhere near Monument Valley."

"So, this is a dead end."

"Yes, it would appear that way. Listen, why don't you come home. We've got to put our heads together on this and come up with a Plan B. Bring Miguel if he wants to come along. Three brains are better than two."

Sydney and Miguel met the pilot at the airport the next day and flew back to North Carolina. Back at the ranch, they sat down with Brian in the living room to decide their next move.

"If we're right about the bunker being near Monument Valley, then how is it possible you didn't see anything on that radar?" asked Miguel.

"There are several possibilities," said Brian. "Kansas is so flat that it's much easier to pick up low-flying aircraft on radar. You don't have any canyons or mesas to get in the way. Out around Monument Valley, there is what you could call *ground clutter.* That clutter can block radar signals, making it impossible to see an object flying at low altitude.

"But we're also in the dark regarding the way their propulsion and navigation systems function," he continued. "They seem able to stop on a dime, from incredibly high speeds, for example. Or accelerate to extremely high velocities, almost instantaneously. If they were to maintain speed until the moment they arrive over the bunker, then there's a good chance they wouldn't show up on radar even at higher altitudes."

"So, we could still be right about them operating near Monument Valley," said Sydney.

"Absolutely," said Brian. "Our inability to detect their arrival on radar does not prove or disprove anything."

"Alright, then what do we do next?" asked Miguel.

"That is an excellent question," said Brian. "I feel fairly confident that the alien bunker must be somewhere near Monument Valley. But it would be nearly impossible to find it in a ground search; satellite imagery of the area has not turned up anything, even in infrared; and tracking the UFO there has proved unworkable. I'm struggling to come up with another option."

Suddenly, the answer became clear to Sydney.

"I have to let myself be abducted again," she said to the other two.

"I'm sorry, *what*?" said Miguel. "How would that help?"

"Brian, could you implant a tracking device in me, like what the aliens used?" she asked.

"Yes," he said. "And then we could use your tracking signal to locate their bunker. Good thinking, but I think this is too dangerous."

"Why?" she asked. "We have no evidence that they're doing any permanent harm to the abductees. I survived my first encounter, psychological trauma aside."

"But now we know from your meeting with Babcock that they have something special in mind for you specifically," Brain said. "We don't know what that might be, but it's quite possible it *would* involve permanent harm!"

"It's worth the risk," she insisted. "And you'd know where I am, so you'd be able to rescue me if they don't just let me go the way they did last time."

Miguel shook his head. "This is crazy. Do you have a death wish? Babcock told you flat out that you could be in danger."

"Okay, then what's our other option?" she demanded. "How do we find their bunker if we *don't* do this?"

Neither one of them could answer her.

"Right, exactly," she said. "This is the only way. If you implant a tracking device in me, then you can use that to locate the bunker. What else would we need to do?"

Brian let out a long sigh.

"*If* we decide to pursue this," he said, "and I'm not suggesting that we *should*, then I think we'd want to minimize the deleterious effects of the experience as much as possible. We should explore possible antidotes to whatever neural inhibiter they're using, to help you retain your memories and muscle control."

"Yes, good," she said. "Maybe a stimulant of some kind. That way, in addition to locating the bunker, I could do a little recon while I'm there. Have a look around, and see what I can see."

"That poses another danger, however," Miguel said. "If they see you moving, then they'll know you did something to counteract their drug. They might choose to punish you in some way."

"Well, I'll have to make sure they don't see me move," she said with a shrug.

"Let's start exploring this," Brian suggested. "Sydney, why don't you start with Dr. Lee and see if he can suggest any kind of stimulant that might counteract the alien neural inhibitor. Meanwhile, I'll look into an implantable tracking device. It's too bad we don't have the tech to commandeer the aliens' device—we won't be able to come up with something so small!"

Sydney called Dr. Lee right away and explained what they were planning.

"Hmm," he said. "We were eventually able to identify the compound they used, so that's no trouble. The hard part will be determining what kind of drug might counteract it. To be sure, we'd have to run tests—inject you, or someone, with the alien compound, and then administer the stimulant and see if it works.

"And while we've been able to *identify* the alien compound, we have no way to manufacture it."

"And that means there's no way to test an antidote," Sydney remarked.

"Precisely. The best we can do is make an educated guess. It would be ideal to develop something that directly neutralizes their compound—thus stopping it from ever working in the first place. But again, we don't have the means to do that, and even if we did, we don't have the time—that would take years."

"No, we can't wait that long," Sydney agreed.

"The next best approach is to use a stimulant that would directly counteract the *effects* of their compound. I'll need to do a little research on this. Give me a few days, and I'll come up with something."

"Great, thank you!"

Sydney and Miguel didn't have much to do for the next few days. Brian was hard at work exploring the best options for a tracking device, and they hadn't heard back from Dr. Lee yet.

But finally, Brian came up with the best solution.

"This is it," he said, sitting down with them in the living room one night. He held out his hand, showing them the device.

"It looks like a drug capsule," Sydney observed, "only thinner."

"So, how does this thing work?" asked Miguel.

"It's a subdermal implant," said Brian. "Typically, they would inject it just under the skin in your hand. For our purposes, we'll want to position it somewhere less apparent—the inner thigh, probably, to make it less obvious to the aliens.

"There are two types of microchips for this kind of application—active and passive. The passive variety does not have its own power source. When you scan it with the chip reader, the radio waves from the reader power the chip, and it emits a signal with whatever information you've programmed into it. But it's unable to emit a signal without the reader, and even then, its range is less than a meter."

"No, that wouldn't work at all," said Sydney.

"This is an active tracker. It has a small battery, which it uses to emit a signal, even without the presence of a reader. And its range is several hundred meters.

"This still presents us with some challenges. The range is better than it would be with a passive tracker, but we'll still have to be close by to detect the signal."

"We ain't gonna be able to find her if we're far away when she's abducted," said Miguel.

"Exactly," said Brian. "You and I will need to station ourselves in Monument Valley with scanners. As long as one of us is within roughly eight hundred meters of Sydney's location, then we've got her.

"The other issue will be timing. We don't know how far underground the bunker might be. But the tracker's range will be much shorter going through the earth, probably by an order of magnitude."

"Which means you need to find me *before* they take me underground," said Sydney.

"Now, wait a minute," said Miguel. "Can't you use a GPS tracker? Don't those have way longer ranges than that?"

"Sure," said Brian. "We could use an app on her phone for that. But I don't believe that would work. First of all, there's a good chance that ship is shielding its EM radiation—which would explain why it wasn't visible on the drone's video footage. That shielding would prevent any type of GPS tracker, including her phone, from transmitting any kind of signal.

"Again, there should be a brief window of time, when they transport her from the UFO to the bunker, when she would move beyond that shielding. But GPS trackers would need access to a cell tower to transmit their location data…"

"And we had no cell service out there," said Sydney, "so we already know there are no cell towers in range."

"Exactly," said Brian. "This device is based on a standard RFID chip—it's typically used for identification. It can be used in place of an ID badge to open doors in a high-security building, for example. I was able to modify it to boost its signal—the original had a range of only about two hundred meters. But that same window of time will still apply—the signal from this tracker most likely will not be able to penetrate the UFO's EM shielding. We'll have to find you while you're being transported from the ship to the bunker."

"If that's true, then why does it have to be implanted?" asked Miguel. "She could keep it in her pocket, no?"

"Yes, that's a possibility," said Brian. "You both remember still being clothed when they moved you into the bunker. But on the other hand, should we end up needing to mount a rescue mission, having the chip implanted could help tremendously once we're inside the bunker with her—so long as they don't find it and remove it first."

"This whole thing is going to be tricky," said Sydney. "You two will need to be ready to go in Monument Valley when I'm abducted. And you'll have to be pretty close to the bunker. This doesn't exactly sound like a sure thing."

"It's not," Brian confirmed. "But with current technology, it's the best we can do. We'll have to sit down with a map, and with the memories you both have of your abductions—specifically the position, orientation, and distance to Monument Valley—come up with our best guess as to your location. Miguel and I should then each take a position within an eight-hundred-meter radius of that location, at opposite sides of that circle, to maximize our chances of detecting your signal."

"Let me walk through the plan, then," said Sydney, "and make sure I understand this. I'm going to need to be in Kansas—Alien Alley is the one place we know we can count on regular UFO visits. But this won't necessarily happen the first time we try it. I'll have to go out to the Driscoll homestead night after night until the aliens decide to show up. And that means you two will need to be out in Arizona, and you'll have to set up shop out in the desert every night."

"Correct," Brian agreed.

"And then as soon as I see the UFO, I'll have to call you to let you know it's on," she said.

"Wait a minute," said Miguel. "How is that going to work if there's no cell service?"

"I'll take my satellite phone," Brian replied. "It works from anywhere on the surface of the Earth."

"Oh..."

"And then they'll abduct me," Sydney continued. "The UFO will take me to their bunker in Monument Valley. And when they take me off the ship, you two will have to locate me before I go underground."

"Yes," said Brian. "Now, there's also a chance that we'll have visual contact with the UFO when it comes into range. So Miguel and I can move toward its location as soon as we see it, and that should improve our chances of finding you. We should use walkie talkies, too, to make sure we can communicate with each other while this is going on."

"And as long as you've located me, then you should be able to find the entrance to the bunker," Sydney concluded.

"At the very least, we should have the possible location reduced to a sufficiently small area to make a ground search feasible," Brian said.

"Alright, and then what?" said Miguel. "We knock on the door and politely ask the aliens to return Sydney to us?"

"Hopefully, this doesn't *need* to be a rescue mission," Sydney replied. "They do what they do, and then they return me to Kansas. That's how it's gone in every single case we know about."

"I still don't like it," said Miguel. "Why does Sydney have to be the bait? We could run this game the same way, but instead of them taking Sydney, we wait for them to take someone else, and she lets us know when they take whoever that ends up being."

"We wouldn't have the ability to track such a person," Brian pointed out.

"Sure, but you just said we'd make visual contact when the

UFO shows up in the area," said Miguel. "We could still find the bunker that way."

"Possibly," Brian replied. "But keep in mind, we don't know for *sure* that we'll see the UFO out there. And without the tracker, we won't be able to pinpoint their location nearly so precisely. The area we'd have to cover with our ground search would be much larger. But we could try this first, and see how it goes, and keep Sydney's abduction in reserve, as a last resort."

"No," said Sydney. "That could be a huge waste of time, and it's even less likely to work than sending me with a tracker. On top of which, we lose the potential to do some recon inside the bunker. Let's stick to the plan."

Miguel opened his mouth to argue, but Brian cut him off.

"Why don't we sleep on it, and we'll discuss it further tomorrow?"

They went their separate ways for a couple of hours. Brian cooked dinner for them. After they ate, Sydney and Miguel went for a walk under the stars.

"Beautiful night," he observed.

"It is," she agreed with a smile.

They walked in silence for a minute.

"You thought about this plan any more?" he asked.

"Nope," she said. "I don't need to. I've already made up my mind."

He didn't reply for a moment.

"Can I ask you something?"

"Of course," she said.

"Why do you care so much? Why is it so important to you to do this?"

"Because whoever is behind these abductions is up to no good, and I have the power to help *do something* about it!"

"Fair enough. But at what cost? You heard that CIA guy—the man in black has something special planned for you. What if they *don't* release you as they have before?"

"Then we'll figure it out," she said. "What we learned from Babcock only *strengthens* my desire to help.

"Look, those CIA assholes murdered my best friend's husband. They kidnapped her children. I was able to help those kids, and that was the right thing to do. They didn't have anyone else.

"Knowing that the people behind these abductions tried to get to Jaden and Malia proves they're cut from the same cloth. They put power before people. Someone's got to take a stand and put a stop to this. We have the power to do that."

"We could call in the government like they did when they rescued us from them gray aliens," he said.

"And how would we know whom to trust?" she asked. "Babcock confessed he's been compromised—he's working for the people who are behind the abductions. And no matter who else we contact, we'd have no way of knowing if they've been compromised, too."

Miguel took a deep breath.

"I can't talk you out of this, can I?"

"Not a chance. I watched as the Malor killed hundreds of thousands of people during the invasion. Even though I was powerless to do anything about it, I've had to live with the guilt, the nightmares. There's no way I'm walking away from this."

"Okay. I get it. But you'd better promise me one thing."

"What's that?"

"That you'll come back to me."

Sydney turned to look him in the eye.

"Look, I ain't never gonna try to tie you down or anything," he said. "I value my independence too much to do that, and I respect your freedom. But truth is, I'm falling in love with you, Sydney Hastings. And I don't wanna *not* have you in my life anymore."

"I'll come back," she said. "You can count on it."

Pulling him into her arms, she kissed him.

"I have a confession to make," she said.

"Oh yeah? What's that?"

"I think I might be falling in love with you, too."

"*Might be?*"

"Yeah... just maybe..."

"You're such a tease."

"I know," she replied, kissing him again.

Back inside, they found Brian in the living room. He'd started the fireplace.

"We don't need to sleep on anything anymore," Sydney announced as she and Miguel took their seats.

"Oh?" asked Brian.

"Resisting this woman is futile," said Miguel.

Sydney smiled.

"Alright, then," said Brian. "We can leave tomorrow. In the meantime…"

He got up and poured them each a glass of Scotch.

"Here's to kicking some alien ass," said Miguel.

The three of them clinked their glasses.

Chapter Twenty: Abducted

The next morning, Sydney drove into town to visit Dr. Lee. He gave her a bottle of capsules.

"Take one of those when it seems like you're about to be abducted," he advised. "It'll take a little while to work its way into your system, but it should take effect by the time you need it."

She gave him the chip Brian had provided her. Once he'd sterilized it, he implanted it under the skin of her inner thigh.

"Good luck out there," he said when they were done.

"Thanks, Doc."

When she got back to the ranch, she found Miguel with Brian in his office. There was an image of Monument Valley projected on the far wall.

"Whatcha doing?" she asked.

"Check this out," said Brian.

"Monument Valley," she said.

"Yes. This is a 3D simulation of the major mesas and buttes in the area. Miguel and I were trying to determine the approximate position of the alien bunker by calibrating this simulation to his memory of the orientation and distance of these formations."

"Ah, neat," she said, staring intently at the projection. "That's pretty accurate... but I think they weren't quite that far away."

Brian adjusted the simulation to bring the background closer.

"Yeah, that's better," said Sydney.

"I agree," said Miguel. "I think that's about right."

"Now, I feel like this big mesa here was farther this way..."

They spent the next twenty minutes fine-tuning the simulation. Once Sydney and Miguel had agreed that it was very close to what they remembered, Brian plotted the point on the map that would match that vantage point.

"Where is this relative to that Malor camp we found?" asked Sydney.

"Give me a second..." He checked something on his phone, then tapped a set of coordinates into the mapping program. "Right about there."

"That's not too far," said Miguel.

"It's about half a mile from where we found the Malor," said Brian. "Not very far at all."

"That's a little strange, isn't it?" asked Sydney. "If they were that close, wouldn't they have detected the Malor, or vice-versa?"

"That's quite possible," said Brian.

"Does that mean they're all working together after all?" asked Miguel. "The grays and these cat-eyed aliens?"

"That's also possible," Brian replied. "Hopefully, we're about to get some answers!"

Later that morning, they flew to Kansas. Sydney deplaned there, while Brian and Miguel continued to Arizona.

Sydney rented a car, booked her room in the usual motel, and drove over to the Driscoll homestead. She met Mrs. Driscoll at her front door and told her what she was planning.

"Let me get this straight," the woman said. "You're *trying* to get abducted again?"

"That's right," Sydney replied with a chuckle. "I am."

"My dear, that is about the craziest thing I have ever heard."

"I know, me too. Listen, unlike before, I'll want to make myself an easy target. I'm planning on basically camping out by the side of the road at night. I noticed you've got an ample supply of firewood; do you think I could use some of that?"

"Take as much as you want," she said. "And let me know if there's anything else you need."

That night, Sydney came back, parked her car on the side of the road, and with Owen's help, set about lighting a giant bonfire.

"Thank you for the help," she said once the fire was roaring. "But listen, you'd better head inside. We don't want to get you abducted, too."

"I hate to leave ya all alone out here," he said.

"I appreciate that, but I'll be alright."

He headed into the house. Sydney called Brian on his satellite phone.

"Hey," she said. "I'm in position; how about you boys?"

"We're here," he replied. "Took a little longer than we anticipated—part of the trail was washed out, so we had to go around the hoodoos instead of through them. But we're ready."

"Great. I'll call you if anything exciting happens."

Sydney took one of the pills out of the bottle the doctor had given her, slipped it in her pocket, and got comfortable in her lawn chair.

Minutes passed, and then hours. She added more logs to the bonfire periodically. A car went by every so often, but by dawn, nothing interesting had happened.

She checked in with Brian again, and then returned to the motel and went to bed.

Two more uneventful nights went by. But on the fourth night, around two in the morning, Sydney noticed a satellite passing overhead.

She kept a close eye on it. It made its way across the sky, doing nothing remarkable. But as it approached the horizon, it stopped.

"Bingo," she said out loud and called Brian.

"I think I've got something," she told him.

"What?"

"I thought it was a satellite, but suddenly, it stopped."

"Yeah, satellites don't do that."

"Hang on," said Sydney. The point of light had reversed direction. A moment later it accelerated and grew in intensity. "This is it! I gotta go!"

She pocketed her phone and moved out into the middle of the road. The light grew ever brighter, dark clouds gathering around it. Sydney waved her arms over her head. The UFO was nearly overhead now.

It stopped. Sydney waited in anxious anticipation, but the spotlight didn't come. The craft moved farther up the road.

"What the hell!" she shouted. "I'm right here!"

The UFO kept moving, picking up speed now.

Sydney got in her car and started the engine. She took off down the road in pursuit. At the end of the street, the UFO kept going straight, but she was forced to turn. She raced to a crossroad and then turned left.

She was moving in parallel to the UFO now but had lost ground. Flooring the accelerator, she tried to catch up.

Glancing at the speedometer, she saw she was going over eighty miles per hour. Luckily, there were no other cars on the road.

Moments later, the UFO seemed to stop. Sydney found a dirt road that led in that direction; she hit the brakes and turned onto it, tires screeching. It was very dark here, and she had no choice but to slow down. But she was headed directly for the UFO now.

It started moving again as she drew closer. She drove as fast as she dared.

Before long, she reached another paved road and could not continue in the same direction. She turned left and then found another dirt road that led toward the UFO. Taking the turn at speed, she plowed into the corn stalks before straightening out and accelerating again.

The UFO came to rest again. She drove directly underneath it, then slammed the brakes, skidding to a stop. The car died.

She got out, waving her arms over her head again.

"I'm right here!" she yelled. "I'm all yours!"

The UFO started moving again, this time across the cornfield.

"Shit!"

Sydney took off through the field. She reached a stream, hiked up her jeans, and splashed across, then took off at a run.

But moments later, the UFO streaked across the sky and disappeared.

"Dammit!"

Feeling defeated, she headed back to the car. She got in and started the engine without a problem.

"Great. Now I don't have the slightest idea where I am."

She took out her phone and tapped in the Driscoll's address. Turning around on the narrow dirt road was tough, but she managed it and headed back the way she'd come.

But as she approached the main road, the car died again.

"What the hell?"

Suddenly, a bright light appeared in her rearview mirror.

She got out of the car and looked back down the dirt road. The UFO was back and nearly directly overhead.

Sydney had to wait only another moment before the spotlight shone down from the center of the craft. Reaching into her pocket, she pulled out the pill she'd left there and swallowed it.

Suddenly, she found herself floating up to the spacecraft. She passed inside, into the dark chamber with the metal walls. The opening in the floor disappeared, and she was staring into total blackness.

There was a buzzing noise, and Sydney suddenly felt groggy but managed to stay conscious. She felt anxious now; her heart was hammering in her chest. A light breeze touched her arm and her hair, and she felt as if she were moving. A moment later, she found herself in a circular chamber, with pods lining the walls. There was a man in one of the pods. He was staring at her—he didn't speak or move, but his face registered terror.

Sydney tried wiggling a finger—she could do it but didn't risk any movement beyond that. Some unseen force moved her across the chamber, turned her around, and backed her into a pod. She felt something prick the back of her neck.

Other than the man in the other pod, she did not see or hear anyone else. She suspected the ship was probably moving by now but didn't feel any acceleration. Over the next few minutes, she noticed a tingling sensation in the back of her neck that slowly spread to her head, down her back, and down her arms. She tried wiggling a finger again but couldn't.

A jolt of fear ran through her body. She couldn't move her arms or her legs and couldn't shift her gaze. Her breathing was normal, and she felt her heart beating very fast in her chest, but she'd lost motor control completely.

For a moment, she felt her anxiety rise—why wasn't the stimulant working? But the answer was obvious. Dr. Lee had warned her it could take "a little while" for it to take effect. It would seem the alien drug had been injected directly into her bloodstream, allowing it to go to work much more quickly.

Minutes went by. Still, there was no sense of acceleration. But after only a short time had passed, she found herself moving out of the pod again, across the chamber.

An instant later, everything went black. She couldn't look down but noticed a glow suddenly emanating from somewhere below her. Now she could see the metal walls and knew she was back in the room where she'd first entered the UFO.

Sydney felt herself moving down, and she passed through the bottom of the craft. She was in the desert. As she descended to the ground, she could make out Monument Valley in the distance.

She stopped for a moment before her feet had touched the ground and then floated forward. Up ahead, she saw the butte with the opening in its face. She passed inside, still unable to comprehend what force was causing her to move.

There was a short tunnel inside the butte, with what looked like a freight elevator at the far end. She moved inside of that and was turned around to face back down the tunnel again.

Someone was approaching—she could see them only in silhouette at first. Her heart leaped into her throat—who was this?

But as he passed inside the elevator, she realized it was the man from the other pod back on the ship.

The elevator door closed, and the bottom seemed to fall from beneath them. She could feel their downward acceleration now and thought that they must have been moving at extreme speed. Moments later, she felt them slowing down, finally stopping with a light thud.

The door opened again. There was a much longer tunnel here, and while there was enough light to see, she couldn't tell where the light was coming from.

She moved out of the elevator, leaving the man behind, and progressed down the corridor. Metal doors lined each side. About halfway down the hall, she found herself floating into a large room. It was dark here—she couldn't see the far walls. There were exam tables here, all empty.

The unseen force moved her to one of the tables, tilted her onto her back, and lay her on the table. There was an odor—she couldn't identify it. In the next moment, everything went black, and Sydney knew no more.

Miguel followed Brian through the Arizona desert. They'd been walking for almost an hour already. The sun was minutes away from setting.

There were many small buttes and mesas in this area—well, small by comparison, Miguel thought. They were much smaller than the formations of Monument Valley but still towered over his head. They wound their way between them.

For three nights, they'd trekked out here and spent the night in the desert. And for three nights, there had been no activity on Sydney's end.

"Alright," said Brian when they reached the southern end of their target area, "I'll be in touch."

"Be safe," Miguel replied.

Brian continued to the northern end of the area. They each had a walkie talkie and a dedicated GPS device, so they could stay in touch and relay their coordinates to each other if anything happened. Miguel also had his cell phone and the RFID receiver

Brian had supplied him. The cell phone was pretty much useless out here, with no Wi-Fi or cell service. But it connected to the receiver over Bluetooth, and the app Brian had sent him showed the direction of any active signal. Right now, it displayed only a blank screen.

Miguel sat down on the ground and watched the sunset. As it grew darker, he lay on his back and gazed at the starry sky. The Milky Way became visible as the night reached full darkness.

The app for the receiver was set to give him a notification if it received a signal, but he couldn't help checking the app every few minutes anyway. It continued to be blank.

After a while, he felt drowsy and got up to walk around a bit and keep himself awake. The hours slipped by with nothing to break up the monotony.

But at two in the morning, he heard Brian's voice on the walkie talkie.

"Miguel, you there?"

"Hey, I'm here—what's up?"

"Sydney's got something," he said. "Be ready."

"You got it!"

Miguel felt his heartbeat increase in anticipation. He pulled out his phone and the RFID receiver. The app's display was still not showing any signal.

Miguel wondered how long it would take the UFO to get here from Kansas. Who knew how fast that thing could go?

He kept his eyes peeled to the northeast, looking for anything that resembled a satellite or shooting star. The minutes dragged by, and nothing happened.

"You got anything over there?" he asked on the walkie talkie.

"Nothing so far," Brian replied.

Miguel felt his anxiety increasing. This was taking a long time. Twenty more minutes passed, and he was growing impatient.

Suddenly, he saw a shooting star streak across the sky.

"Hey, did you see that?"

"What?"

"Shooting star just went by, looked normal from here, though."

"I missed it," said Brian. "I've got no activity here. I tried calling Sydney, but she's not answering."

A few more minutes went by, then Brian's voice came over the walkie talkie again.

"I've got a signal!"

Miguel checked his phone. It was still blank.

"Nothing here," he said.

"I've definitely got something—it's directly south of my position. I'm moving toward it now. If you head due north, you should find it!"

"I'm on my way!"

Miguel hurried into the night. It was dark, but the moon had risen, providing ample light to see by. He kept the receiver app open on his phone as he moved. He'd gone only a few hundred feet when it picked up a signal—due north.

Within minutes, he saw lights up ahead but had no view of the source of the light. Seconds later, he rounded a rock formation and caught a glimpse of the UFO dead ahead. He backpedaled, hiding behind the rock to assess the situation. But at that moment, the spacecraft rose into the sky and streaked off into the night.

Miguel moved cautiously to its former position; he didn't see Sydney anywhere. He pulled out his walkie-talkie.

"Brian, are you there?"

"I'm right here," said a voice behind him.

Miguel started, turning to see Brian approaching.

"You scared the shit out of me!" Miguel said, his heart now pounding in his chest. "Don't ever do that again!"

"Sorry," Brian said with a grin.

"Where is Sydney? Did you see her?"

"No, the UFO was floating right here when I arrived. I waited to see if she'd come out, but then it took off. They must have taken her off before I got here."

Miguel checked his phone.

"The signal has disappeared," he said. "But the butte with the tunnel to the elevator must be very close."

"Yes," Brian agreed. "Let's have a look around."

They searched the area very cautiously, keeping their eyes open for any unwelcome surprises. There was a butte close by.

"This doesn't look right," said Miguel. "Too wide."

He turned slowly, taking in his surroundings.

"There," he said finally, pointing to the east.

Brian followed him. There was another butte, taller and narrower than the first.

"I think this is it," he said.

They started moving around its perimeter. Miguel found a depression in one side of it. He took out his phone and turned on the flashlight. They examined the surface.

"Look here," said Brian, tracing his finger along the rock.

Miguel saw a thin line running vertically up the butte as if someone had cut into the surface with a fine saw.

"This doesn't look naturally occurring," said Brian.

"The tunnel to the elevator is inside here," Miguel told him. "I'm certain of it. This is where they took me."

"Sydney must be in there," said Brian.

"Yes, she is," said a voice behind them.

Miguel and Brian turned, Miguel pointing his light toward the source of the sound. A man was standing only a few feet away, the hood of his sweatshirt pulled over his head, covering his face in shadow.

"Who the hell are you?" Miguel demanded.

"You may call me Salvatore," he said. The light caught his eyes, and Miguel gasped—the pupils were slits, like a cat's—precisely like the man in black, but this was someone else. "Your friend is in grave danger, and it is up to us to save her."

Chapter Twenty-one: The Bunker

Sydney opened her eyes. It was dark. Where was she?

It took a few seconds for the memory to surface. She was inside the underground alien bunker.

This didn't look like the same room she'd been in before—there were more exam tables, and they were arranged differently. Most were empty, but a woman was lying in one; she was naked.

Sydney realized that she was naked now, too, although she had no memory of her clothing being removed.

She was able to wiggle her fingers—the stimulant must have taken effect. Slowly sitting up, she took in more of her surroundings. This room was only dimly lit, and she could not see beyond the exam tables.

Swinging her legs over the edge of the table, she dropped silently to the floor. She found her clothes folded neatly under the exam table. As quietly as possible, she got dressed, then tip-toed over to the other woman.

She was young, probably in her early twenties, with dark brown skin and short, dark hair. Her chest gently rose and fell with her breathing. Sydney didn't want to risk trying to wake her for fear that she might scream. She'd probably be unable to talk or move, but she didn't want to take the risk.

Crossing the room, she found she could see the area a few feet ahead of her, although she still could not locate a light source. The wall suddenly loomed out of the darkness.

Sydney walked along the wall for ten paces, twenty, and then after thirty paces found an opening. There didn't seem to be a door, but she could not see beyond the entrance. Turning back, she could still see the exam tables. She walked through the opening and found herself in the hallway where she'd first arrived. There appeared to be a metal door in the space through which she'd walked, but when she tried to touch it, her hand went right through it.

The walls seemed to be some kind of stone, but they were perfectly sheer and smooth to the touch. There were doors along both sides of the entire corridor.

Sydney hurried to the next door and moved through it. Inside was another room with several exam tables, but nobody was there. She went into two more rooms, finding them empty, then found a man in the third room she tried.

She moved across the room to him as quietly as possible. He was Chinese, maybe fifty years old, and completely naked. She could see that he was breathing, but his eyes were closed, and he seemed to be asleep.

Sydney continued down the corridor, peering into every room she passed. A few were empty, while she found people in some of the others—no more than two people in any room.

Near the end of the corridor, she found a room that differed from the others: It was brightly lit. The walls and ceiling were polished metal. The space was empty, except for half a dozen exam tables. There was a woman on one table, but she was clothed and strapped to the table.

Sydney rushed over to her. The woman opened her eyes and gasped.

"Sh—please, don't scream," she whispered.

"Who are you?" the woman asked quietly.

"My name is Sydney."

"You're not with *them*? The people who run this place?"

"No—they abducted me."

"You got out? How are you able to move around?"

"It's a long story. Do you know how long you've been here?"

"It feels like forever... I have no idea. Weeks. Months, maybe—I have no way of measuring time. They took me a few days after the invasion."

"Have you been awake the whole time?"

"No—I was in a different room when I got here—it was dark, and I couldn't move or talk then. And they kept me naked, just like the last time this happened."

"You've been abducted before?"

"Yes, but I've never been able to remember much from that time. Just the dark room. And the aliens..."

"Like the ones from the invasion?"

"Yes, exactly like them."

"Have you seen anyone this time?"

"Yes—but they're not aliens."

"What?"

"They're human, just like you and me!"

"*Are you kidding me*?! Humans are working here?"

"The first time this happened, I thought aliens had abducted me—I could swear I saw a few of those gray ones. But it's all foggy... This time, I've seen only regular people. Doctors and nurses."

"No aliens?"

"None."

"Have you seen anyone besides medical personnel?"

"No, I don't think so... wait, yeah, I did see a man once. I think he was a security guard or something—he was wearing a black suit. And sunglasses, which was strange..."

Sydney gasped.

"What is it?"

"Did the man take off his sunglasses? Have you seen his eyes?"

"I only saw him once, through the door there, and it was only for a few seconds. He didn't take off the sunglasses."

"Have you seen any other abductees?"

"A few—they come and go. I've been in this room the whole time. Sometimes they bring people in here for a little while. They're always unconscious, though. And they never stay long.

"Except for these two kids—they've been in here as long as me."

"Kids?"

"Well, teenagers, really. A boy and a girl. They just took them out a few minutes before you got here. They'll probably come back soon."

Sydney considered the situation for a minute.

"I'm going to unstrap you, and we're getting out of here," she said.

"What? Are you crazy? They'll just catch us and tie us down again."

"Maybe, but we should give it a try," said Sydney. "I came all the way down the hallway, and I didn't run into anyone."

"Where are we going to go?"

"There's an elevator at the other end of the corridor. We can take that back up to the surface. I have friends up there who will be waiting for us."

Sydney released the woman's straps and helped her get to her feet. She seemed a little unsteady at first.

"Are you okay?"

"I'll be alright," she said. "This is the first time I've tried to walk in... well, as long as I can remember."

Sydney led her across the room. They moved through the door, into the hallway.

"Wait," the woman whispered, grabbing her by one arm. "We should take those two kids with us!"

"It's too dangerous," said Sydney. "We have no idea where they might be!"

"Gotta be in one of these rooms, don't they? They're just kids; we can't leave them here!"

Sydney took a deep breath.

"Okay. I've checked all the rooms on this end of the corridor, except that one across from yours, and I haven't seen any kids. Hold on a second."

She moved across the hallway and poked her head through the opening, backing out immediately, her eyes wide.

"What is it?" the woman asked.

"Looks like the command center," she said. "You're right—humans are running the place. Five or six people were sitting at work stations along the opposite wall. I don't think they saw me.

"Let's go!"

Sydney led her halfway down the corridor toward the elevator, then stopped and checked one of the rooms. She saw the Chinese man she'd found earlier.

"Okay, this is about where I started. Let's check the rest of the doors going this way—I'll take this side, you take that side. But be careful—just stick your head through the opening—we don't want them to see us!"

They crept along the corridor, checking inside each room. The first two on Sydney's side were empty. When she checked the third room, she saw people lying on two exam tables—they looked young.

"I think I found them," she said to the woman. "Let's go inside."

They moved into the room and hurried over to the two people.

"Yep, this is them," the woman confirmed.

Sydney gasped. Lying on the exam tables were Jaden and Malia Kwan.

"I don't believe it... How can this be?!"

"Welcome, Ms. Hastings," said a voice from behind them. Sydney turned. It was the man in black. "I'm so glad you could join us."

To be continued...

Printed in Great Britain
by Amazon